"**A madcap morning-radio team hanging with Sinatra,** intimate father-and-son conversations over drinks at the Friars Club, and a young, blond, blue-eyed 'mystery woman' from another realm swiveling everyone's head: Come on, Ross Klavan was raised on this canvas. It's in his DNA. No wonder I felt in such expert hands."

— **David Pollock**, author of *Bob and Ray, Keener than Most Persons*

"**In this extremely entertaining romp through New York in 1969,** a fast-talking radio host and a garment-industry crook collide—and much amusement ensues. Klavan's light touch and sharply drawn characters echo Carl Hiaasen, and are also very much his own."

— **Emily Bazelon**, author of *Sticks and Stones*

"**A schmuck can be an unconscious dope or an intentionally malignant prick.** Klavan keenly and hilariously describes the lives of a network of schmucks growing up and fighting with one another in a tumultuous period of change, 1969. I laughed out loud and also wept reading this fast-paced novel of a Jewish Holden Caulfield."

— **W. M. Bernstein**, author of *A Basic Theory of Neuropsychoanalysis* and *The Realization of Concepts*

"*Schmuck* **is delightful reading from beginning to end,** but be forewarned. There is often seriousness beneath a tale whose Yiddish title means roughly 'a dope.' It deals with social status and family, the lingering effects of World War II on those who fought in it, and love or what passes for it. It's Jewish New York (or New Yawk) and will make you laugh one minute, wince another, but will let you find yourself in it, no matter where you come from or who you think you are. Hats off to Ross Klavan! Let's make it morning!"

— **John Bowers**, author of *The Colony*

SCHMUCK

SCHMUCK

A Novel

ROSS KLAVAN

GREENPOINT PRESS

NEW YORK, NY

ISBN 978-0-9886968-3-9

Library of Congress Cataloging-in-Publication Data

Designed by Robert L. Lascaro, LascaroDesign.com
Book text set in Minion Pro, text drop caps and cover title
set in Road House

Greenpoint Press,
a division of New York Writers Resources
greenpointpress.org
PO Box 2062
Lenox Hill Station
New York, NY 10021

New York Writers Resources:
· newyorkwritersresources.com
· newyorkwritersworkshop.com
· greenpointpress.org
· ducts.org

Printed in the United States
on acid-free paper

This book is for Mary Jones.

"Our real choice is between holy and unholy madness:
open your eyes and look around you—
madness is in the saddle anyhow."

— Norman O. Brown, *Apocalypse and/or Metamorphosis* (1991)

PROLOGUE

1945 — The End of World War II

COMING BACK FROM THE PACIFIC, back from The War, when he first eyeballed the Golden Gate Bridge— that's when he got rid of the Japanese skull.

A real Texas cheer went up from all across the troopship. Everywhere, from the top deck where the rust broke through the cracked gray paint to down below where the smell of vomit was so thick it rippled in the air and caught you in its stinking web, everywhere you could hear the whoops, the hollers, the throat rattles and, by God, they shouted, by San Antone, Jesus Christ and holy, holy shit! They were home.

The troopship cut steadily toward the bridge. Elkin had been in the army four years, in the Pacific in combat 18 months. He was 21. And now as the men cheered and shouted and some danced and some leaped up on the ship's thin railing, Elkin joined in. He was calling to nobody across the ocean, smacking someone on the back, hugging another G.I. he didn't even know, and then they were jumping up and down and shaking each other. Elkin was small and thin and the hugging and backslapping knocked his glasses crooked. The Japanese skull was in his duffle bag. A souvenir. He was carrying it home to his firstborn son—if he ever had a firstborn son—because his possible firstborn son would definitely want to know about The War, what had happened in The War.

And Elkin would tell him. But now, on the ship, Elkin made his voice into a deep, comic jazzman's growl and shouted, "Lemme outta heah, Momma, so I can grab-ass every broad I see!" and other G.I.'s laughed.

Elkin would tell his possible firstborn son that he had been on a patrol on Guam in '44 and that they had found the Japanese soldier already long dead. Most of the flesh was rotted away, the gut open like shit in the grass, the face gone and the head offering itself up as a skull. The body didn't even stink anymore. Sgt. Cole kicked at one of the dead Jap's boots and the rotted foot came partway off. Nobody said anything. Elkin didn't know why he didn't care but he didn't and he wasn't sure it might not be a show-off stunt for the other men, but he kneeled in the dirt and pulled away the skull and saw that the top of the head had been mostly blown off. Inside the skull, lining the bone, there was still a little bit of grease, some gray matter, what was left of the dead Jap's brains. Some white worms, too. Elkin would tell his firstborn son about this and also he wouldn't be afraid to admit that he was glad, even more than glad, that they didn't find any live Japanese on this patrol. He might even add that he'd had enough of live Japanese for the rest of his life.

Elkin pulled the bayonet off his rifle and scraped away what was left of the brains. It was like cheese gone bad on the blade. He flipped it into the dirt. Nobody said anything except for Cpl. Crouse, who said, "Elkin, shit," and shook his head and spit but it was so hot that nobody cared. They were glad enough to be finished with the patrol. Perretti took off his steel pot and walked five steps and dragged out his dick and pissed on a tree. He didn't like Jews, Perretti. He'd once called Elkin a "kike" and said he didn't like the way Jews smelled. Elkin finished scraping out the Japanese brains and then he made a haunted house sound like "Whoooo-hoooo!" and as a joke held up the skull and pushed it back and forth at McCarthy, who swiped at it and said, "Knock it off. Put that fucking thing away."

McCarthy usually called Elkin a "four-eyed Jew" but it was joking. He didn't do it now because the patrol put them all on edge.

Anyway, that's how Elkin got the skull. He set it by his cot and used it as an ashtray. If he thought about the skull's human-being past—the mundane stuff like how the skull had once looked, talked, eaten, whistled, kissed, had yearned not to end up as an ashtray—he didn't think about it for very long. Mostly, he wanted all the Japanese soldiers to die so he could go home. He felt that way when the unit was shipped to Okinawa to prepare for the invasion of Japan and he felt that way when the radio in the squad tent announced that a "superweapon" had been dropped on the Japanese city of Hiroshima and there was absolute, dead silence in the tent until somebody said quietly, "It's over." And it was.

Now, as the troopship was shadowed by the Golden Gate, the G.I. celebration had become the ship. Every metal plate. Every bolt. Screams, cheers, chants, whistles, there was nothing else. Then, one G.I. ran over to where the duffel bags were piled in a heap like baggy green sandbags, lifted one of the duffels, ran back to the rail and, with a cowboy whoop, sent the duffel bag spinning overboard and into the Pacific. All along the corroded gray railing, the men who saw the bag go into the ocean joined in a single voice, cheering. That's the way. It's over. Other men grabbed their duffels and tossed them over the side. From the ocean there was the sound of distant artillery fire as the duffel bags slapped onto the surface. One after another. Like they were throwing away The War. And Elkin had his duffel bag in his hands now, too, saw his name "Elkin" and his serial number stenciled in faded black on the side and that was that. He lifted the duffel bag, held it over his head and then hurled it into the foaming ocean. Gone now and sinking were his extra fatigues, his web belt, his boots, his copy of *The Great Gatsby* which had gone unread and, of course, his Japanese skull.

Afterwards, he was a little sorry the Japanese skull went into the Pacific Ocean but right now he didn't give it much more thought.

Not the skull or the Jap it had once belonged to or the dead G.I. he'd tried to pull out of a crashed B-29 whose charred arm had come off in Elkin's hands like a piece of hamburger or the Jap sniper Elkin spotted while on guard duty one night whose rifle had jammed when he had Elkin in his sights. That didn't matter. What mattered was that he was alive and in one piece and that he was home. He thought about how on Guam he had gotten the letter that said his mother had died and he was sorry she wouldn't be there when he got back. Soon, he'd be mustered out and he'd get on with his life. Elkin had been thinking about this day since that moment in The War when he realized he might actually live through it. And holy moly! It was a new world. He was here, he was back, he was ready to roll.

They were all screaming now and dancing and seeing how far they could throw the duffel bags and the troopship let loose with its horn and San Fran was right there and Elkin started doing some of his funny voices. He shouted in a broad Japanese accent to thank the "Amelicans for croming to visit us" and then shouted in an equally broad German accent that "Ja, ve vould like to zank you, alzo!" The G.I.'s around him laughed but Elkin couldn't tell whether they were laughing with him or at him or just laughing because they were still alive. He made a note to include the voices in his act.

Because now that he was still alive there was definitely going to be an act. Just like he'd dreamed.

Show business. That's the ticket! That's the next stop! That's what he'd dreamed. Radio! If he lived through The War, he was going to be on the radio. A new life. He couldn't wait to start. Jokes. *Kibitzing.* Comedy. He was alive. He was ready. He was on his way.

*　　*　　*

Max Rosenbloom, Jr. had been back home from The War for a month and already his old man had put him to work "helping by hurting" as the old man joked, creating accidents.

He was living with his parents in their Bensonhurst walk-up just like before he shipped out and that was OK, sure, but to tell the truth, he was a little sick of it. It was time to start over. Yeah, but still. He didn't have the moola to get his own place and the only work he knew was the old man's textile salvage business and killing the Japanese. He was pretty good at both.

Now it was night, on a Brooklyn street that never seemed to see morning, lined with low, darkened walk-ups and warehouses. It was a ripe place to get clobbered. Max Rosenbloom, Jr. was walking alone, heading for the docks, and because he was six-four and knew a couple of things, all he was thinking was that he had to talk the old man into giving him more to do, more responsibility and more money. He wanted to get married. Have kids. Max Rosenbloom, Jr. was thinking about how one day he would have a wife and a large house, but mostly he would have a daughter, a beautiful daughter to spoil and dote on. That's what he had dreamed about during The War. Max would sit outside with his wife and his gorgeous daughter and his old man and they'd all laugh about this and that but keep some of it pretty tight-lipped so no one got in trouble. The old man would make sure of that.

When they retook Corregidor, Max had killed one Jap with a bayonet and had had to kick the body off the blade to get it free and later that same day he'd shot a Jap officer in the face. He'd been in a tough outfit, "behind the lines" they used to say, and a lot of them didn't come back. But Max did. That's right. They had jumped out of a plane and snuck up on the Japs and killed them with Thompson submachine guns and then when things quieted down most of them would turn around and walk off and vomit from the tension and the rabid death stink. Max parachuted in weighing 230 pounds and when he walked back out of the jungle he weighed 80. They lived off the land if you could call it living.

Walking toward the docks, Max mulled over how he hadn't really been afraid in The War, he hadn't been much of anything, all he had been was hungry and bone-dead weary and sometimes sick with malaria. But now? Well, now when he started to think about it he thought he should have been afraid. He was 19 when he was on

Corregidor, he hadn't known enough to be afraid. Now, he was 20 and he wasn't so damn dumb.

There was Larry Passoff up ahead, sitting on a crate.

Larry Passoff was a 4F pencil-neck geek with a perforated eardrum so Larry Passoff didn't go to The War. The War for Larry was Bensonhurst and newspapers. He helped out Max's old man and Mr. Passoff, Larry's own father. At first, Max wondered whether that eardrum really had a hole in it or whether Larry Passoff's old man got a hole in his pocket from greasing someone's palm to keep Larry safe. After a while, though, Max didn't care.

They nodded to each other when Max got close but they didn't say anything and Larry Passoff went inside the warehouse where the door was already open but only just enough to squeeze in and Max squeezed in after him.

Larry had done his job already. Just so. Very careful. The rolls of textiles were set at one end against the wall and he'd spread and piled the trash and cuttings against the other side, the far wall. Max could make out the shapes. The warehouse was dark and the air reeked of dust from the rolls but they wouldn't be inside for very long. Larry was washing it down with kerosene and getting ready with the candles that he'd wrapped in celluloid.

They walked out and were about two blocks away when the warehouse window exploded and the fire flashed through the darkness, flickered on glass and brick, letting them know that everything was going to be OK. Without speaking, Larry Passoff went to the pay phone on the corner, dropped a nickel and called the fire department. By the time he finished calling in the fire, Max was gone.

Soon, Max would go back to the warehouse with the old man and they'd run their fingers over what was left of the textiles and smell which rolls were too charred or stained by smoke and which rolls could be resold, and they'd buy them cheap from the warehouse owner who had asked the old man to help out in the first place. Insurance money would be collected and Max would go with the old man to resell the rolls of textiles at probably 100 percent profit.

But, damn it, once that was done, Max promised himself he'd get up the guts to ask the old man for a piece of the business. The old world was gone, goddamnit. It was time to head out on his own. It was time to get married. He wanted to move out of Brooklyn and, with the help of a G.I. Loan, get a house. Get a wife. Have that little girl, that beautiful little girl. He was gonna get it up to ask the old man, goddamnit, he was.

This time, Max promised himself, he wouldn't chicken out.

1969

The End of Everything Else

CHAPTER ONE

ELKIN DROVE PAST THE HUGE BILLBOARD that read "Elkin and Fox, the 10 Funniest Guys in Town!" and thought that Fox, his partner, was a complete *schmuck* who was in the process now of destroying his, Elkin's, career.

Destroying both of them, really. The team. The billboard showed their disembodied faces, each wearing that overly wide happy face smile that Elkin snapped on any time a camera was turned his way. He wasn't smiling in the car. He was clearing his throat, humming, screaming, singing, making voices, trying to wake up. It was five a.m.

In the car with him was Dr. Huckleberry, Coach Bruce Bruise, Miss Emma Reel, Mr. Nosh, Senator Flip Denizen, Chip Chopper and all the other characters who graced the show, all funny voices courtesy of Jerry Elkin who now "gargled laughter" as he thought of it, warming up his voice as he drove into the city. It was still dark. And Ted Fox was still a schmuck.

"The team of two zany madcaps with the gift of gab that means gold" is what *Variety* called them. Since 1954, "Elkin and Fox" had been the highest rated morning radio show in the country. Actually, only Elkin was zany or a madcap—a short, bald man with glasses who was constantly watching his weight, or "constantly watching it go up" as he told *TV Radio Mirror*. Fox was the straight man. Just over six feet tall, swept-back black hair, rock solid, camera-ready features that were usually mistaken as the source of his magic touch—a face that made it easy for him to fuck every housewife on Long Island and then move on to the secretaries who hung out at the Miramar Bar across the street from the station.

But it wasn't the face. It was the voice. Even Elkin was in love with that voice. The son of a bitch didn't even need to be on radio, all he needed to do was speak and every woman in the city would have followed him naked into the desert for 40 years. He was the best straight man in the business—Elkin told that to *The NewYork Times* and he meant it. In front of the mike, they could read each other's minds. Every weekday morning they went in and ad-libbed four hours of radio and records with Ted Fox as the handsome *goyisha* straight man and Elkin as the funny-looking little fat Jew (said Elkin) and together "Elkin and Fox" brought in almost two-thirds of the station's commercial income. You laughing this morning? You're listening to "Elkin and Fox."

Said the ads.

Then, two days ago, through Elkin's manager and Ted Fox's agent, a call came in from The Coast that MGM was tossing around ideas for an Elkin and Fox movie. The handsome guy, the funny-looking little schmuck, it was perfect. Let's talk about it. A knockdown Martin and Lewis.

"I'm not a knockdown anything." Ted Fox didn't go for it. Didn't want to listen, didn't want to talk.

"What? Why? Ted, you can't keep doing this," Elkin said. "Ted, you're the handsome guy. *I'm* the funny-looking little schmuck."

It wasn't the first time. There had been offers of a TV sitcom, TV voiceovers. Two years ago there'd been talk of another movie deal. They'd talked, they'd been offered, this was only the beginning.

Except that schmuck Ted Fox. He wouldn't sign. He wanted to stay right where he was.

"Oh, tell me why, Ted Fox," Elkin said out loud in the car, talking pinched and out of the side of his mouth. "Perhaps you're just... frightened." And here he threw in a quick OOO-eeee, some horror-movie music just for a kicker.

Then Elkin answered himself in his best Ted Fox music-of-the-spheres voice, "Yes, I am, Jerry. Frightened enough to sink us both."

Elkin listened to the car radio squelch and die as he drove through the Midtown Tunnel. By the time he hit East 46th and found a parking space, he was so pissed off at Ted Fox that he was now rehearsing how to march in and go right to Studio B and before they even started the show Elkin would quit. Break up the goddamn team. See how you like that, Ted Fox.

It was Friday. End of the week. OK. Maybe he'd wait until after they finished the show and then walk. Elkin didn't want to ruin the show that would be his last with Ted Fox. They'd make their way through the four hours and then, finally, Elkin would give the team's usual sign-off, "Elkin and Fox! Let's make it morning!" and when the On Air light went dark he'd turn to Ted Fox and say, "Ted, listen. I've had it, it's over. It's been a great ride. And by the way, fuck you!"

Could they sue him for that? Not Ted Fox. The station. There was something in his contract that said he could be sued for the loss of potential commercial income if he did something like...well, something like walking in angry and quitting. Like he was about to do. Loss of potential income? You gotta be kidding. OK, but what were his rights? Why should Jerry Elkin be held prisoner by some schmuck like Ted Fox? Fox would do fine once they broke up. He was one of the most talented radio guys Elkin had ever heard. And himself, Jerry Elkin? Well, Jerry Elkin was going to get on the goddamn phone even as the words "Let's make it morning!" still hung in the air and he was going to call Marty Horowitz, his manager, and find out if there was any possible way he could get out of the contract and say "Goodbye, Ted Fox!"

Elkin took the elevator to the third floor and then the shortcut through the newsroom. Four news guys were already knocking away at their typewriters in the weird low yellow light with the syncopated tapping of the teletypes bringing word of burned babies in Vietnam, an entire family lying dead on the floor in Red Hook. A faint broadcast smell of plastic and wires and cigarettes coiled through the air. The light, the smell, the muted sounds—it always made Elkin feel like he was home. Every radio station smelled that way, every studio. One of the news guys called out, "Elko! Let's make it morning!" without looking up and Elkin did a dragged out "Gooten morgan!" in his Viennese Dr. Huckleberry voice as the sports announcer yelled, "Elko! Hey there!" Elkin did a funny trip-step, a near comic fall beside the sports announcer's desk but he said nothing. The sports announcer was a schmuck, Elkin thought, a bullshit tough guy named Steve Leo who claimed to have a steel plate in his head from his antics as a Navy frogman during The War. Yeah, sure. Charlie-fat-chance.

Ted Fox thought Steve Leo was a fake, too, and Ted Fox should know. Handsome, tall, beautiful voice, gorgeous wife, two lovely kids—who wrote the story on this guy? And Fox was also decorated during The War, a hero, still had a small piece of shrapnel in his leg from the battle for Guadalcanal. Then, on a gray afternoon last year, in the Miramar Bar across the street, Ted Fox had downed five J&Bs on the rocks and suddenly told Elkin that one night on the island, in the rain, he'd heard a sound in the jungle and opened fire and in the morning a patrol had gone out and found a dead pregnant woman in the bushes. Then Ted Fox started to cry and Elkin had had to drive him home.

So, don't say I never did anything for you. That, and dragged you out of half the upscale gin joints in town when Elizabeth called, Mrs. Fox, wondering where her wandering boy had gone after work and why he hadn't come home. Out with sponsors? Meetings? Where?

Yeah. That's what Elkin was thinking, steamed and ready to pop as he opened the double airlock doors to Studio B.

Surprised that the room was dark, he flicked on the lights and shouted, "Jesus Christ!

"Jesus!" he said again. And added, "Holy shit!"

Elkin spun around. He stepped back into the long hallway and stood there. He said, "Goddamn it" and heard the magnificent God-blessed voice of Ted Fox behind him call, "Aw, Jerry, don't be like that," which made Elkin stride off in fast, stomping steps. Back through the newsroom, banging his thigh on a gray metal desk corner, ending up finally in the little enclave where they had the refrigerator, the cups, the sugar and what Elkin called The Pot of Perpetual Coffee.

It probably wasn't the first time that Ted Fox had banged some broad in the studio, but ("Jesus Christ!" Elkin said once more as he poured a coffee) it was 5:40 in the morning and they had to start prep for the show. Five forty and there was handsome, golden-throated Ted Fox with his pants around his thighs on top of some babe on the table where the newsman sat when he came in at the top of the hour. I can't take it, Elkin told himself.

"You're not gonna believe this."

"I believe it," Elkin said.

Sgt. Al, Aldo Colavito. The longtime producer of "Elkin and Fox." Squat, barrel-chested with thick, tattooed forearms. They called him "Sgt. Al" because he'd led a rifle platoon through Europe during The War. He'd liberated Buchenwald and maybe that's why he was always saying that getting tattooed was the stupidest thing he'd ever done.

"You know Ted's got some broad in the studio?"

"Still?" Elkin said.

"She's probably gone but we gotta get in there."

"He's gotta stop," Elkin said. "I mean, I admire the man's skill but Jesus."

"I'll tell him," said Sgt. Al.

"No, I'll tell him," said Elkin.

And he was enjoying the painful burn in his hand as he took his coffee cup and headed back through the newsroom toward Studio B all bucked up to read the riot act to Ted Fox and this time when the fake tough guy sports announcer Steve Leo said, "Knock 'em dead, Elko!" Jerry Elkin stopped at Steve Leo's desk and said, "Here's a lesson for that schmuck Ted Fox and for you, too. Don't shit where you eat."

Then Elkin set down the coffee cup, touched his fingertips above his head, spun around twice on his toes and danced several graceful, comic ballet steps back toward Studio B.

＊　＊　＊

Now, as the car service took him back to the Island, Max Rosenbloom Jr. started to chuckle and the driver was chuckling, too. Partly, it was the beheading. Why that struck him as funny he didn't know, but it did. Max was going home from JFK where he'd landed this morning coming back from Haiti where he'd gone because one of his business partners had gotten his head lopped off.

Also, the driver was listening to "Elkin and Fox," who Max loved, and they were doing a Coach Bruce Bruise routine where the thick, dumb coach was trying to understand what Ted Fox was talking about when he announced a sale at Bloomingdale's.

Max had gone to Haiti to "make arrangements." Get the body back. Talk to officials in Port-au-Prince, talk to the wife. It was really too bad. Yael Gerlitz was a pretty smart cookie and definitely not a schmuck, an ex-captain in the Israeli army with a lineup of three indented machine gun holes in his belly to prove it. Max had sent Gerlitz to do a deal on a warehouse full of children's clothes that had been accidentally sprayed with some kind of defoliant and Gerlitz had said on the phone that he thought they could get the poisoned clothes for a song, then double the price in a resale to China.

"I want you to push this for me," Max Rosenbloom had said. "This is real money and we can use it."

Max Rosenbloom explained why. His daughter, the little girl he'd dreamed about having all through The War. He was going to send her to Paris. The Sorbonne. He'd figure out what he had to do to get her there and then he'd do it. His little girl, his Sari, was going to be a woman of the world, Max Rosenbloom had said, and he wanted Yael to know it.

That was the last time he'd spoken to Yael. A day later, Max got a call from a woman at the American embassy saying that Yael Gerlitz had been found near a textile warehouse with his hands roped behind him and his head cut off, probably by a machete. Police were looking into it "but, frankly, don't count on any answers," she said.

When Max called the wife, Rivka, there was a long pause before she said, "I knew this would happen," and Max was about to say, "What? That he'd get beheaded?" and he wondered why getting your head cut off would occur to anyone. But he kept his mouth shut and said, "I'm terribly sorry," and promised that he would send her that month's pay and a month extra.

On the car radio Ted Fox was trying to do the Bloomingdale's commercial but Coach Bruce Bruise kept breaking in with the weather, telling Max it was 65 degrees and sunny, which Max could see through the car window. Then, on the radio, a sound-effects door slammed and Jerry Elkin came in, trying to get the Coach out of the studio so Ted Fox could finish the commercial. Max smiled and nodded.

His mood lightened. It was just what he needed. Max Rosenbloom adjusted his legs in the back seat because now, at 45, he was a thick 6'4" and nothing seemed built to house him, with his hard, jutting gut and legs that his wife said were "like pylons," a word she got from the crossword puzzle. Still tight-muscled, though. Max Rosenbloom lit up a Kent. Also, probably because of the Scotch and the cigarettes and because he was comfortable with shouting, when Max Rosenbloom opened his mouth to speak, his voice sounded like gears grinding without oil, guttural, like his trachea had been slashed and sewn back together by some discount hack. Max liked to think he could be tough if he had to. He liked to think people were afraid of him and, well (he thought), they had good reason to be.

It was Friday. He was heading home to meet with Boris Jampolsky. This was the Russian that poor headless Yael had talked about so much. An old friend. Maybe you have a place for him, Yael had said. Well, OK, now there was. Max didn't trust easy but this Boris came highly recommended. And maybe the Haiti deal could be saved. Max had invited Boris out to the house to make things a little more comfortable since he might turn gun-shy at the prospect of doing business that could make your body end at the neck.

On the radio, a door slammed again signaling that Coach Bruce Bruise had left the room and then Elkin and Fox gave their spirited "Let's make it morning!" and the show ended and the news came on. The newsman said that the U.S. had been secretly bombing Laos and Cambodia and he quoted *The New York Times* on the story, American G.I.'s were fighting to take a place called Dong Ap Bia in Vietnam and politicians were going around and around about the hard hats who'd stormed an antiwar demonstration in lower Manhattan and beaten up high-school and college students while the police stood by watching.

That made Max Rosenbloom think about his son who was a sophomore at BU. They didn't talk anymore and the kid didn't come home. Max still sent him money. Listening to the news, Max Rosenbloom thought how he'd helped the kid out plenty, probably saved his young ass. And had Max ever gotten so much as a thanks? Don't hold your fucking breath. When the kid turned draft age, Max had advised him to give up his student deferment and take his chances with the draft lottery, betting that if he got a number that was even moderately high, coming from the neighborhood he came from, the goddamn Army wouldn't come fter him and the kid could rest easy. He'd been right. It had worked. Max Rosenbloom knew how to work it. Max knew a thing or two.

When the radio news ended, Max said, "Turn it off and pull in here."

Didn't matter, because the car service was already pulling into his driveway.

The Jaguar was parked and so was the Rolls. That meant Yvette was home, Vee Vee he called her, his wife. So was his daughter, Sari. For just a moment, staring at the cars, at his house, everything else dropped away—Port-au-Prince, the beheading, making arrangements to bring home Yael's body, secret bombings, his lousy son, a big deal maybe gone south. Max Rosenbloom was just glad to be home.

Vee Vee met him inside the foyer.

"I can't imagine," she said.

Max nodded and dropped his bag. "Don't try." Max kissed Vee Vee lightly on the cheek, listening to the shower running upstairs, up the split-level, and noticing that Vee had taken down the velvet rope that kept the living room off limits except for special occasions.

"You want something? Drink?"

"I'll wait for Boris," Max said.

Vee went to the kitchen. She still had the most amazing blue eyes he'd ever seen on a woman, blue like two holy jewels that could pierce and cut or make you go down on your knees to kiss her belly. And that was what he found so tough to take. Vee, his beautiful Yvette, blond and blue-eyed and from a top Jewish family in Philadelphia that owned a good solid serviceable furniture company, who swiveled men's heads, who understood business, who knew how Max Rosenbloom made his bones. Vee was now a size 16 and she wore it with a kind of wild, murderous hatred that was poised just below the surface.

How the hell had that happened? Why? Max always told people, "A man wants to give his woman nice things, buy her everything she wants," and her closet upstairs was crammed with dresses and outfits from Pucci and Halston and Laurent, the best around, every week she added more and more. Everything was packed together in a kind of crushing jamboree of bright reds and greens and swirling colors and violet or brown squares, amazing designs. Beautiful. Except she couldn't wear a one of them. Because they were all size eight. Like when Max had met her at Temple U. And when Max quietly asked her why she did this, why she kept clothes she couldn't wear, Vee said, "My metabolism will speed up, Dr. Corey said so, you'll see."

Max had no idea what she was talking about.

The shower was still running. Well, OK. Sari could do whatever she needed and only Sari knew what that was for sure. She was 18, getting set to graduate high school, to go off on her own, off to Paris, like Max Rosenbloom had promised, unless maybe....

Sari would have to....

Maybe Sari would never....

Sari reminded him of Vee when he'd first met Vee, except...

Except there was magic in Sari. Vee had been smart, beautiful, sexy, but Sari was from some other realm. When men looked at Sari it was like she had emerged through the invisible wall that made mystery mysterious and appeared suddenly, proving that some dreams about women actually do come true. Men didn't fall for her, they tumbled, and they didn't so much tumble as turn to smoke. They went dumb. They heard wordless promises and saw signs. One look at Sari and the bus-stop world vanished into cool, smooth flesh and perfume. Max had seen it. Even Yael. Two weeks before the man got his head lopped off, Max had listened to Yael try to explain his love, no, his fascination, no, his obsession, no, "Help me, Max," he'd said and Max Rosenbloom had grabbed him by the shoulder and said, "It's OK. You're a good man."

Max Rosenbloom no longer tried to explain it. It was true. As real as the thick, wool-pile carpet in the living room and the art collection hanging in the hallway that Max and Vee had put together scouting the auctions with Max showing Sari the ins and the outs. Whatever it was and for however long it lasted, Sari was ecstasy and Max loved it. Even though it was starting to drive Vee nuts if it hadn't already.

The doorbell. The new guy.

Boris Jampolsky came into the house like he owned it but that was OK. Max Rosenbloom didn't want some goody-two-shoes schmuck to be doing business down there around a bunch of machete-swinging idiots. Boris could've been any one of Vee's younger cousins—not tall, not short, solid handshake and underneath the Brooks Brothers suit, well, good, another young Russian yid you didn't want to mess with. Max smiled, sized him up quick. He was just the right cocktail of smart and dumb. Max liked the kid right away and went one-two-three with all the proper etiquette when he introduced Boris to Vee.

"Enchanté," Boris said in Russian-accented French and he took Vee's hand and bowed slightly.

That's when Max decided to put in the finishing touch. Knock him for a loop. Boris was his and they'd get along just fine.

"Hang on," Max said.

He tilted his head up toward the upper floor of the split-level where he could still hear the shower running.

"SARI!" Max shouted. "SARI! COME OUT! I WANT YOU TO MEET SOMEBODY!"

Voice a growl, a guttural cannonade. "SARI!"

Like when he'd yelled "GRENADE!" that time on Corregidor and hit the dirt, which was why he only had his cheeks pocked with tiny shrapnel scars instead of being dead like Chase, who'd been nearby.

"SARI!"

There was a long pause, water still running. Then a thin, echoed rhythm of shifting currents. Then a young woman's voice came from under the fall. "I'm in the shower!"

Words that were sung, a lilt from across the boundary.

"DOWN HERE!" Max screamed and grinned as Boris said quietly, "There's no need" and Vee stood silently with blue eyes icing over and Max shouted again, "SARI! GET OUT AND COME DOWN!"

They heard the water stop.

They heard the rustle of cloth.

They heard the door click open.

And then Boris was staring up at her, at the legs, at the perfect rise of her calves as the light danced around her, at the towel wrapped around Sari, at the shoulders and the curve of neck where the wet hair lay in swirls, at Sari. Her face. At Sari, because now Boris said, "My god...."

"Look at her!" Max said. "Look at her!"

Then nobody said anything.

Until Max said, "Look at her! Isn't...she...beautiful?"

CHAPTER TWO

LATER THIS SAME EVENING—the evening of Sari's shower—Jerry Elkin gave some thought, once more, to the Japanese skull. But that was later. Right now, he was thinking that his partner, Ted Fox, was a schmuck and that his own wife, Marsha, was gonna get it, too, because she kept at him, and at him and at him, all the time saying that because of Ted Fox, Elkin was flushing his career right down "ol' hungry Mr. Toilet." As Marsha said.

Elkin slammed the door when he left the house shouting that he was going out to get the evening paper if anyone wanted to come and Jake, his son, yelled back, "Wait for me!"

In the car Elkin told him, "Some women are crazy and I hope you don't marry one." Jake had heard the closed-door arguing but his parents had been arguing in whispers so he'd stopped listening.

It was Jake who made Elkin think about the Japanese skull. To pluck out each thought of his wife, Elkin began to talk about The War but nothing serious. In the Volvo, he started showing Jake how to break down the clock when the Jap Zeros came at you during a B-29 mission, how to signal that there were Japs "at three o'clock" or Raiders at "six o'clock low" or, the worst and most treacherous, when they came at you from "12 o'clock high," down at you out of the sun so you were fighting them blind.

That's when Jake said, "Didn't you once tell me you had a Japanese skull for a souvenir?"

"A Japanese skurr? Oh, boy!" Elkin said in a broad, comic Japanese accent. "Ret's not talk about it!" He tried to start a conversation about movies.

"You were bringing it home for me," Jake said. "Or, I mean, whoever was gonna be me, I guess." Too bad. Jake was sort of sorry he didn't have a Japanese skull. The kid next door, Fred, had a Nazi helmet with bloodstains inside and his friend Steve down the block had his father's OD green medic's kit with a piece of dead skin still stuck to the scalpel.

"I read something in a book," Jake said. Then he told Elkin about this book on the battle for Iwo Jima and how there was a page at the end that said if you had any Japanese skulls, taken as souvenirs, please return them to such-and-such an address for the sake of the Japanese families and the souls of the ancestors. No questions would be asked.

Elkin didn't speak for the rest of the ride to the store.

Now, Elkin was parked in front of Frederick's Soda Fountain watching Jake walk inside to get the *Daily News*. Schmuck, he said to himself. Why the hell did you have to tell him about all that for? The skull and everything. One goddamn Japanese skull and a kid's mind is on the roadside. When Jake was a little kid, Elkin worked up a dance routine for the two of them, a cane-and-top-hat number to the song "Me And My Shadow." They practiced funny voices together and Marx Brothers routines. But did Jake ever ask about that? Hell, no. He asked about skulls. Elkin was thinking that the kid, now at 18, was a damn good-looking kid, almost up there with Ted Fox, and he kept himself in shape, too, but underneath all that there was something....

Jake got back in the car. He was staring straight ahead and there was a little knowing smile on Jake's face that Elkin, not wanting to, wanted to knock off and kick.

"What's funny?" Elkin said.

Jake shook his head.

"I'm not starting the car until you tell me what's funny."

"Nothing's funny."

"Maybe I can use it on the show."

"Go," Jake said. "Drive."

Elkin was in the middle of saying something else. He was in the middle of "Come on, you don't want your old dad's ratings to slip and then we'll all be out on the street," but only got halfway through when a girl like no girl he had ever seen came walking out of Frederick's alongside a young man not much older than Jake who looked like men he had seen all too many times before.

The sentence died out. Elkin said to Jake, "Jesus, look look look!" nudging him with an elbow to see the girl. "Va-va-va-VOOM!" Elkin finished.

"Goddamn it," he said then. "That is one beautiful little chippie!" Only he said it in a Yiddish accent doing one of his most popular characters, Mr. Nosh, the supposed owner of the downstairs deli. "Boy oh boy oh boy oh boy!"

Jake wasn't looking. He crunched down low in the seat so that this astonishing girl wouldn't see him sitting in the car with his father. Sari Rosenbloom was almost out of sight, walking with a guy who was definitely not from high school and who Jake quickly convinced himself he could take if he had to. They got into a black BMW and drove off.

"Holy moly!" Elkin said. "That wasn't just beautiful, that was *whooo-wheee!*"

Jake sat up again in the seat but he kept staring dead ahead toward the cyclone fencing of the park across the street.

"Well, it's like you always tell me what's at the halfway point in a sitcom, Dad," Jake said. "Mom. Dad. We're getting married!"

"What are you talking about?"

"That girl," Jake said. "I'm going to marry her."

Elkin whistled and did Dr. Huckleberry's Viennese Freud voice: "And vhat is de nature of dis dream?"

"No joke." Jake knew who Sari was. She was legendary even if in school she never quite achieved the quality that touched her in outside life. School was just school. For kids. The Sari magic needed the light and lies and possibilities of the outside-school world.

"I just talked to her," Jake said.

"You've gone mad! You've gone nutsy!" said Dr. Huckleberry.

Elkin started the car and made the turn past the park to the road home.

"Dese dreams are gobbling up your brain!"

Jake was a good kid but there was something taking cover inside him, with its teeth bared, like whatever it was he really wanted in life wouldn't show itself, might spring out and kill everyone around for miles.

"What is it with you?" Elkin would sometimes say. "You've got to want something, want it badly, really desire something."

And Elkin would tell him about coming home from The War and what he wanted, how much he wanted it. And he got it, too, oh boy, except now Ted Fox was ruining it. Once, though, he told Jake the story of the Japanese skull. Only once. That time he was listening to himself and then he never talked about it again.

Elkin sometimes came out from hiding in his darkroom in the basement, taking a break from the one and only peace he could find, and there nearby was an out-of-breath, sweating, stinking Jake torturing himself with push-ups and sit-ups and shadowboxing and karate kicks and blasting The Rolling Stones as background music. There was something angry at the core of it. Jake, as a little boy, would come home likely as not with a bloody nose or a black eye or a split lip, which is what he was getting instead of applause as a budding smart-ass.

And Elkin would tell him, "Nobody likes a smart-ass, smart-ass! And I should know!" But Jake wouldn't explain what was what. "This isn't about somebody calling you a Jew bastard or a kike, is it?"

Elkin would sometimes say, "Cause if it is, I hope you decked him." But soon he started saying, "Stop, Jakee, stop. Stop trying to answer everything with your mitts."

Finally, he couldn't take it anymore. For three days, Elkin forced Jake to come home immediately after school and they locked themselves in the basement where Elkin taught Jake the rabbit punch, the knee in the groin, the shin kick, the throat grab, the things he'd been taught in the jungle on Guam and Okinawa. Elkin would always feel very proud of himself and strong afterwards and little Jake would go off to school as another trained Jap killer. Only he hadn't killed any Japs. And he hadn't held onto the bones, the insides, the bodies of those who'd been killed by Japs. And he hadn't been nearly killed himself. And Elkin, without wanting to and fighting against it, Elkin who during The War had touched a fear and terror in himself that was so deep, so vivid and essential that it was like growing a Fear Spine made out of Terror Vertebrae, Elkin would sometimes think of his son, Jake, and say, "He doesn't know." Exactly what it was Jake didn't know, Elkin couldn't quite say. But it made Elkin feel that when the shit hit the fan, the kid would always be "the kid."

So now, as they drove away from Frederick's Soda Fountain, Elkin began thinking about maybe having Mr. Nosh fall in love on the show tomorrow, and he was trying to think of who Mr. Nosh would go ga-ga for when he heard Jake say, "That girl back there? I got her number."

"You're in trouble now." Maybe Mr. Nosh would go after Miss Emma Reel. That would work, that would be funny.

"I'm being serious," Jake said.

"I've warned you. That's the worst way to be."

"Like I said. Mom. Dad. We're getting married!"

"There you go," Elkin said. But what he was thinking was, With that girl? That chickadee that I just saw? Yeah, *bubala*. You? Marry that girl?

As we used to say, Elkin was saying to himself…

Charlie-fat-chance.

A couple days later, Elkin was thinking about jabbing a pencil point through his ears, he was so sick and tired of hearing about The Girl. Nothing else came out of the kid's mouth. Elkin heard the kid talking to himself with daydreams sailing across his eyeballs. Elkin said, "Don't you have a life to live?" But the kid was living a life, Elkin could smell it on him—the kid's life was The Girl. What to do with her? Where to go? On this date, he wanted to be Dylan on the street with that girl on the album cover, a freewheelin' guy. Jake's phone calls to friends, which Elkin listened in on, had a little bit of lipstick to them. OK, but don't give him a lecture, Elkin told himself, not another one of those yeah-and-another-thing moments. Elkin sometimes thought the kid sounded like a pipsqueak schmuck, a little giddy babe, when he talked about The Girl. And Elkin wanted to say, "Jesus Christ, just take her out already! Anywhere!" because Elkin had seen her and he knew: If this girl's lucky numbers keep coming out right and she doesn't get pregnant, hit by a car or develop an obscene abscess or cancer, she'll never end up with the Son of Elkin. Some clown who owns his own country is gonna step in and then poor Jake can say bye-bye to the girlfriend. The whole thing was doom and tears from the get-go.

Oh, and Jake didn't miss any of this either, didn't matter if Elkin kept his trap shut. Up in the morning, eyes still dreaming, Jake already had the argument with his father going in his head. Fuck you! Schmuck! You'll see! All of it zooming right toward Elkin, the old man. And this day coming up? With this girl? This was one goddamn important day, Jake knew—don't blow it, don't blow it, don't blow it.

Real life. That's what Jake could show her. The world was in bones and pieces, a smoking pile that was aching for him to sort it all out. Some way, any way. Jake could take her to safety, he'd been on the edges. The thoughts pulsed through him as he pushed-up, sat-up, karate-punched, sweated it all out. What did his old man know? Nothing. The other world. The old world. World War Two. Making funny voices. Doing commercials, selling shit. Nothing.

OK, man, OK, baby doll, Jake said to himself. Let's go.

Jake took Sari to Gerde's Folk City in the Village. They drank rum-and-cokes and smoked cigarettes and Jake nestled into his character, a kind of 1969 hipster beat. He talked a jigsaw of Hendrix, Stones, Beatles, *Irrational Man*, Norman O. Brown, Leary, Kerouac, Burroughs, Dylan. Smoke rings were blown, cigarette smoke dragoned through his nose. The only thing was that when Sari got up to go to the toilet, she was stopped twice by men who whispered something to her that Jake couldn't hear and then the bartender leaned in close to Jake, jerked his head in the direction of Sari and said, "Hey, Pancho, are you sure you can handle that?" And while Jake tried to think of an answer somebody yelled, "Phil Ochs!" who happened to be sitting in the crowd and then the clapping started and Phil Ochs got up on the little stage and gave them all the glassy eye. He bobbed his head, did a wrist-to-mouth, and then he nodded to Sari.

"This is for that honey babe right there," Phil Ochs said. And dropped into one of his songs damning the war.

When Jake and Sari walked to the Mexican place on Thompson, Sari got the big hairy eyeball from every man who passed by, old, young, movie stars, Quasimodo, fringes, Army jackets, athletes, wheelchairs, didn't matter. In the restaurant, while Jake was eating some kind of taco or tamale (he couldn't tell) wrapped around melted cheese and drinking Corona beer, a man from another table came over and stuck his sweaty, money-grubbing businessman face in front of Jake and said, "Excuse me." Then he seemed to make Jake disappear while he turned to Sari and said, "I apologize. But you're so beautiful that I'd like to kiss you. I've never seen anyone like you. May I? Just once. On the top of the head."

Sari didn't answer and the man moved in close and planted one—a big flower-lipped, wet one—right on the top of Sari's head and then he whispered "Thank you" and left the restaurant.

Eyeballs dribbling blood, ears spinning on their stems with steam pouring out—Jake was positive that was going to happen to him and Sari would look on in horror and he wouldn't be able to stop. Throwing up wasn't out of the question, either. He was going clammy fighting the upchuck moment. Jake struggled for his 1969 hipster beat cool, hoping to get another chance and finally he settled into a smile at Sari and he spit out, "My thoughts, too."

Recover, he told himself, get a grip. A quick switch to talk about the war and Nixon followed by a sympathy shot, the real possibility of running for your life. But just as Jake began his rambling fantasy of flight to Canada and lonely exile, a guy in a ratty Army shirt and greased Apache hair stumbled into the restaurant and began shouting that everyone there was a "middle-class motherfucker! Keep feeding your faces, you fucking trash!" He yelled at the restaurant, the people, the beers and the tacos. "Keep eating while children die under your bombs!"

That took care of any other sound. And it was sort of true, Jake was set to tell Sari, made even worse by the fact that it was coming from a guy who was out of his fucking mind. Two waiters started to move in but by then the man had keeled toward the table, balanced and halted, a thin, shaggy reed poised right in front of Sari, staring down at her in an expression of genuine wonder.

Nobody talked. Not until Sari quietly said, "It's all right."

She smiled. He nodded as if he had passed into some new form of understanding. Then he walked out.

"Wow," Jake said. "Man. Can you teach me that trick?"

"There is no trick." Sari touched him on the point of the nose and went on eating.

"C'mon," Jake veered close to a whine. "Explain it."

"I can't," Sari said. "And if I did, that would make it go away."

Jake now was noticing that being with Sari was a little like what it must be like to walk down the street with God, except that Sari really existed. It went like this: You were walking along with God. You were proud. God was your friend. "My pal, God." You had outdone every person who stopped and gawked. The only thing was, standing next to God, it always made you feel like sort of a total schmuck. And maybe that's what people were really thinking: "Hey, look at that schmuck walking with God!" Because what else could you be by comparison, walking down the street with the Great One?

So Jake began to ask her about herself, trying to make Sari more earthly.

Jake wasn't the first person to try this. Like God, Sari knew how to keep it mysterious. She knew she was "a mystery woman," she said so flat out. When Sari actually gave Jake a solid answer, she said things like, she'd been accepted by Barnard but probably wouldn't go because her mother wanted her in Paris at the Sorbonne and her father was working on it. That would be very exciting, she said, because they kept having riots where people threw cobblestones at each other.

"My mother wants me to fly," Sari said.

"You mean, like a stewardess?"

Sari let him feel stupid for a moment then said, "Like a princess. Like a queen." Her mother, Sari said, was very wise, a very wise woman. Very strange, too. But she knew things.

"Just like I know things," Sari said.

She didn't go out with many boys her own age. Her mother didn't like it. The man Jake had seen at Frederick's Soda Fountain? A business partner of her father's named Boris. They had been out to dinner, Boris, Sari and Max, and afterwards Boris had asked Max if Sari could go for a drink and Max had said, "By all means." Then Max had given Boris a wide smile, like the smile he'd given when the Jap Zeros came in low strafing their position on Corregidor. So low that Max could see the Jap pilot's face as the rounds kicked at his foxhole, and Max had smiled and stood up like he didn't care if he was a target, a man of 6'4," and then Max Rosenbloom had opened up with his Thompson rat-tat-tat and goddamn it if he didn't hit that Jap son of a bitch dead-on and then Max had put on the smile again. The one that he put on now for Boris.

"I'll be waiting up for her," he'd smiled at Boris. "Not my wife."

And Boris had promised he'd be a good boy.

When Sari finished the story about her father, Jake said, "That doesn't mean he knows things."

"My father says everybody in the world is a different kind of nuts. That's the only way to understand it."

"Everyone's nuts?" Jake said. "Even you?"

Sari gave him the unblinking eye for that, then turned to look out the window of the Mexican place. This nailed a guy who was passing by, a guy decked out in an English policeman's coat and a leather cowboy hat. He stopped on the sidewalk and stared at Sari. Sari stared back at him. Then she stuck out her tongue and made a face and the man hustled away. And after that, Sari turned to Jake and burst out laughing and in the impossible promise of her eyes Jake could see that for some reason, suddenly and just for that one moment, he was being invited in on this cosmic joke-for-two and—Sweet Heaven!—a thank-you-thank-you-thank-you feeling welled up inside him. That ended all conversation for a while until Sari said, "Your father's famous."

"Well known," Jake said. "Not famous."

"My father listens."

They had already exhausted that part of the conversation about "what did your father do in The War?" so Sari shrugged, did a small shimmy of who cares with her shoulders, then leaned in close and asked Jake about his plans for the future. Dull question but Jake was sure he caught the trick. A challenge. Jake to Sari, mystery man to mystery woman.

"Not sure," Jake said. "See things."

The line hit with a clunk, Jake heard it. So he tried to blow air into the body, explaining that with the country exploding, he just wanted to be around to see what went down, see it for himself.

"See an exploding country?"

"You know what I mean, I know you do. I can see it."

That got Jake back with his 1969 hipster-beat-cool again and he dove into a ramble about "all the things that have happened." JFK dead in Dallas, Oswald, Bobby, Malcom X, King, Medgar Evers, the head of the Nazi Party, that guy in the Congo, and then the war and all the riots and all the cities burning and Jake told about how his cousin had called him from Washington D.C. after King was shot and said, "You won't believe it but there's two tanks guarding our street and you know the soda fountain we go to? Man, there's soldiers outside it, sentries, and, Jake, those guys are the same age as us," and how after the killing his mother bought new locks for all the doors and windows in the house and Elkin and Jake spent an entire day screwing them in, Elkin cursing every turn. Then Jake went down to Washington and drove through the streets where the riots had burned and the place looked like the photos of Berlin at the end of The War.

"Hey, like, man, maybe there won't be a country," Jake said. "Don't know. Maybe they'll drop The Bomb. But I'd like to drive around. See where everything's happened."

Jake couldn't gauge how he was doing but when he talked about what was going on he always got hooked in, got to sit in the lap of history, got the feeling that something was going to change, something big, *something*, but he didn't know what. He hoped whatever it was, it would mean that he didn't have to get a job.

"Not a regular job, anyway."

When he was done with this part of his conversation, Sari just nodded. Then she said, "I'm going to change my name."

She told Jake she was going to be Sari Rose-in-bloom and that her mother had promised to help her put the papers through. Jake told her that was pretty cool and said if she actually did it, he'd change his name to Jake El Kin and they could move to Spain.

He was doing just fine and dandy, Jake was certain of it. To top it off, he now announced to Sari that he was about to give her a guided tour of The World To Come.

Jake had no idea what this meant but it sounded good. First idea: He walked Sari around The Village so he could think of a second idea. Street after street. Spice and garlic, incense and cigarette smoke, the air so cool it drifted right in and broke your heart. Jake showed her Cafe Wha? and with the music pouring out on the street he did his Dylan voice singing, "And Revo-LUTION in the air!" and they walked past the Village Gate where Jake explained about Jack Kerouac and Ginsburg and Mailer and Burroughs and how Norman O. Brown could bust the roof off your head and how he once saw Jean Shepherd perform live at the Limelight.

"Shepherd's wild, man, the greatest radio performer ever," Jake said.

"What about your father?"

Jake kept walking. They didn't talk for a while. They did a little more walking and suddenly Sari caught on.

"You forgot where you parked the car, didn't you?" she said.

"I don't do things like that."

When they turned the corner to Sullivan Street, a big guy in saffron doing the beard-and-beads holy man came out of a store where they made their own shoes and said to Sari, "I saw you pass by before. Did you lose your car?"

"I know exactly where it is," Jake got the rise of the Schmuck Feeling and his voice came out like a whining cartoon mouse.

"Let me help you find it," the holy man was snorting at Sari. "You're a majestic creature."

Jake hacked, cleared his throat, then grabbed Sari by the arm and rushed her across the street.

"Are you drunk?" Sari said.

"Keep searching!" the holy man yelled after them.

"Maybe you should call the police," Sari said. "They'll find it."

Jake started to lecture her about spontaneity, chance, opening yourself to the accidents of the universe, facing your own death, Eros, Thanatos, Zen mind and Jungian (as opposed to Freudian) dream theory. This got them from Washington Square, back along Thompson and over to Bleecker. From Bleecker back to MacDougal he lectured Sari on radical uncertainty, the relativity of Truth, psychic reality and the function of the orgasm.

"There it is!" Jake said suddenly. "Right there where I left it!" Dumb luck. Jake knew he was exactly what his father called him, "One lucky little Jew who's perched on the edge of the Canyon of Fools."

On the drive home, Sari was silent. When Jake asked her if anything was wrong she said, "No, just thinking," and when he asked her what she was thinking about she said, "Oh, just the night and the world and myself." Sari opened the window and let the rushing wind catch her hair. "And maybe you." Then she tossed her hair with her face to the wind and her eyes closed and as Jake watched her, he almost put the car into the center barrier.

This was like the first time he saw her—goddamn it, she made every time like the first time he saw her! Oooooh. He loved her! But everybody loved her! He scrambled after himself: revolution, war, protest, peace, Zen, that's right, man, there's a New Day Comin'… no, no, no, he could feel himself slipping. He was becoming a Broadway show tune. Jake didn't know whether to belt out a song or commit suicide.

At the house in King's Point, Jake walked Sari to her door and they both said, "Well, good night" and Jake moved close and went to kiss her.

Sari reached out and put a hand on his cheek. But that wasn't what did it. It was the way she looked at him. Whatever force there is that drives the universe patted Jake on the head and winked at him and Jake thought his knees might buckle. Then, with Sari's hand still on his cheek, Sari said, "I want you to call me again sometime."

She went inside.

CHAPTER THREE

A PERFECT DAY: the sky was that hazy New York summer blue, the reflection of a billion panes of glass and exhaust smoke with just enough of a breeze. Perfect, Vee Vee Rosenbloom thought, a perfect day to tell Sari she was never to see that boy again.

They were having lunch in Rockefeller Center, the outdoor café. Vee always felt safe there, what with the Prometheus statue and the buildings standing guard all around up at street level, like if Max Rosenbloom had windows and if Max was made of glass and steel and stone. Also, until Sari was 15, Vee had taken her ice skating at the outdoor rink every year. (Then they switched to a mother-daughter lunch at Bendels.) So there was a shared history, a past to be wrapped in and worn, which would make it difficult for Sari to get smart and talk back.

"Mother, I think you're being ridiculous."

"Look at me, Sari. No. Don't look over there. Here. At me."

She held Sari's gaze for a moment, then Vee sat back and checked the faces of the men at each of the nearby tables, the way a duck hunter scouts the marsh. "Let's stop things before they start. I'm not saying there's anything wrong with this young man. But there's nothing right with him, either."

"He's my friend. I like him."

"Are you sleeping with him?"

"No."

Vee put her elbows on the table and drilled Sari, the showdown of blue eyes to green. "I'll ask you again."

Sari was game for it, she leaned in closer now, too. "Not yet," she said. "And it's none of your business."

Vee hadn't cottoned to this Jake from day one. Not from the first date. Too sure of how his face was put together, for a start. And now? If he wasn't over at the house in the afternoon, he was there in the evening. Or she was out somewhere with him. And Vee knew exactly what the little schmuck was thinking when he looked at Sari. And what he was thinking when he looked at Vee.

"Well," Vee breathed like she'd just heard the all-clear sound. "Well, at least there's that."

When they'd walked through the Rockefeller Center café, all male eyes had skittered after Sari like rats following a piper. Some of the eyes had not turned away, some left and returned, tossed a glance and then pulled away. Or tried to pull away.

Now, Vee Rosenbloom shopped the faces without caring that Sari was getting upset. "I have an eye," she said as she scrambled through her purse for her cigarettes, offered one to Sari and they lit up. "A woman only gets one chance in life, Sari. Your chance is about to come. You should sprout wings. You should fly."

"You've told me that."

"You don't know yet. You think you do but you haven't tasted it. There are men in the world. Men, Sari. Princes and counts and men who can make your life…."

Sari tilted back her head and spat smoke. When she did, she

saw that the two men two tables down were mesmerized by her. She caught their eyes and smiled back at them. Vee turned to see, went wild inside, then scanned back to the faces that had survived her searching sweep.

"I didn't want to bring your father into this but I'm going to."

"Daddy likes Jake. I think so, anyway."

"Daddy will do what's best for Yvette and Sari." And that's when she spotted exactly who she was after. Her gaze was a tossed net: a young man in a light Brooks Brothers suit. Vee stared at him until the gentleman caught her eye and then Vee Rosenbloom smiled. And crooked her finger at him, as in: Come here, my little man.

"Those people," Vee said. "What they have. It means nothing."

"Which people are you talking about, mother?"

"Mr. Elkin. The boy's father. He's a paid clown."

"He's famous."

"He's well known," Vee said.

"Daddy listens all the time."

"And tomorrow Mr. Elkin could be out on his *tuchus*. And Daddy would listen to someone else. Mr. Elkin has no business to pass on. Nothing of value to leave. And by the way, that little *chazer* wouldn't know what to do with it, anyway. It's done. Do you understand? In fact, it never began."

The blood was in Sari's face but Vee's timing was perfect and just as Sari's lip began to tremble and her eyes clouded over, the young man who'd received the pointed finger was standing by the table.

"You asked to see me, ma'am?"

Vee let him hover there for a moment, letting him get a good close up look. "Anyway," Vee said to Sari so that the young man could hear. "In a few months, you'll be in Paris. At the Sorbonne. Your father's almost got it done for you."

The sound of it, Paris, the Sorbonne, was like hearing ice cream make music. Sari didn't say anything.

"You'll be a princess to the world," Vee Vee Rosenbloom said.

Then she told the young man to sit, what are you just standing there for?

The young man was named Wilson Talbot and his father was a partner in Talbot, Creed and Grimes, the massive Wall Street law firm that had once enjoyed ties to the Kennedy Administration. Vee Vee told him she kept a framed photograph of the martyred president on the wall in the playroom downstairs along with a leather-bound volume of his speeches that she sometimes thumbed through. And silently she was applauding herself: Can I pick them? Or what?

"If you don't mind my saying so, I'm shocked," Wilson Talbot said. "This young lady's beauty actually gets more…."

And when he caught the tiny explosive glint in Vee's blue eyes, "When I saw the two of you sitting here I said to myself, mother and daughter or sisters? Difficult to know from across a crowded room."

"We could be sisters, "Vee said. "But I'm the mother."

Vee Vee smiled and Sari smiled, too, but Sari said to Wilson Talbot, "You don't look like you had a mother. You look like the offspring of a tennis court and a yacht." Jake would have said something like that. Tan, clipped, smells like Nixon, Jake would have said. Run for your life.

Wilson Talbot blinked a couple of times then let out a loud laugh that made every other man in the room take notice of him and where he was sitting and who he was sitting next to.

Sari gave a slight, apologetic shrug. And Wilson Talbot went into a long explanation about this year, his first year out of law school and how his father was keeping him hopping at the firm so he didn't get any big ideas about himself. Sari made her face a billboard of charmed beauty. Vee wrote out their phone number in King's Point, slid it across the café table and said to Wilson Talbot, "Give a call."

It took Wilson Talbot a moment to understand that he was being handed the heave-ho but Vee's glacial blue eyes had caught more movement in the brush. Sometimes it was good to let them fight over Sari and sometimes it was better to pick and choose. So, Vee let the other man come over. Wiry, throwing sparks, a force field that happened to be balding, this one stood beside Sari and glowed. Everyone looked up. The force field looked down and made Sari the only person in the entire city of New York and Sari knew it, she knew it like she knew the heat was on.

"I will make my acquaintance," the man said in a thick European accent. "I am Bernardo Chinita and the light that shines forth from this woman must be captured in stone."

Horns and sirens and the roll of traffic filled the silence until Vee Vee said, "I know who you are."

"Please, if I may," said Bernardo Chinita to Wilson Talbot, and Talbot gave a sudden start, then jumped up from his chair too quickly so that he stumbled. Vee grabbed him by the hand. "I meant what I said," and she shot Wilson Talbot a smile that made him feel he didn't exist and actually had never existed. Talbot started the long, lonely walk back to his own table.

Chinita sat down. He stared at Sari in a way that Sari had never been stared at before, his eye practiced, as if Beauty had released not only its secrets but its every small, intimate detail to him over and over again. Then he said, "I will give you my card. You will call me. You will come to my studio. You, too," nodding at Vee. "I want your mother as witness."

Sari could hear him sounding like Jake Elkin imitating one of the characters from Elkin and Fox and she crushed back a giggle. He was probably as old as her father. Still. She was hoping he would draw her naked. He had looked at her that way, his eyes did more than see, she knew it, not the usual stunned boy's reverie. This was no frightened leer.

"I will draw you. And from the drawing I will," his hands were like Balinese dancers as he traced a woman's shape in the air, "I will make the stone flesh, your flesh."

Chinita clapped his hands and laughed like this was a fantastic idea. He was out of the chair so quickly that Vee couldn't remember if he'd actually sat down.

"And someday you will be able to come and visit yourself. In the Louvre. The Prado. The Metropolitan." He nodded to each of them. "It has been a pleasure."

And he was gone.

Sari stubbed out her cigarette in the ashtray and Vee Vee dropped hers on the ground and gave it the sole of her shoe. Then suddenly, Vee hissed and popped. The viciousness that she sometimes thought of as her "Sari feeling" snapped its bracing and she almost bared her teeth when she said, "Do you see? Do you see what I'm telling you?"

Then Vee said, "You're leaving home, Sari. Fly. Wings. Please. Don't end up like me. It's for you...and you should...you...."

For a moment, Sari was frightened, watched her mother's eyes lose focus as she searched the faces at the outdoor café.

"I'm having an affair," Vee Vee said now.

"What? With who?"

"With Carlo Gambino," Vee said.

There was a long silence. Then Sari leaned in close. "The guy who's the head of the Mafia?"

Vee Vee Rosenbloom nodded "yes" and looked like she might cry. "It's over between you and the Elkin boy," Vee said. And Sari couldn't tell whether Vee Vee Rosenbloom was lying, was telling the truth, was putting in the boot, or was going totally out of her mind.

"She's driving me nuts over this kid," Max Rosenbloom said.

Louie's Oyster Bar and Grill in Port Washington was sometimes called "Dirty Louie's" but Max Rosenbloom didn't tell Boris anything about that, and even Max didn't know the reason why.

"Sari's not ending up with him, I know that. But for Mrs. Rosenbloom? It's like a stick in her eye."

Maybe because the floorboards were rough and the place was dark. The steaks were good, though, sizzling, the way Max liked them and the martinis were strong with the vermouth only passing a shadow over the glass. "Anyway," Max said, and he told Boris how he liked to sit by the back window here and look out at the water, the dock, remembering when his old man would take him to Sheepshead Bay in Brooklyn and tell him about life and how to nail people in business.

Then Boris Jampolsky was telling Max about his own father. Solomon Jampolsky, a Jew, decorated in the fight for Stalingrad. The battle lasted almost half a year. A million casualties, army and civilian.

Max nodded. "They're tough, the Russians." Back then, Max Rosenbloom had thought that after the Japs were beaten they'd go to war with the Russians and now he was thinking again that they would go to war with the Russians sometime soon, maybe in, oh, say, five years.

"He was made colonel," Boris said. "That's only reason I could leave. Special visa to Tel Aviv. Whole family."

"I was made a major," Max said. "Major Wicks got hit and they couldn't find anyone else who could read a map. How's your steak?"

The steak was a piece of blissful Eternity. Boris thanked Max for taking him here to this wonderful Louie's. Boris thought the Russians would probably go to war with America in three years and he was hoping that Louie's would survive the nuclear blast. Louie's and all of New York City, too. Other places. Actually, everywhere he'd seen in America. Because Boris Jampolsky wanted to stay here and to stay he needed a sponsor and a job and that's who was sitting across from him now.

But that was only part of it. There was another reason, a secret reason, that Boris hoped there would be no mushroom cloud over Louie's or New York. Boris was waiting for the right time to tell this to Max, when maybe he knew Max wouldn't get angry and Boris wouldn't find himself back in Tel Aviv driving a cab, shouting at some schmuck in traffic on Dizengoff Street. But Boris was in love with Max's daughter, Sari.

Just a drink after dinner that one time. Boris had only gone out with her that once and even that wasn't a date. But Boris, at 23, thought of himself as a man of the world, a man who had seen things, and he'd seen enough to know he'd never seen anyone like Sari Rose-in-bloom who had already told Boris she was changing her name.

Max Rosenbloom was talking and Boris Jampolsky was thinking. "...make another trip down to Haiti...."

Sari had Russian Soul. Fantastic. Nobody he'd ever met in America had Russian soul. Not only that, nobody he'd met in Russia had Russian soul, either. And in Israel, they had thrown off soul and replaced it with a kind of antic certainty that the world was crazy. But Sari. He could see it at the center of the girl, in the deep of her strange, endless green eyes. Oh, it was there, Boris could feel it, he was in love.

"...to send Sari to Paris...."

Now, I hear the girl's name even in my waking fantasies, Boris was thinking. Every morning, Boris Jampolsky awoke in his musty, one-room Coney Island apartment and he tuned his little transistor radio into Elkin and Fox, the radio funnymen, to better learn about English and America. In the car with Max Rosenbloom, too—he listened there. They both laughed together, Boris and Max. Like an American family. One day, Boris was thinking, he heard Elkin and Fox making laughs and then someone, the Sgt. Al, brought them, on air, a cream cheese bagel for breakfast. Who could believe, the funnymen ate the bagel on air and kept on talking with their mouths full of food! Did you hear such things in Moscow? No. In Tel Aviv? No. Try talking with your mouth full of food, announcing the next piece of military music.

Boris was so much in love, that now when he tuned in again to Max Rosenbloom he heard Max saying, "...that deal and I think we'll have to be a little bit like acrobats."

Boris had no idea what Max was talking about. He said, "Of course," and then asked for another vodka and told Max, "I'm sorry. Is that an American slang?"

Max downed the olive from his martini and smiled. He liked this kid. He was OK. Too bad that Yael had lost his head, but Boris had gone to Haiti to resurrect the deal on the warehouse full of poisoned children's clothing and come back without much fuss or crap. Not only that, if the deal worked, it would send Sari to the Sorbonne and save Max from getting it in the neck financially.

"What I mean is," Max said, "we'll have to watch our ass on this one. Not act like some *schmendrick* who's wet behind the ears."

Boris nodded and made himself look like he'd heard everything.

"I think the way to do it," Max said, "is to stay clear away from any import-export. Get somebody else who can handle that, maybe Larry Passoff. I'll take you over there."

The wheels were spinning. Max Rosenbloom loved this part. He loved sparring with the bidders at auction. He loved looking at the creamy paint on the canvas even if he had no idea what it meant. He didn't care, he loved it. He loved the touch of the cloth, the smell. He loved his cars. Sari. Boris watched him and thought Max Rosenbloom reminded him a little of his own father. There was something about the feel you got from both of them, like at some point in their lives, they had decided that if anyone came out of this alive it would be them. And one other thing: they didn't care if they turned out to be wrong.

"How is the well being of Sari?" Boris was watching those wonderful little boats, gently bobbing against the dock.

"Good, she's good, thanks for asking," Max Rosenbloom said. "Except for my wife and that kid. Jake. I'll send you to Larry on Friday, I'll set it up, so clear your day."

Boris turned back and nodded and Max stared into his eyes for a moment. "Larry Passoff," Max said. "I just told you."

"Please, sir, yes," said Boris. "I know."

OK. This Boris. Max was still thinking he was a good bet but there was something along the edge, he couldn't quite see it. Down in Haiti, Boris got the scoop on plenty. He did a good job on the poisoned children's clothing. Nobody on the Port-au-Prince end wanted to ship this stuff directly to China. They'd tried that, one shipment, anyway, and their contact on the other end went to prison. For a few weeks. Then he went to a big, empty field where the police put a bullet behind his ear. That might explain what happened to Yael, the machete business and all. Maybe a little, friendly warning. Or maybe not. Max couldn't tell what it was outside of a cut with a machete. But what Max Rosenbloom was thinking was that Max Rosenbloom was the one who had the balls to do it. To bring those poisoned clothes here or to Atlanta, anyway, just outside Atlanta. He'd set up a separate company, something that didn't bear the name Max Rosenbloom. So, they'd ship that stuff to some empty warehouses down south and then, under another company name, somebody else (like Larry Passoff) would ship the stuff to China. Max Rosenbloom had killed guys in China. They could go fuck themselves.

But, see, that would split it off from any connection to those schmucks in Haiti who had a hard time staying alive. Max wasn't sure what was wrong with the clothes. Yael said "sprayed with defoliant" but Boris said "treated" with some chemical that made the kid's clothes fireproof and unfortunately also caused a couple of different types of cancers. But Max Rosenbloom suspected that it really wasn't as bad as all that. No, what Max thought was that something else had actually gone wrong. Like the clothes were fine. Like somebody just didn't pay off somebody else who should have been paid off and so now there was going to be a holdup and a lot of bullshit red tape. There was some talk the government was getting curious, here and down there. But that could be handled, too. It was just another scam like everything else.

"We'll see if Larry wants in," Max Rosenbloom finished explaining. "We'll bring the stuff here and after that? I'm not involved and I don't ask."

"I'm in love with your daughter Sari," Boris blurted.

But his life was spared for now because Max Rosenbloom was above and beyond earshot, standing, looming over Boris and heading off to take a piss.

CHAPTER FOUR

AWEEK LATER, Jerry Elkin was driving past the huge billboard picture of himself and that schmuck Ted Fox at five a.m. and he was thinking that he needed to have a long talk with the kid about this girl, Sari, the one the kid kept calling his "girlfriend."

And how about that little *schvantz*, huh? How the hell did he get that chick? Elkin got a brief shot of pride in the kid and said "Well, well, well" out loud, seeing the big Ted Fox face on the billboard and deciding that there was something Ted Fox-like in the kid's whole set-up. That brought him down. Fucking guy, he thought. I gotta have a word. The kid was gonna fuck up his whole future with that babe.

Elkin did the Mr. Nosh Yiddish voice and said out loud, "A *goil* is not a job, *Yankele!*" and after that he did the funny voice of Chip Chopper and his traffic report saying, "And oh my word! A kid's life has cracked up on the LIE and I think I see ambulances!"

Then he called out, "Ted Fox! I HATE YOUR FUCKING GUTS!" and Elkin laughed wildly.

He started singing in the car. Warm up the pipes. The new Sinatra, "My Way," and by the end of it he was belting out the song in a hilarious nasal twang, a sort of Bloomingdale's New York accent.

Utter rage was now propelling both Elkin and the car to the city. For a moment, Elkin hoped his vitriol wasn't hurting him, damaging his heart. This morning, after the show, he was really gonna do it. He was gonna tell Ted Fox they were quits and then he'd head uptown and march bravely into the office of his manager, Marty Horowitz, and start putting together the necessary papers for a divorce. That was it. It's decided. No turning back. Today's the day.

Three hours later Elkin had forgotten all about quitting and he couldn't remember his son's name.

He was in love with Ted Fox and the show was on a roll.

It happened right as the rush hour was ending. They were heading for the home stretch. Elkin and Fox were working like some kind of perfect Radio Universe, like they had been born with one body (the Ted Fox body hopefully) but they had both Elkin and Fox brains. The airwaves tied the streets of the city together in a net of comic magnificence.

At one point, their producer, Sgt. Al, had to leave the studio and stand in the hall because he was laughing so hard but the hall was filling up with secretaries and time salesmen and some guys from the newsroom, even that fake tough guy sports announcer, Steve Leo. The station's general manager, Elmer Hoight, was in the hall. A live audience was blooming. Things like this happened, yes, they happened quite a bit, it was why Elkin knew Fox was the best radio man on the air and why *Time* Magazine had done a piece on them called, "Laugh 'til it Hurts."

But today? This morning? Baby, nothing would ever be the same, this kind of work was the Everest of Laughs, a new set of nerves would have to be plugged into the funny bone to make way for it.

The bits they did with live commercials, say, with Dr. Huckleberry talking about Bali Bras, went on so long that the salesmen crowded in the hallway—guys who'd sold a minute of airtime and were now getting a five-minute comedy routine for the bra company—looked to the ceiling and gave thanks. With every line the timing was exquisite. Elkin's funny voices were so dead-on perfect that he began pushing it, at one point getting Fox to do the straight man for Elkin's Coach Bruce Bruise on one mike while, on a second microphone, Elkin did Lester Flop, his comic radio-station general manager. A three-way.

And the music! They played as many cuts as they could fit in from Sinatra's new "My Way" album, not only this "My Way" song but his covers of The Beatles and Simon and Garfunkel and Jacques Brel. Because Elkin and Fox could make a record. If it was on their show, goddamn it, you had yourself a hit. And when they broke for the news and sports Vic Damone called up and begged them to play "To Make A Big Man Cry" and Elkin said, "Vic, if we can fit it in, we will," and then he listened for a moment and said, "OK, OK, stop crying, Vic," and they hung up and Ted Fox said in a fantastic baritone, "Wowee-zowee!" and they went back to work.

Then it was time to close. Elkin and Fox stepped near to the microphone and said in a single, joyous line, merging into one incredible voice of it's-a-wonderful-world, "Let's make it morning!" and the tone sounded, the news came on.

And it was over.

Ted Fox winked at Jerry Elkin and Jerry Elkin gave Ted Fox a light tap on the shoulder. The audience standing in the hallway applauded as Elkin and Fox, without another word, got ready to leave the studio.

Elkin was out there, now, beyond the sound barrier, sailing on his performance high. He was holding onto it and almost at the door when the newsroom secretary pushed her way through the clapping salesmen and the cheering news guys and the goggle-eyed admirers and said, "Jerry, you've got a call on line two."

Elkin's palms went up in a who-is-it? gesture and the secretary said, "It's a Mrs. Rosenbloom. She says it's important."

"I don't know any Mrs...." Then Elkin felt like his underwear had suddenly shrunk. When the secretary said, "She says she's Sari's mother," Elkin made a swift slashing movement, finger across the throat, and mouthed the words, "NOOOOO, I'm not here." The secretary nodded. Elkin swiveled around to Ted Fox but just as he did....

"Hello there, my liege!" Ted Fox said.

And Elkin chimed in, "My chairman, you've arrived!" in a German accent.

And Frank Sinatra said, "You two laugh monkeys are the best show in town."

Sinatra let them all gaze upon him there in the doorway of Studio B but Sinatra knew when enough was enough. "You can call from the airport," Sinatra said, and he motioned with his head for Elkin and Fox to follow.

Elkin and Fox had met Sinatra a couple of times before, hell, they'd even worked with him about five years ago during a big benefit at Madison Square Garden. But Elkin and Fox had never been in Sinatra's private jet being told they were going to Vegas for an hour or two just to "break up that Monday feeling," as Sinatra said.

It was sort of like riding in the best hotel room in the world, Elkin thought, if the six-star room had broken free and been launched into the air. Hearing the ice clink around in your Scotch glass with the ice in the glass of Frank Sinatra? Elkin's gratitude for Ted Fox was complete now. He couldn't wait to get home and tell his wife about this. But more, Elkin would get particular pleasure telling his son. Yeah, that's right. Here's for every aching, itching word you've blabbered about that little Sari girl, here's for Sari-this and Sari-that and how could anyone be like this, so beautiful, and walk the fallen planet Earth.

Yeah. Hey. I'm with Frank Sinatra. Sinatra's the greatest

singer of his generation, maybe of every generation. Terrific. Great performer. Great actor. That's right, pal. Sinatra said "come fly with me" and here I am, with one of the greatest artists of all....

...Well, Elkin thought in a sudden, intruding, silent, New York gangland accent, one of the best mobsters to ever belt a line or phrase a stanza. And Elkin abruptly started to worry that this little escapade was going to land Elkin and Fox right in front of some congressional investigating committee, where the two of them would name names and plead for mercy and afterwards be found in several rotting pieces in various dumping grounds if they were ever found at all.

For a beat, Elkin was sorry he'd come along. For every thought that crossed his mind. He would go to Vegas, be a gentleman, then tell Ted Fox they were *finito* and head back to New York. He'd talk to Jake about the girl, save him. And there was something else: why hadn't Frank Sinatra been in The War? That was the other thing. That had always irked him. He played all these tough-guy movie roles but when the shooting started? Sinatra was crooning to bobby-soxers at the Paramount. And Elkin and Fox, who didn't even know each other back then, they were on various islands in the Pacific praying to Heaven that the next Jap bomb was meant for someone besides themselves.

OK. Here's another thing. The trip obviously (and Elkin and Fox knew this all too well) meant they'd have to be working. Sure, Sinatra would fly them to Vegas for an hour or two but what did Frank expect on the way out? You got it, baby doll. Elkin and Fox were the two schmucks working the jet like a flying lounge that was packed with the toughest audience you could find, doing a routine about how station manager Lester Flop (in Elkin's voice) wanted Coach Bruce Bruise to get more game footage in the sportscasts while the coach was trying to explain that "this is radio, Mr. Flop!" and Lester was answering, "I've listened to Elkin and Fox. I know flop radio!"

And Sinatra was loving it and laughing.

Not just laughing, Elkin saw. But laughing his ass off.

"You house mouses! You slay me!" Sinatra laughed. "I'm gonna put a word in Dino's ear, Sammy, too. We gotta get you two freaks to open sometime."

And for the rest of the trip to Vegas, Jerry Elkin was more in love with Ted Fox than ever but now he was in love with Frank Sinatra, too. Not only in love but in awe of the man. Like he was sometimes in awe of Ted Fox. And Elkin knew that later he'd right himself and his vision would clear up and he'd hate himself again. But here and now, as the plane touched down in Vegas and Sinatra poured Elkin and Fox another short one, if Frank had asked Jerry Elkin to shine his shoes Elkin would have said, "I learned to do it great in the Army, Frank. Let me show you a few tricks."

Sinatra gave them each fifty bucks and set them loose in Caesars Palace. They gambled for about 15 minutes and by then the money was mostly gone. So was Sinatra. He hung with Elkin and Fox until they lost it all and then Sinatra said, "Watch your wallets, boys and boys," and told them duty called, he had to be off, he'd drop by the studio again soon. For a while, Elkin and Fox strolled around taking in the ornate fake Roman décor and the huge, round pool and the immense fake Roman façade. Then a cocktail waitress found them and passed across complimentary drinks from Mr. Sinatra. Also word that the Sinatra jet was theirs and would take them home in about an hour. She smiled. Ted Fox said to the cocktail waitress, "You're far too miraculous for this, let's run away together in Frank Sinatra's jet."

"Let me change," she said.

"And ruin perfection?" Ted Fox said.

And he disappeared with the girl.

Elkin now realized: he was dead and he'd gone to Ted Fox Heaven. Maybe one day he'd find a Jerry Elkin Heaven but not today. The whole day seemed like some kind of blessing: the fantastic mesh of the show in the morning, Sinatra, the trip to Vegas. Even being here with cocktail angels who were the property of Ted

Fox. And Elkin was thinking that if someone suddenly kicked him in the ass and told him he was dreaming and that he should stop dreaming he'd....

That's when the little wiry guy in the dark suit came up to Elkin, asked if he was Jerry Elkin and said he had a phone call. The room, the lights, the music, everything was still spinning as Jerry followed him through the casino.

"Jerry Elkin," Elkin said into the phone. He was in what seemed like a closet to the side of the reception desk and the room seemed blasted in a low, green fluorescent light.

"Mr. Elkin, this is Yvette Rosenbloom."

Elkin began humming into the phone. "That's the new Sinatra," he said. "Sorry. I got it running around in my head."

"Vee Rosenbloom," said the woman's artic voice. "Sari's mother."

"I don't..." Elkin started to say. But then he did. "Yes. My son Jake...."

"That's why you and I are going to talk."

"Has something happened? Is Jake all right?"

"Oh, you're so concerned. So, so concerned. Has something happened? No. But it's going to. As my husband would say, sure as shit."

The "sure as shit" business brought Elkin back to Las Vegas and Frank Sinatra. He got hold of himself. He didn't like this broad's tone.

"Let me ask you something. How did you track me down here?"

"I have my ways."

"I guess that explains it," Elkin said. "Listen, Mrs. Rosenbloom. This is going to have to wait until I get back. I'll have my wife call you in the morning, you can explain everything, how's that?"

"You don't have to try to impress me," Vee Rosenbloom said. "I know you're a star, my busy, busy man."

"Mrs. Rosenbloom. This is probably difficult for you to

understand. But I'm working. I'm at work."

"Sir, I just said. Don't try to impress me. I'm not impressed."

"Why can't this wait until I get back?" Elkin said.

"What I am is very, very upset about my daughter's future and we are going to sit down, sir, and we are going to nip this thing in the bud."

The click? That, he expected. She had that "I'm going to hang up on you" lilt in her voice. Elkin held the phone for a moment thinking once more that he was Jerry Elkin of Elkin and Fox and he had just gone to Las Vegas with Frank Sinatra so how could some she-wolf of Auschwitz still give him a hard time? Elkin became Mr. Nosh and said Yiddishly, "*Oy yoy yoy! Ve* got trouble!" then said to himself quietly, "Schmuck," not sure of how many people fit the bill right then. But when he came out of the little office and looked around Caesar's Palace, everything had changed and the entire room gave him the sickened feeling that some too-sugary pieces of candy were clinging to his teeth.

And where the fuck was Ted Fox?

Elkin told the blond at the desk that he was supposed to go to Frank Sinatra's jet. She asked him his name, made a call, listened, smiled widely and told Elkin, "Your car will be outside in five minutes, Mr. Elkin."

He smiled back. Then he said, "You're far too miraculous to work behind that desk. Let's run away together in Frank Sinatra's jet."

"Mr. Elkin," said the blond receptionist. "You may be the only man in Las Vegas who can't find himself a hooker."

Everything else worked better. The car was outside and he was headed for the airport right on time. "So at least that worked out right," Jerry Elkin said to himself. Slumping down in the limo seat, he made motor sounds with his mouth.

Elkin thought of telling the pilot to fly him to L.A., to Hawaii, maybe even back to Guam, because, shit, it was probably beautiful and The War was over. It was sort of beautiful then, too. Sort of. Fly me there! Elkin started to think of Guam as a strangely exotic tropic paradise, not the balls-deep-in-mud shithouse with the rain that cascaded from dark sunrise to black sunset. Which made it tough to spot the snipers.

That didn't last. Elkin could hear the sword of Yvette Rosenbloom's schmuck-like voice in his head. (Gotta talk to the kid, Elkin was thinking.) It sliced at him the entire trip back to New York. (The kid's gotta get smart.) And that schmuck Ted Fox?

He kept on snoring, asleep on Frank Sinatra's flying sofa, alone.

* * *

Sari wouldn't listen. Vee Vee Rosenbloom was thinking about that. And this Mr. Elkin wouldn't listen, either, he wouldn't even return her calls. Vee Rosenbloom didn't have to put up with that, no siree. But mostly, Vee Rosenbloom didn't have to take what was being dished out by Max.

"Fantastic! Remain exactly in that position!"

Sitting very still, upright, Sari was having one of those moments when Sari couldn't find Sari. Posed on a battered wooden chair hoping her yellow T-shirt and jeans didn't make her look too girlish, she felt it: the blood-and-bones Sari, not the dream. But that other mystery Sari was coming into focus. Bernardo Chinita was making Sari's face appear on the pages of a large sketchbook. Full portrait this time, but in drastic, loving detail. Then a full page for her nose, from this position and from that, another for her eyes, her ears, then a full portrait from a different angle. Chinita danced around her, inspecting, holding, drawing.

"You are magnificent!" Chinita said. But every now and then he would rip a page out of the book and toss it to the floor as if Sari's secrets had eluded even him, the man Vee told Sari was "the real genius artist of Spain."

Vee sat off to the side. The loft looked like battalions had rolled through and done their worst. Two stories high, unfinished wooden floors scarred with paint stains, canvases piled on top of canvases, canvases leaning against the walls, drop cloths hanging from racks of paintings, crusted paint cans set out across the floor like little colorful cities and a high window and all of it made Vee feel she was an appreciator of great things. No, she was also a maker of great things. She had made Sari whose magnificence was now being honored. Worshipped.

"To the right, just so," whispered Bernardo Chinita.

Vee Rosenbloom had been in many an artist's studio with Max when they went out to buy art. With Max, she was an appreciator of great things but she was also a bringer of great amounts of money and she always got that special twinge, knowing that this woman, this man who had painted such a wonderful piece would now cut off his or her right arm if that's what it took to get Max to just—please, please, please—open his purse.

"Now, stand, please!" said Bernardo Chinita.

Max. Well, he was a man, he couldn't see it. They had really had it out last night before going to bed because Max was missing the utter vileness of this little Jake schmuck who was after their daughter.

"She's got her head screwed on fine," Max said. "Nothing's gonna happen."

"It's already happening," Vee was angrily shifting through her closet of size eight dresses. The colors swept by like some untouchable cosmic rain. Too small, too small. "She's very young. She doesn't know."

"You think Sari doesn't know?" Max said.

"She's just a little girl. Still. In some ways."

"Sari's got the world on a string," Max said. "You ever want to find Sari, just follow the broken hearts."

"NO!" said Bernardo Chinita suddenly. Sari was standing now and Chinita was sitting on the floor with this sketchpad, looking up at her. He uncoiled to his feet with a soft "ahhh" like standing had given him tremendous satisfaction and he said, "I'm sorry. I cannot continue. Your garment. Your shirt, your pants. Take them off."

Sari turned to Vee.

"Absolutely, positively NOT," Vee said.

"Mother...."

"She will be in the Prado, Louvre, the Metropolitan," Chinita said. "The jeans and the shirt are for those looking at art. Not for the art, itself."

"She's still a child."

"Mother...."

"With apologies, then." Chinita began to gather up his ink pens, his pencils, he was putting them away as in: finished.

"Wait," Sari said. This man who was looking at her. He honored mystery, he wasn't trying to crack it open and see inside.

"When you leave my studio, Mrs., think to yourself that you have robbed not only your daughter but those who now will never experience her in stone."

Vee said nothing. Sari began to sink down into a teardrop curve, her hands at her sides. For a clock tick, maybe. Then, from beyond the horizon, from the domain that only Sari knew, she stood up straight, grabbing at the bottom of her T-shirt and suddenly lifted it over her head, the yellow disappearing into a crumble of cloth on the floor. A small bead of sweat ran down her flat, tight belly and she glared at her mother. You asked for it. You have it coming. Things are going to be different. It wasn't really a smile that followed, it was more licked lips after tasting first kill. When she began dropping her bra straps down from her shoulders, Bernardo Chinita did a "hssssss," picked up on trouble and stopped her.

"Step behind that curtain, over there, my sweet one. Some privacy. You will find hanging some bathing garments. Please. Change for me."

Sari was off, almost skipping behind the curtain.

"Much better, I'm glad you understand," Vee said to Bernardo Chinita, who made a slight motion with his hand, then gave a slighter smile and only the impression of a bow. When Vee dipped her head in answer, she was thinking how she could really strangle Max.

"You know what," Max had said last night. "She'll be going bye-bye anyway soon. To Paris. So let her date whatever high school kid she wants, it ain't gonna last."

"If you can swing Paris," Vee said.

"I'll swing it. I got a deal coming up. I'll pay whoever I gotta pay."

Sari was back now, dressed in a two-piece bathing suit that was swimming with cartoon fish in blue and green. And Bernardo Chinita grabbed his sketchpad and pens again, was studying her, circling her, saying, "That's right, now both hands out and left leg back, exactly," and Sari was following directions. Her arms went out, her long, smooth left leg went back. Chinita paused, nodded at her, and went on drawing.

Vee watched. She was hoping that Sari's body—now perfect, too perfect, enragingly perfect—would never suffer the indignities of the nameless hormone problem that made Vee fat. It probably would, Vee thought, but she hoped it wouldn't even though it would. And if not the hormones, then the someday babies who would kick out her shape and rage away her beauty. That would probably happen. She hoped it wouldn't but it would. Or the anxiety! Oh, God, how that would drive the girl to the fridge at one, two, three a.m., cursing herself. Vee hoped it wouldn't happen, though. She was hoping that Sari would take wings and fly.

And the fight with Max last night? Max had said, "The kid's father, the radio guy, he's pretty funny, you know. I like when he does that Mr. Nosh. Also the…"

"Is that something to do for a grown man?"

"He's a comedian," Max said. "What?"

Vee was bayoneting him with those bright blue eyes. "OK. So, listen. And laugh," she said. "But when the fun stops, then you've got a little schmuck with a father doing ha-ha-ha and no prospects for the future."

"Vee," Max said. "There is no future. Sari's not gonna marry him. And she knows what she's doing. She's Sari."

Vee Rosenbloom had been frustrated and angry and jealous when she'd gone to sleep last night. This morning in Bernardo Chinita's studio, all that roiled inside her, was whirling, marinating into rage and plans to set the world right. She was Vee Rosenbloom. She would find a way. The funnyman was going to wake up screaming. Max, too. And Jake? He was dust. It's only beside my Sari that this little schmuck shows any light. But now....

"Now, my sweet one," Bernardo Chinita said. "Would you do me the honor of removing your top?"

Sari looked at Vee.

"And your bottom, too," Bernardo Chinita said.

And Vee Vee Rosenbloom was thinking, Nobody knows what I can do. Don't make me mad. You and Mr. Nosh and you, too, Max Rosenbloom. And you, especially, you little Jake schmuck. I know things. And you're going to hear me out.

"You're going to be in the Louvre, Sari," Vee said now. "The Prado. Or the Metropolitan."

Sari reached behind and undid the bathing suit bra then slipped out of the bathing suit bottom. Bernardo Chinita dropped to his knees.

Letting her eyes skim along Sari's breasts and the curve of her waist and hips inside her arms and how flat her small belly was, flecked with just the lightest sunshine of down, Vee Rosenbloom pitied all of them. She was going to take this girl and hurl her against the world.

"The never-ending perfection," Bernardo Chinita was shaking his head. His face was level with Sari's pussy and Vee thought, just for a moment, that she saw Bernardo Chinita dip slightly forward and breathe in deeply. But soon he was drawing her. Every part of Sari that he hadn't seen so far. On paper, Bernardo Chinita was rushing bliss through the veins of his pen lines, tracing the image of the small sandy triangle of hair between Sari's legs and then, moving in slow motion, he was touching her on the hip, brushing his fingers down her thigh, telling Sari to turn around.

"No one can be the same after knowing you," said Bernardo Chinita. "And when the work is done, everyone will know you. And nothing will be the same."

CHAPTER FIVE

HENNY YOUNGMAN SAID HELLO. So did Jack E. Leonard and Abe Burrows. Even the sports announcer, fake tough guy Steve Leo, called out, "Hey, Elko! Stop by when you get a chance!" So, Jerry Elkin hoped his son Jake would enjoy—all right—be impressed by going to lunch at the Friars Club.

"There's a Mrs. Rosenbloom on the phone for you," the receptionist said.

"Sari's mother?" Jake said.

Elkin grunted, "Mmmm. No take call," like he was sidekick to the Lone Ranger. Jake's jacket shoulder crunched firmly in hand, Elkin shoved the kid forward to a table.

Back in the old days—he'd taken Jake here as a little kid— Milton Berle himself had walked by and pinched the kid's cheek, saying to Elkin, "There are laws in this state about what you can do with children." Everyone laughed like the line was brilliant. But usually? Going to the Friars Club was too much like work. Ted

Fox wasn't even a member. He told Elkin, "Too many Jews." Was he kidding? Who knew? And Elkin thought, Come to think of it, the food did remind him a little of being in the Catskills, another place he tried to avoid.

Still, it was a fancy former residence turned comedians' club that members called "the Monastery." So, now, when Elkin entered this faux place of worship, passing beneath the arched ceiling and faux candle lit hall, when he was seated near the photo of Bob Hope, Elkin felt he was on his own his turf, The Comic Turf. Comedy would protect Jerry Elkin. He was safe.

"A Gibson," Elkin told the waiter.

"Just a coffee," Jake said.

"Coffee?" Elkin said. "Have a drink."

"I'll have a Brandy Alexander."

"A Gibson for me," Elkin told the waiter. "And the fag drink for the kid."

The waiter laughed. Even Jake laughed. "OK, OK," Jake said. "A Gibson."

And then when they were drinking and comfortable with one another, Elkin said, "Two things. Get a haircut. And I want to talk to you about this girl."

When he got back from the trip to Vegas "with Frank," as Elkin said, Jerry Elkin had told his wife about the call from Mrs. Rosenbloom and Marsha had said, "Stay out of it."

A call like that, The Rosenbloom Call, as Jerry Elkin now thought of it, was supposed to go wife-to-wife, Marsha had said. So this Rosenbloom woman obviously knew what she was doing, a real Annie Get Your Gun, she knew how to rankle and scare. "When she phones *me*, then…." but Marsha hadn't said then *what* and that ended the conversation.

A day later, Jerry Elkin was coming in the door of his house at around 3:30 in the afternoon after having drinks to ass-kiss sponsors (along with Ted Fox) and he'd happened to run into Jake, who was leaving. Nobody planned it. It was nobody's fault. Jake opened the door. There was Jerry Elkin about to stick in his key. And Elkin picked up on it right away and did a funny mime of a guy poking around, trying to find a door that had just disappeared and then with a huge grin he'd looked up.

And then he wasn't smiling. She was standing right there. Sari. The girl. It was the closest Elkin had ever been to her.

What Marsha said to Elkin that night was, "Stay away from her."

And the next morning Marsha said to Jake, "Keep her away from your father."

So now, in the Friars Club, Jerry Elkin said to Jake, "Look. This girl. She's a princess, I can see that. But it's too much time. In fact, if you'll pardon me for asking, what else is it exactly that you're doing with your life? Besides fooling around with her."

Jake took out his cigarettes, tapped one on the table, then lit up.

"And stop smoking those goddamn things."

"Yeah. Right after I get a haircut."

"You're gonna make yourself sick," Elkin said. "You know why I stopped smoking my pipe?"

"Because you threw away the Japanese skull ashtray?"

"Because I was afraid I'd get cancer and they'd have to cut off my tongue and then I'd get on the radio and every show it would be, *heemeemdmdmemmdmd*. And then what would we do? We'd be out on the street."

There was laughter from where Abe Burrows was sitting but it was laughter at something else. Jake could still smell Elkin's sweet pipe tobacco and the way it had made him carsick as a kid and he was thinking about the Japanese skull ashtray while Elkin, the weekend photographer, was thinking that he would like to take pictures of Sari Rosenbloom naked. He was thinking that he would like to do a lot of things with her naked and that he shouldn't be thinking these things. Not about his son's girlfriend. Clam it, Elkin told himself.

"Your mother says you don't do anything but her. On the

phone. Out. What are you doing to yourself?"

Jake caught himself just before his voice bleated out like a five-year-old. Instead, he blew cigarette smoke through his nose.

"Two things," Elkin said.

"Get a haircut…."

"And did you knock this fucking girl up?"

Jake said, "Jesus, no." How could he? A paw was what he'd laid on her but that was all.

"This is your life I'm talking about."

Now there was laughter from where Henny Youngman was sitting.

"She's my girlfriend." When Jake walked around with Sari Rosenbloom, what? The whole world was his very own Friars Club, his own Elkin and Fox. He could explain that, it would be easy but it would also be what a jerk sounds like. OK, he'd try something else and…

"You're jealous," Jake said.

Elkin wanted to bust him in the teeth. "Unfortunately for you, that doesn't matter," he said. "I'm still right."

A drum roll of clanking knives and forks. The room filled up with the thick smell of scrambled eggs.

"Well, if this is what I want to do, then this is what I'm doing."

"Wait a minute, what?" Elkin said. He did a funny take, banging on his skull like the marbles were loose in his head. Sometimes, Elkin thought it would be great to get rid of Ted Fox and teach the kid how to straight-man. They'd team up. He hated talking seriously to the kid. 'Cause every time he talked seriously to the kid he caught that look in Jake's eyes that said I. Am. Going. To. Cut. Your. Fucking. Balls. Off. How's that, Dr. Freud?

Anyway, Elkin thought. Here goes.

"I'm going to tell you something," he paused for effect. "You're alone in life."

From the booth at the far corner of the room, the fake tough guy sports announcer, Steve Leo, called out, "Elko! Elk-a-reeno!

Come on over here, damn it, and bring that handsome kid."
Elkin shouted back, "You're a star, Steve Leo! A star!" And in his
Yiddish Mr. Nosh voice he went on, "but if I sit with you, darling, it's
AFTRA scale plus ten!" and then quietly, under his breath, Elkin said,
"and you're also a major schmuck, but we'll worry about that later.

"Anyway, like I was saying," Elkin said to Jake, "you're alone."

"I know I'm alone," Jake said.

"No, you don't." Elkin snapped it out too fast. Well, shit,
anyway, the kid didn't know. Elkin was sure of it. But, hey, listen,
Elkin thought. You can't tell anybody anything. Would it make
any difference at all in this kid's life, in anyone's life, if he, Jerry
Elkin, said, "When I was around your age, I was on a troopship to
the Pacific. I broke up with my girlfriend when I left. I didn't want
there to be any connections. And I tried not to make any friends
because I didn't want to lose them. Because, you know, going overseas, we all figured that The War would last forever and eventually
we'd all be killed. And that, as they say, is that."

Wouldn't mean zilch. Even now, Elkin sometimes had the
troopship feeling, like The War had sewn its own cellular system
through his heart. But if he looked back at that time and imagined
it, even Jerry Elkin couldn't believe it had really happened. Never
mind that, sometimes he couldn't believe he was Jerry Elkin of
Elkin and Fox. Maybe he was just an ugly little Jew with a potbelly
and glasses who wasn't half as funny as he thought he was.

But even so, the real question was: what did Sari Rosenbloom
look like naked? Was she the kind of woman who had those small
dimples in her….

"Everyone's alone in life," Elkin said quickly. "You've got to
look after yourself."

"You sound like you're doing one of your stupid commercials."

"No, dummy, it's just the opposite. The connection between
people? Got news for you. Ain't as deep as they say. And where it's
deeper, it doesn't matter because, well, you can't do anything to,
see, because…"

Oh, for Christ's sake! Elkin was voice-overing in his brain: Stop me, already, you little schmuck, I can't take myself anymore. The world's not a serious place or maybe it's so serious that there's no possible seriousness to explain it so, c'mon, let's just go over there and *kibitz* around with...

...Elkin suddenly nodded his head and said, "Look, over there, there's Soupy Sales," as he waved to Soupy and got a wave back.

"Wow," Jake said and he meant it. Jake had been a star at school after Elkin appeared on Soupy's show and took a pie in his face that totally fucked up a pair of glasses.

"OK. Let me put it this way," Elkin said. "Here's the real difference between men and women. Women think everything is a relationship and they have to learn to be alone. Men know everyone's alone. Sometimes they learn to have a relationship. Some of them. Sometimes, like I said. That's the difference between men and women. See? So, what I'm trying to tell you is..."

"You know what? I could live a million years and never meet anyone else like Sari."

Elkin caught Steve Leo's eye. The fake tough guy sports announcer was motioning to him, "Get over here!"

"And I don't care if it's crazy," Jake was going to choke, "it's all crazy, everything. Nothing makes sense. Not really. Not when you really look at it."

"Stop saying things are crazy when I'm saying things are crazy," Elkin said. "Jesus. It's driving me nuts."

"I want to be with her and that's that."

"OK, OK, listen," Elkin said. "Here's what I'm trying to tell you. You're acting like a fucking girl. And that little broad is leading you around by the nose."

"That doesn't make sense," Jake said. "See, that's really crazy." And he threw his napkin down on the table, jammed back his chair. "Just crazy." On his feet, Jake stomped back through the cathedral of the Friars Club trying not to cry. Behind him, Henny Youngman and Abe Borrows and Soupy Sales erupted in laughter and Jerry

Elkin shouted, "Aw, wait a minute, damn it, come back here!" but Jake was already at the faux monastery's front door.

The receptionist called out to him, "There's a Mrs. Rosenbloom on the line again for Mr. Elkin...."

But Jake was gone, through the heavy door and out into the sunshine, the street outside.

"There's a Mrs. Rosenbloom for you, Mr. Elkin!" the receptionist shoved the phone at Jerry Elkin as Elkin did a hotfoot past her and skipped out the door.

Elkin could zoom in on the back of Jake's Navy blue jacket as he went out of the Friars Club after the kid, a quick heel-and-toe down the street toward Park Avenue, passing the construction project near the corner of 55th, the one with the huge American flag hanging from the girders. That's where the trouble started.

Elkin was calling, "Aw, come on, Jake!" and one of the hard hats up on the building frame shouted "Hey, El-KIN! Yo! Let's make it morning!" Elkin stopped and looked up. The hard hat broke into a meat-faced smile and waved, then began a sing-song chant of "El-KIN! El-KIN! El-KIN!" and Elkin felt, for an instant, that he was losing his balance. He teetered back because now there was another sound, something that mingled with the hard-hat chant, the traffic rush and the horns. It was like a gigantic bellows working short-long-short-long-short-long—El-KIN! El-KIN!—and then suddenly the street was crowded with people carrying signs and chanting, "Out now! Out now! OUT NOW!" Protesters. Antiwar. Elkin, his name insanely mingled in their chanting, figured the protest was probably rushing to meet catastrophe at a larger demonstration outside the U.N.

Everything else happened too quickly. Jake was walking ahead of him. Then there was a crazy swirl of energy and color and guttural ranting around Elkin. And then construction workers seemed to be falling from the sky, parachuting, raining or jumping down from the scaffolding and the girders. And Elkin saw what was happening but the suddenness turned Jake to ice. Jake stood there. He couldn't move.

There were quick shots of what was going on. A fist crushing the flesh below someone's eye then hammering a young man and then a young woman, maybe three, four times. Hands tearing open the front of a shirt. Cloth bundled in grasping fingers. Cloth and buttons suspended in air. Someone lying on his side on the pavement choking and steel-toed boots dancing on top of him. The tin-can ring of a metal hard hat hitting the asphalt. From very close by, a woman screamed in a sound without any shape, no "ah" or "oh" or "aw." And a deep voice started shouting, chiming in, "Hey! Hey!" All of it churning, mixing with the blare of taxi horns and the sea sounds of traffic coming from Park Avenue.

Because Jake was now standing still, Elkin was able to catch up to him. And Elkin caught up just as the police arrived, three of them on horseback. Hoof beats in Manhattan, the swift other-century clip and clop bouncing off the metal and the glass. And the riot cops were swinging their long nightsticks right and left in wide arcs that came down on the heads and arms and shoulders of the kids who were protesting the war.

Jake was rooted, wide-eyed and dummy-like when Elkin grabbed him by the back of the arm and pulled him onto the sidewalk. As he hauled the kid back, a police horse passed so close to Elkin that he could see the gleam on the horse hairs and the auburn flank of the animal looked beautiful while its spinning, crazy eyes made the soul gyrate and pop. It wasn't so great, either, that the cop way up above was chopping with his long riot stick on this side and that, like he was taking off pieces of skull and bone. Elkin saw the whole world put its arms up, hands up, hunch down, bend to protect itself and fail. Elkin heard screams. Elkin saw blood. Elkin saw a young woman reel away, slamming into a car, crying, howling, holding the crushed side of her face.

On the sidewalk, Elkin rammed Jake maybe too hard against the marble façade of a building and that was the last thing he remembered for a while. Some weird energy went sparking between his ears. He stepped away from the kid now and standing near a parked car, standing right at the edge of the action, Elkin started shouting. Throat dry, he was shouting, "YOU FUCKING FASCIST BASTARDS! FUCKING PRICKS! LET THOSE KIDS ALONE!"

Jake couldn't believe it. Elkin couldn't believe it, either. Outside of himself, watching himself, sure, but not only that, Elkin was cheering himself on. "FUCKING FASCISTS!" He turned around to Jake. Who shouted, "Dad!" as Elkin shouted, "GIVE ME SOMETHING TO THROW! LOOK AT THOSE COCKSUCKERS! LOOK WHAT THEY'RE DOING TO THOSE KIDS!"

Jake yelled "Dad, come over here!" but when Jake took one step away from the side of the building, a head of tangled long brown hair poking out from a checkered logging shirt fell in front of him, went down on hands and knees as a cop tapped a quick one, nightstick to neck. And Jake didn't move anywhere after that.

"FASCISTS!" Elkin shouted. That got some attention. A construction guy in a silver hard hat and suspenders like red ski trails over his big mountain gut stepped to where Elkin was screaming. He gave Elkin the torch of his searching eyeballs and raised his heavy fists and what Jake could see was that Elkin had his own fist, too, hidden by his side, and if Jake wasn't wrong, Elkin had a set of keys sticking through the fingers, like the eye-poking tips of a weapon. The two of them squared-off for a moment, stepping right, shifting left. They were fear-smell close now, close enough to radar the rage, close enough to hit. A pretty good bared-teeth grin, that's what Elkin thought he was giving, hoping that he could still pull it off. During The War, he'd been a tough guy for about three days. After that he'd only been scared of dying.

That's when the hard hat said, "Hey! You're Jerry Elkin!" Elkin's lips stretched tight across his teeth and he wanted to look around and say, "Where? Where?" another old comic stand-by. The hard hat started doing a voice. An Elkin voice from Elkin and Fox: Coach Bruce Bruise. He was shoving it in Elkin's face. The big, dumb coach voice—stolen from Elkin—now sprayed at Elkin from a couple of inches away.

"WE GONNA MAKE A FEW YAHDS!" this fake Coach Bruise was laughing. And didn't he know what a shit-hook job he was doing? He was doing the voice badly!

That's when Jake stepped forward. Like he was riot-stupid, diving into the chaos. This might be the time, Jake was figuring, that he might have to use something that his father had taught him so long ago, one of the few lessons that he'd actually taken to heart: not how to sing, dance or time a joke, but how to kick somebody's knee out. Jake moved to Elkin's side ready to pounce forward. And the hard hat saw him. Maybe he didn't like the odds, maybe it was all the kid's push-ups. Or the sit-ups. But the hard hat bounced a look from Jake to Elkin, back and forth, and then he just turned and walked away. Jake took his father by the shoulder, pulled him back, as the riot crackled its way down the street, carried along on a current of its own rutting, mad energy.

Jake said, "Step back here, you're gonna get hurt," even though by then the riot was separating like a flock of frightened killer birds, the fighting flying off in different directions and dying out as quickly as it had started.

"Did you see what they did to those kids?" Elkin said. Jake had never seen the old man's eyes like that, behind the glint of his glasses, sorrowful, witness to some terrible future and struggling to tell about it.

"Fascists," Elkin said. "Pricks."

"Let's get the hell out of here," Jake said.

"Yeah, c'mon," Elkin said, and then he suddenly shouted down the street, "AND YOUR FUCKING COACH BRUCE BRUISE VOICE STINKS, TOO, YOU SCHMUCK!"

"Unbelievable," Elkin said.

"No, it's not," Jake said.

"Just unbelievable," Elkin said again.

Jake felt like he could believe it just fine. The action stunned him, he'd have to admit that, OK, but not the fact of it. This was the story all over. The country was coming apart at the seams. Read the paper, watch TV, look at what's going down in the street, what did his father find so fucking unbelievable about it?

"Are you hit? Are you hurt?" Elkin put his hand to the kid's chin and turned his face, ran a hand down along the kid's arm.

"I gotta ask you a favor," Jake said.

"Just remember what I told you. Look out for yourself," Elkin was checking Jake over for contusions and cuts and the kid was saying, "Yeah, yeah, I hear you," but then without warning Jake said, "Listen. I'm gonna bring Sari by the station."

Elkin stopped checking. The surprise made him use his Chip Chopper voice and do a tittering "Whoa Boy!" but then Jake said, "You know, to watch you work."

"This is just what I'm talking about, damn it, " Elkin said. "No. Don't bring her around. Jesus. Don't you listen to anything?"

Jake went on, "It's important."

Elkin was considering that this Sari-in-the-studio might not be a bad idea if he was going to take his special pictures of Sari Rosenbloom. Naked would be best but if not? Well, he'd ask her to….

"She'll get a real kick out of it," Jake said. "C'mon."

"Impress her with your own stuff," Elkin said. "The show is mine."

"Oh, great, just great," Jake said. That's when Elkin started going back over his "What I've Been Trying To Say" routine but by the time he'd finished, Jake was already crossing Park Avenue. The kid did a skip-step to miss being killed by a Checker cab and then he was standing on the center island, waiting to get as far away from Elkin as he could.

Morning. Five a.m. As his Volvo swept by the huge billboard with his picture saying that he and Ted Fox were "the 10 Funniest Guys in Town!" Elkin was chattering out loud that now he hated that schmuck Ted Fox more than ever and he hated that fucking Mrs. Rosenbloom, too, and now he was sorry that he had run across Park Avenue, chasing Jake and yelling, "All right, Christ, if it means that much to you!" Mostly, he was sorry he'd agreed to let Sari Rosenbloom come to the studio to watch Elkin and Fox do the show.

But Jake insisted. He had to bring the girl by. What Jake didn't explain to Elkin was that the ante had to be upped and big guns pulled out because some asshole artist had talked Sari Rose-in-bloom into stripping for him.

"What! I knew it!" Jake paced the kitchen digging the phone into his ear. "You're so fucking smart," Jake yelled at her, "but this little *putz* talks you out of your pants."

"He's an artist," Sari said.

"HE'S A SCHMUCK!" Jake shouted because it wasn't fair. Some middle aged, balding Spaniard knew how to get Sari naked within 20 minutes. She'd show her beautiful ass to this son of a bitch but when Jake tried to take a step beyond anything involving only mouths and fingers he either got tears or an apology or a promise of "soon" or the giggling explanation that she wanted to remain a "woman of mystery." And Jake was in love with her. And more than that. And he had told her so.

Not knowing any of this, Elkin had told Jake, "I was just pissed off 'cause of those cops, is all. Sure, I'd love you to bring her in," and all he could think about now driving past the billboard was how much he hated Ted Fox and the fact that this girl was coming in to watch them work. And what if she liked Ted Fox more than him?

He'd have to be great. Elkin, you have to be on your best behavior. You have to be careful, that's what he said to himself.

This slowed things down. His Dr. Huckleberry voice, a Viennese accent, was just the slightest bit off but then he fluffed a live commercial, hitting the word "contemporary" and fucking it up so many times that he started to snowball and Ted Fox had to drag him out of it. Also, he missed a cue coming back after the recorded spot for the musical "Hair" and when he and Ted Fox ate their breakfast bagels on the air, Elkin started to choke and

Sgt. Al had to pound him on the back while they segued to Barbra Streisand.

"You all right?" Ted Fox said during the news.

Yeah, Elkin thought. And pretty soon, you will be, too.

Now, in the studio as the show wound down to its final hour, Jerry Elkin imagined he could hear a sudden silence from outside and across the hall in the newsroom. The typewriters stopped. The tickers died away. Mayor Lindsay's recorded voice turned to syrup and fell silent. There was an odd hush in the hallway, too. A vapor of some sweet, magnificent perfume made the air alive. In the studio, a strange rainbow aura was beginning to surround the airlock door. Musical notes stretched and deepened. Elkin would swear to it. And then Jake entered Studio B—first waiting in the hall for the red On Air light to go dark—and along with him, as promised, came Sari Rosenbloom.

"Holy moly," Ted Fox whispered.

The problems began immediately after everyone was introduced.

When the mike opened after the news, Ted Fox told the audience, "We have an exquisitely miraculous visitor in the studio this morning, what is your name, dear?" and he introduced Sari Rose-in-bloom, as the young lady was careful to pronounce her name, then followed with some charming chit-chat that ended only when Elkin forced his way to the turntable and put on Mel Torme. When Mel was through they segued into the Eastern Airlines spot, but Ted Fox came out of it saying, "Come fly with me, Sari Rose-in-bloom!" and Jake threw a pen down on the table so that the four million people listening heard the clatter of plastic rattle-and-roll.

Elkin made some jokes as Chip Chopper, playing the innocent bumpkin who had never seen a girl so pretty, but it was like the hook-of-hate came out and dragged him off stage because the routine fizzled. Then they went to another commercial. Ted Fox was now fixated on Sari, who was propped on the stool nearby with her legs crossed, and Ted Fox said, "Without any stockings, it's like the sunlight is bouncing right off the smoothness of that beautiful leg and sliding right up beneath your skirt.

"Pardon me, I apologize, that's so crass," Ted Fox said quickly. "And yet so true. See what you're doing to me?"

Jake stomped off into the hall to catch his breath.

That's the way it went until the end. Right before sign-off, Ted Fox handed Sari Rose-in-bloom a piece of copy, saying "Sari, why don't you join me in reading this delicious Russian Tea Room spot, since you're so busy raising my hackles and my caviar," and Elkin grabbed the paper from the girl and as Mr. Nosh began intoning, "*Luz* me have a look, *dahlink*! Since *dey'll* probably *drop us* as a sponsor next *veek*."

Sari Rose-in-bloom laughed. Ted Fox slipped a hand into his shirt and made it look like his heart was pumping big and fast.

Finally, when Ted Fox and Jerry Elkin leaned in for the sign-off, "Let's make it morning!" Elkin belted out his own name but Ted Fox roared in with a gleeful, "Ted Fox and Sari Rose-in-bloom! Let's make it morning!" and he gleamed as Sari's smile went wide.

And why not, Jake was thinking. She was smiling like a woman who was the central naked model for some blowhard sculptor. And now smiling wider as the lynchpin for the zaniest radio comedy team in the entire U.S. of A. The whole thing was a mess. He should never have brought her in.

Elkin caught it, too. This had to stop. She was the kid's girlfriend and hopefully the soon-to-be subject of Elkin's own widely acclaimed photography show, "The Most Beautiful Woman I've Ever Seen Naked." Elkin watched the unbearably handsome Ted Fox making goo-goo eyes at this little broad and he said...

"A couple more shows like that and we'll be lucky to be working in Fresno."

"Oh, not true, my liege," Ted Fox said. "Ask this lovely young thing. You'll drop in again, won't you?" he said to Sari Rose-in-bloom.

When Jake and Sari took the train back out to the Island, Jake sat silently listening to Sari talk about how funny his father was, how talented, you must be so proud, and that Ted Fox is a really handsome man. What an incredible voice! She was laughing as she told him all about Ted Fox.

And what about Ted Fox? Jake was asking her. Because in that one quiet minute when Jake hit the hall, Ted Fox had finagled with Sari long enough to give Sari his "special" phone number and then he'd invited her to dinner two weeks from today.

"Oh, Jesus fucking Christ!" Jake said, then tried to keep his voice below the metallic bump-and-grind of the L.I.-double-R. "Does my father know about this?"

"Maybe I told Mr. Fox I had a boyfriend and I couldn't go," Sari said.

And Ted Fox, after watching Sari's skirt sway back and forth as she left the studio and thinking about where that lucky beam of sunlight had bounced, Ted Fox was in love with his partner Jerry Elkin, in love with the kid he'd known since the kid had learned to walk, and now he was in love with Sari Rose-in-bloom, like it or not.

Ted Fox was gonna give Sari Rose-in-bloom a call. Or maybe, one day, he'd go over to see Jerry. And afterwards for this Sari, well, he'd just drop by to pay a visit.

Elkin didn't calm down until he turned into his own driveway. He cursed that schmuck Ted Fox all the way home on the crowded anonymous ribbon of the LIE, then swerving off on Exit 33 he began cursing Jake from the exit to where the big shopping center was splayed out and finally, by the time he hit the hill at the top of his own block, he had lapsed into a sneering Sari-Rose-in-bloom voice, a soft, raspy, female whine of, "*Oh, Mr. Fox you're just so funny, Oh Mr. Fox, Oh, oh, oh!*"

But the driveway made it all better. Just resurfaced, the paving was smooth and dark and perfect without so much as a leaf or a loose stone. He threw the car into park and killed the engine. This is my driveway, Elkin thought. The house itself had an unassuming comfort to it, nothing ostentatious, that wasn't Jerry Elkin. Low, colonial, you wouldn't take it to be the home of one half of Elkin and Fox. It was the home of a man who did OK for himself, sure, who worked for a living, who'd survived The War and had a couple of good breaks. This is my home, Elkin thought.

When he came in the front door, he took off his jacket and went upstairs to his bedroom and said hello to his wife, Marsha, and knew that he was glad to see her. This is my wife, Elkin thought.

"We're having dinner with the Rosenblooms on Saturday," Marsha said.

"WHAT? Nooooooooo!" Elkin threw himself on the bed, kicking his feet and banging his fists in what he hoped would be a comic but true expression of his feelings.

"And this happened how?" Elkin cried.

So, Marsha began to tell him. This Vee Rosenbloom was a master of the twist. One moment Marsha was determined to meet this Rosenbloom woman only in Hell, and the next moment she was taking down the Rosenbloom address and marking the dinner in her date book.

"This can't be happening," Elkin answered.

"You know why it's happening, Jerry?" Marsha said. "I'll tell you why it's happening, Jerry. Because, Jerry, she heard the girl on the radio. She heard Sari on your show."

CHAPTER SIX

"H E'S COMING OVER THE HOUSE," Max Rosenbloom was saying about Jerry Elkin. "And we're gonna have a lousy time."

"Jerry Elkin's coming over?" Larry Passoff said. "The radio guy?"

"Like I said. His kid keeps sniffing around Sari," then Max Rosenbloom was telling the whole story to pencil neck Larry Passoff, the 4F from the old neighborhood. How Vee was throwing this party as a trap. A way to give the Elkins a good shot in the *kishkes*. A party so that Jerry Elkin and Elkins for the next several generations to come would never want to mingle with the Rosenblooms again. Max thought it was a terrible idea and he said so, too, which meant that the only thing accomplished so far was to make Vee blow her stack and get angrier than fuck.

"That Vee, if you don't mind my saying so, is some piece of work," Larry Passoff said.

"She's calling this Elkin kid her boyfriend."

"Who is this boyfriend?" very suddenly from Boris Jampolsky.

"Won't last," Max said.

The three of them were in Reuben's Restaurant trying to get a waiter to know they were alive and sitting there. The place was packed. Who can hear anything in here? Larry Passoff yelled and Max didn't tell him that was just the reason he'd suggested Reuben's. Also he liked the corned beef with chopped liver and onion but not so much the classic Reuben sandwich because the sauerkraut sometimes made the bread soggy.

"What?" Larry Passoff said. "I can't hear you, f'chrissake."

In the service, during The War, a guy like Larry Passoff would've been called worse than a pencil neck. He was too thin and his teeth were too big. No sense of class. The ears and the nose bristled with a froth of graying black hairs, his shirts were cheap, he always missed a couple places shaving and he always seemed gas-pain cranky.

"You know, this place, either here or when they were in another location," Max said, "this's where Arnold Rothstein talked about fixing the 1919 World Series."

"You're not going to fix the World Series!" Larry shouted. "Forget it, OK?"

"Not me! Arnold Rothstein!" Max yelled. "My old man told me!"

Larry looked around for a waiter and said "Jesus" under his breath.

Boris was sitting next to Max and they were across from Larry. "More quiet place would be better."

The waiter showed up. A little old guy in a uniform that made him look like a skinny jockey who'd lost his horse. He tossed down silverware so that it clattered on the table.

"Let's have it," the waiter said, pen hovering over the order pad like it was poised for spear fishing.

"A corned beef…" Max started to say and the waiter said, "C'mon, c'mon, maybe I should come back next week when you've decided."

Max smiled. "I'll give you the order now, you'll probably bring it next week."

"You'll get it when I give it," the waiter said. "OK. You. Pencil neck. Go."

Matzoh ball soup was ordered, corned beef, Boris asked for the Reuben and the waiter said, "A classic for the Russian spy, good, go on," and soon they were wiping their mouths clean of mustard and dressing and drinking seltzer so they wouldn't explode. With the pickles, for some reason, maybe it was the salt, Max noticed the noise in the room getting worse, louder, and with his mouth full of rye he said to Larry, "Here's the deal."

There was the good chance that Larry could hear him and the near guarantee that nobody else would get a word they were saying. Max always liked to outline these kinds of deals in a public place where he was just another guy bolting down lunch. He started laying out the details. How Max would bring the poisoned children's clothes into the country and how a new company would then be set up so no one would know that this was the same batch. Then Larry Passoff— only if he wanted to, of course—would buy the clothes and then do what he wanted to do with them. Like maybe sell them overseas.

"Which laws have we broken so far?" Larry said.

Larry Passoff was slurping his matzo ball soup as if this was a major part of listening carefully. Max was watching the little swirls of chicken fat catch light on the surface.

"See, the idea is, we each just carry a little piece of this deal," Max said. "If we split it up smart, no one's the wiser."

Larry Passoff grimaced. "Hey. This is important to me," Max Rosenbloom said. "Larry. It's for my little girl."

Max talked about sending Sari to Paris. He laid out the whole idea again. When he saw Larry wagging his head a little, not really taken with the whole plan, he told Larry that he, Max, would make it even easier. Max Rosenbloom would have Boris rent another office in yet another company name and maybe Larry could then use said office without using his own name or company and he could do what he wanted, just don't tell Max that he'd sold the stuff to Europe or Asia which is what he should do. Then they talked about the money and who would get how much.

"Everything's gonna work," Max said. "Larry, how long have you known me?"

"Yeah, yeah, yeah," Larry said. "I know you."

"So?"

"So nothing. So I'll think about it."

"Think, what's to think? What's to fucking think?" Max said.

"People aren't so stupid as they used to be, Maxie," Larry Passoff used the name from the old neighborhood just to give Max a shot.

"What's that supposed to mean?"

"Like I said. Let me roll it around for a day or so."

Max picked up the tab. Outside on Madison Avenue they all shook hands. Larry Passoff promised he'd get back to Max tomorrow, next day at the latest, and he started walking off south, downtown, turning his pencil-neck body around the corner on 37th Street. Max and Boris watched him go and Boris was thinking that he loved America and these ways of doing American business when Max said, "Go after that piece of shit and tell me what he does. I want to know everything."

Boris took off a smart distance behind Larry Passoff. He was thinking that when Max Rosenbloom was in a better mood, he'd ask again about Sari's boyfriend. But carefully. With Max, you always had to be careful.

★   ★   ★

During The War, on Guam (Elkin was telling them in the car), it once rained for six months straight, or that was his recollection, anyway. The jungle crushed them with dripping trees and muck that bubbled, the jungle handed them snakes and spiders the size of your crawling hand and rats as big and hairy as dogs which came running in packs, scrambling through the leaking squad tents, across the boards and under the cots. Inside, the men went after them with machetes.

"That's the way I feel about this cocktail party," Elkin said.

"It'll just be the Rosenblooms and us," Marsha said. "And Jake and Sari. They just want to talk."

Elkin said that during The War, there were 12,000 Japanese still on the island when he landed and the Army was calling it a mop-up operation.

"That's this cocktail party," Elkin said.

He drove the Volvo in silence the rest of the way with Marsha propped stiffly beside him and Jake lounging in the back blowing smoke out the window.

"Look at these houses," Elkin said.

"Don't start," Marsha said.

"See our house says, 'The talented Jerry Elkin of Elkin and Fox lives here but he's not showing off so don't get mad.' But look at these…."

Driving toward the Rosenblooms' place? The houses began piling upward like chips in a winning game. Cruising along the winding suburban roads, among the evergreens and dogwoods, the car was soon passing the great white columns of Civil War style mansions or sprawling ranch houses or the very contemporary angles of glass and steel set back on wide lawns where every blade of grass looked individually clipped. These homes announced themselves.

"These homes," Elkin said. "They're telling us, We make more money than Jerry Elkin and Jerry Elkin can't even begin to figure out how we do it."

"We won't stay long," Marsha said.

Elkin was good and steamed by the time they got to Sari's street. When they pulled up to the curb, Elkin twisted the key to turn off the engine and surveyed the Rosenbloom driveway. He said to Jake in the back, "Does Max Rosenbloom have five cars?"

"The Jag and the Rolls," Jake said. "That's all."

"There's five, no, six cars here," Elkin said. "What's going on?"

And when they were all out of the car and in the street, Elkin said, "I'm doing this for you, Jake. So, *Yankele*, you owe me one."

A doorbell was rung on a white front door with a big brass knocker and a small round window. "Listen to that," Elkin said. "It's like a funeral bell tolling for a wasted evening." Muffled laughter pushed through from inside the house. Elkin looked down at his feet and said to himself that these feet could simply spin around and run away but that wisdom passed and then he said to himself, as he had in The War, "This is where I am, it's real and I'm going to make it through." He felt this way working with Ted Fox sometimes but only when the show was going into the toilet.

"When they open this door," Elkin said, "it'll be like lifting the lid on a giant coffin. We'll see dancing death and destruction or maybe just boredom and the march to oblivion."

The door opened. Elkin stopped studying his shoes and looked up. There in front of him was the woman this shindig was all about. There inside an actual house (not a cloud castle or a secret forest hideaway). There was Sari Rose-in-bloom. Elkin began to say something funny but the words refused to leave his brain. And Elkin thought that somehow this Sari Rose-in-bloom, just by being there, was making it seem, suddenly—just standing there—that every impossible good thing about living on Earth was actually true. He'd been a fool to doubt it.

That lasted until Elkin stepped inside. This was no shock to Jake, an experienced Rosenbloomer. Jake knew what was going to happen. Elkin was swept into a room that was a Las Vegas floor show designed by the King of France. A yellow-tinged carpet seemed to come up to his knees, and Elkin was staring at a gold-framed oil painting of a bald man in wire spectacles that had eternal-flame lights set on either side on the mantel below. Antique furniture from a hundred different periods picked up the light with perfect surfaces. Far off in the dining room, there was a crystal chandelier so grand it might have been brought up from the Titanic. But what surprised Elkin was Sari Rose-in-bloom. She stepped back, too, inside her home, and when she did, whatever aura there was about her, whatever special brightness surrounded her or pulsed inside, or drew men on, vanished. Maybe the room stole it from her. She was a good-looking girl, but that was all.

"Ah, so the show can finally begin!"

That voice! Elkin jumped the way he'd jumped at every loud sound when he'd come back from The War. Vee Rosenbloom. Sari's mother. Who now said, "Jerry, it's so good of you to stop by and bring laughter," and she took both of his hands in hers and gave him the blue-eyed diamonds of hate. Marsha thought Vee was coloring her hair badly and that the dress she was wearing with its size and its impossible collection of colors made her look like a continent populated by cartoonists.

"My father," Vee said, pointing out the painting with the eternal lights.

Elkin nodded to the painting. "Please to make your acquaintance, my liege," and Vee turned away so Elkin wouldn't catch the diving hawks that came screaming from her features with that remark.

"I think we got off on the wrong foot," Vee was saying.

"Which foot was that?" Marsha said.

"Do you have any daughters, Mrs. Elkin?" Vee Rosenbloom said. "I promise you. It's no hayride."

"Are the kids getting married?"

"No, no, no, no, no, no, no," Vee said. "Like I told you. As long as the kids have grown so close, we parents should get together, just to see if we can get along and be social." Her voice sounded like you could bake cakes on it. "And Jerry was so kind to allow Sari to visit the studio. So why should only our daughter have the pleasure of meeting that talented Mr. Elkin of Elkin and Fox?"

"Jerry! Jerry Elkin!" This came from near the dining room table, toward the back of the room. Elkin waved back but who was he waving to? A small crowd gathered but they were a blur of shirts and blouses and cleavage and spectacles. Somebody's hair grease gleamed but Elkin couldn't find the source. "You're my favorite,

I listen every morning!" Another voice, this one like the crush of an oncoming tank. Max Rosenbloom. Elkin felt himself sinking. He was getting smaller. Max Rosenbloom now appeared out of nowhere at Elkin's side. Gargled glass and spent shells were in the rumble of Max Rosenbloom's words.

"How's this sound?" Max Rosenbloom started doing the voice of Mr. Nosh, the Yiddish deli man, but it came out a spent balloon version of the character, Mr. Nosh sounding like he might choke on his own pastrami.

"Great, Max, great," Elkin said. And again Elkin thought, That voice! Elkin was gazing way, way up into Max Rosenbloom's face. The shrapnel pockmarks and the deep brown eyes that were always looking for how to bull their way to anything they wanted. And this Max was shaking Elkin's hand in a grip that was light to the touch, a grip that told Elkin's fingers this Max had to be very careful not to shatter any bones.

"Come on over here," Max Rosenbloom said. "There's some people you should meet."

Guided by the Max Rosenbloom hand that could have been a giant mushroom, Elkin was moved through the Rosenbloom zone in a daze. He caught a fading glimpse of Sari kissing Jake hello and then saw the two of them disappear. Seven or eight or ten other people seemed to gather around for the tragedy, two other couples, maybe four, probably around Elkin's age…and there was an older man. Elkin was losing his grip. He felt their heat when he shook their hands, registered the condition of their teeth, for some reason, but the names? No, he absolutely, positively could not remember them, fuck them and the horse they rode in on. And where was Jake? Why had Jake forsaken him?

Then, while staring down the cleavage of somebody else's wife, Elkin was told that Sari and Jake had gone downstairs to the playroom, as Max called it. He wondered if Jake was fucking that incredible girl, the center of the Jerry Elkin photography show, while all the so-called adults were up in the living room flapping their jaws and laughing and keeping him off balance—him, Jerry Elkin.

He caught himself. He was Jerry Elkin. He wished Ted Fox would appear right there beside him, that was the way it oughta be. When he was mobbed with Ted Fox around, there was no problem. Then, Jerry Elkin felt like he was Kong batting away flies. But there was no Ted Fox around now, so Elkin snapped his fingers down by his sides a couple of times to bring himself back to reality, make himself Jerry Elkin again, and soon he was tossing off lines, making inane comments to the wives, acting like Max and Vee Vee Rosenbloom were lucky to have, in their very living room, the greatest guy in the world.

"Thank you for asking," said a guy who took Elkin by the arm. "Those little staples in the matchbooks? I manufacture them," which he must have fit in between tennis and sunbathing, this *chazer* was so fit.

"A noble pursuit," Elkin smiled.

For just a twitch, the tennis guy's grip tightened. Then he said, "You're making fun. Which is your gift. But Jerry. Do you know how many matchbooks there are in the world?"

The tide came in. Others crowded around him. They asked him what time he got up in the morning and how he could do all those voices and how he thought up his routines and what's Ted Fox really like and would he do Mr. Nosh right now, just a few lines, and was he as funny at home as he was on the air? Elkin threw off his chiseled answers, he saw the questions coming before they were asked, but when he heard Vee Rosenbloom tell her friends, "Oh, I just never said anything to anyone, I don't like to brag, but Jerry and us, well…we're very close, the kids are very close," he wanted the entire room to disappear in fire. Then he heard Max say to him, "You're in my car every morning, hey! Come on over here, I got a couple of ideas for you."

"But then I'd have to pay you," Elkin laughed and he went back to speaking with a little man who was built like a flesh light bulb, a guy with a grinning mouth, liquid lips and skin that had been spotted by the sun. Elkin thought the guy's name was Stu Edelstein but he wasn't sure and so he avoided using it. But this possible Stu Edelstein was a fucking billionaire. And he'd made his money by figuring out that if you put little cellophane sheets between slices of American cheese, then a lot, and I mean a lot of people would rush cheese-ward to the store with money in their hands.

Elkin was about to insult him but then Vee Rosenbloom called from someplace close in the room, saying, "C'mon, Jerry, I want you to meet somebody. This is a funny man. He can help you."

Elkin called back to her, "Can't take any more funny on my show, the walls will burst," and he went back to speaking with an overweight, attractive woman with a Jackie Kennedy hairdo who wanted to fetch Elkin another drink. And when Elkin laughed, "No, thanks, please, you'll drink me under the table," she got up close to him and whispered, "And what would I do with you there?"

Marsha tried pulling him away. "There's a back entrance, we can run," she was saying quietly. But it didn't work. They swelled around him. Welled up and poured across him. Elkin tried to back away but there was no room to move. And somewhere he understood that this Vee Rosenbloom knew the secrets of how to hurt. She knew that if she threw Elkin overboard, like a Japanese skull, that he would land in the ocean of his audience and they would be real. Not just "out there," unseen anymore. Elkin, too. He would no longer fly invisibly through the airwaves into their imaginings. He'd have a body. He'd have to buy shoes and deodorant. He'd be talking about when he went to bed and when he got up. He would dissolve.

Then right in his ear Elkin heard a shouted, joyous, "Hey, Mr. Comedian, you're a comedian? OK. Say something funny."

Everything went dead. A vicious quiet. Elkin turned. Beside him was Max Rosenbloom. Vee Vee was right beside him, egging him on, giving Max a couple of quick secret knocks with her elbow.

"What's your name again?" Elkin laughed.

"I told you, but I'll tell you again," Max smiled. "That's my Rolls and my Jag parked outside. This is my house."

"Say something funny, go ahead," Vee wasn't laughing. She had her hand on Elkin's herringbone shoulder. "Oh, come on, is it asking the world?"

"Is it?" said the possible Stu Edelstein. "Would it cost you an arm and a leg?"

Elkin jerked his arm in a spasmodic "I'd like to say yes, it would" movement and the martini he'd been drinking suffered a storm at sea. "Jesus," he said, now trying to step on and leather-sole a dash of spilled vodka into the thick yellow carpet. Vee Rosenbloom watched him with an expression that had last been seen on the men who captured Eichmann.

"I'll get the maid to get a sponge," Vee said softly.

"Jerry!" the matchbook man was calling to him. "Do Coach Bruce Bruise! Do Mr. Nosh! Do Chip Chopper! One Chip Chopper for chrissake!"

"C'mon, Mr. Funnyman," Max Rosenbloom said. "Do it. Say something funny."

"Why won't you be funny for us, Jerry?" Vee Rosenbloom said.

"I thought we were here to talk about the kids," Elkin said.

"Don't you want to be funny?" Vee said. "Let the kids be the kids. We'll have our laughter."

"Wait a minute, wait," Elkin said. He held up his hand and put his martini glass on the sheen of a brown wood surface nearby. "Let me ask you…"

"Not there! What the hell's wrong with you?" Max Rosenbloom said, sweeping the martini glass away. "That's from eighteenth-century France, f'chrissake." His thick fingers wiped away the wet circle, rubbed at the wood to make it feel better.

"The guy who owned it last probably got his head cut off," Elkin said.

"That's not funny," Max Rosenbloom said. "You don't know."

"I tried," Elkin said. "You told me to be funny."

"Jerry!" said a barrel chest with a bright red polo shirt. "Say something else!"

Max Rosenbloom left the living room in a walk that Elkin thought might make the room rattle. When he was gone, the red polo shirt guy started an unbroken jabbering with Elkin, but Elkin had stopped listening after he heard the phrase, "Ben E. Fahr, the Underwear Tsar."

Then Max Rosenbloom appeared again, pushing a fresh martini glass in Elkin's direction and Elkin wanted to thank Ted Fox for the workouts in how to keep up with drinkers. He made a little motion with the glass, a salute, being very careful not to let things get out of control. He sipped.

"We're your listeners," Max Rosenbloom said. "So what we're asking is, to listen."

"Max, please," Elkin said. "Let me ask you: what do you do for work?"

"I'm a textile jobber," Max said. "Salvage."

"Well, see, what I'm saying is," Elkin said, "being funny is what I do for a living. It's my work. So what you're asking me to do, at your fabulous party on a Friday evening, is work."

Max blinked at him.

"I'm not asking you to work," Elkin said. "I didn't come over and say, 'Hey, Max! Job me some textiles!' Did I? 'Salvage me some textiles, Max!' No."

Max Rosenbloom went still and solid as the New Jersey Palisades and Elkin couldn't help staring at him. Raising his eyebrows, Elkin twisted his head around to give Max the same cartoon-broad clown smile that you could see up there on the "10 Funniest Guys" billboard. The comic face went off like a grenade in the room and there were shouts of "There it is! Jerry Elkin!" from the other guests. And finally, Max Rosenbloom smiled.

"See," he said. "You *are* a funny guy. You shouldn't be embarrassed by it."

"We should all sit down at the table," Vee Rosenbloom said. Elkin caught a shot of Marsha speaking to the Jackie Kennedy hair, and making motions with her eyes as in, "Let's go."

"Oh, this is so embarrassing," Marsha said then, "but I didn't realize this was a dinner engagement. I thought Vee said 'cocktails.'"

Vee turned her face slowly to stare up at Max Rosenbloom.

"We have to go," Marsha said. "We made other plans. A rain check, if you've got one. Next time at our place."

That pinpoint explosion went off again in Vee's arctic eyes. Elkin caught it. He knew for certain that his wife had hit the wire on something she shouldn't have been fooling with but just then he wasn't sure what.

Vee Vee started nudging Max and Max Rosenbloom was taking the cues so now he was allowing himself to tower forward. Elkin could have sworn he'd heard Vee say, "He's making fools of us, Max," but maybe it was only happening between his own ears.

"Not staying? For dinner?" Max said. "You know, we had a guy like you in my outfit during The War."

"Probably transferred in from the Schnorrer's Brigade," Elkin said.

"No, he got killed jumping out of a plane."

"I'll make a deal with you," Elkin said. "You don't tell me your war stories and I won't tell you mine."

"Mr. Rosenbloom had a very tough war," Vee Vee said. She turned to Max and went on, "He's making you look like a schmuck."

The woman who wanted to get under the table with Elkin came over and said, "Oh, Vee, leave him alone. He's a busy man. He dropped by. He was funny. What else do you want?"

"I want to know what his son's intentions are with my daughter and I want to know what prospects that boy could possibly have for the future."

"Where's Jake?" Elkin said.

Vee sideswiped Max Rosenbloom with her elbow again. "Max, please," she said. "He's embarrassing me."

"You're kidding, aren't you?" This was Max. "Stay. Eat."

"At least let Jake have something," Vee said. And to Max, quietly, "He's making me cry, Max. Look at me. Look at the tears."

Elkin backed away. He heard himself lie again and now Marsha revved up her little scene and began lying about how it was all her fault, she should have said something about dinner. Various noises of disappointment symphonized in the room, voices that said, "Make him stay, Max," and "You promised dinner with Jerry Elkin" and Vee's notes cutting through all of it, "See, Max, I told you."

Then it faded. Elkin headed for the little stairs that led down to the "playroom." Behind him, what he heard loudly was the in-shape tennis buff saying, "Well, Max, he certainly gave it to you up the *patoot!*"

Elkin stepped gingerly downstairs thinking he'd been ambushed by these fuckers, all of them, the Textile King and the Underwear Tsar and the Cheese Cellophaner. And that Vee Vee! My God! This Max Rosenbloom survived the war for that? Elkin was gonna save Jake, get the hell out of there, then he'd spring for a terrific meal at North Shore Grill or maybe they'd drive into town and go to Sardi's. But even if they heated up TV dinners, for the people in this horrible house—fuck 'em, all of 'em. Let them eat their own lousy *chazerai* without Jerry Elkin of Elkin and Fox. By the time he was in the hall near the playroom, he was mad enough to go tight-chested and short of breath.

Elkin looked behind him. For just a second or two, he thought Max Rosenbloom might follow.

The playroom where Sari and Jake would be was off to the right. On the wood paneling of the hall were photographs of Sari Rose-in-bloom as a little girl and Elkin immediately thought of posing her naked and then even more immediately tamped the images down like pipe tobacco. Another photo. President Kennedy. And a photo of some little boy, a little kid, standing beside a lake and looking very unhappy.

Elkin could hear the TV. He braced himself for what he knew he was going to find, Jake and this fantastic Sari in some incredible fuck position. Elkin turned to the doorway, then stopped when the most ungodly stink of greasy fish was carried down from the kitchen and through the lower hallway and Elkin was glad he was missing some kind of home-cooked healthy fish meal, probably badly done. He shook himself out of it and poked his head into the playroom. What he saw there slapped him even worse.

Both Jake and Sari were clothed but they were sitting on the floor in the sweetest cuddle that Elkin had ever seen. Sari's back was to Jake, she was seated between his legs. Jake had drawn up his knees and wrapped his arms around her. The TV light flashed across their faces like a sun glint off a lake. The two kids were glassy eyed at the television but even more, they were lost in the comfort of their bodies. The touch of each other. Promising and peaceful. Jake made a small motion to touch Sari's hair. She moved a little to make it easier for him. They didn't know Elkin existed either in the doorway or anywhere else. Childlike but sexual, it had everything that you hoped might exist in the...

Elkin had the strongest inclination to rush into the room and start kicking the both of them. He pushed that down in the pipe with the photos of the naked Sari. Then Elkin drew out a long, "Uh, kids...." and both Jake and Sari moved just enough to smile up at him.

"Dinner ready?" Sari said.

"See that's the thing," Elkin smiled.

He began to lie and explain.

As Elkin and Marsha drove down the Rosenbloom driveway, Elkin was checking the rearview, trying to spy Jake. OK. So the little fucker wanted to stay on. So stay on. Have dinner with that awful crowd. You be my gift to Vee Rosenbloom, Elkin was thinking. And that's when he saw her, Vee, in the rearview.

She came out of the house and down the slate front walk in a blitz of hustling steps and she planted herself there on the grass. Shouting something. Jabbing the air in the direction of Elkin's car.

"That woman is out on the lawn," Elkin said.

Marsha rolled down the window and adjusted the side-view mirror.

"And there's Max," Marsha said. "They're pushing and pulling. Fighting, I think."

In the rearview, Elkin saw Max shouting and whipping his arms wildly and Vee was starting to slap him. Max was shaking her. Vee kept pointing toward Elkin's car as it drove into the distance and Max Rosenbloom clamped down on her arm, finally dragging her back up the steps and inside. At the front door, their guests were now crowding around them, witnesses and onlookers.

"Look there in the kitchen window," Marsha said. "Wait. Now all I can see is somebody looking down that woman's dress."

"That's Jake."

"Jake's not bald," Marsha said.

"He will be," Elkin said. "I'll make sure of it."

Before they got home, Elkin was doing a Max Rosenbloom voice, the rumbling tank treads talking to a buoyant Chip Chopper about how he'd just met Jerry Elkin who was one talented son of a gun if Max did say so himself. Elkin knocked on the dashboard like he was knocking on a door and then Mr. Nosh came on the scene, asking why the hell they'd gone to that party in the first place. What did that woman want? asked Mr. Nosh. This Rosenbloom? Maybe they should consult Dr. Huckleberry. And how about that Sari? Mr. Nosh said. That's one heck of a sweetie pie, *whooo-weee*, I could chase her around the room until I fall down.

"Yeah, yeah, very funny," Marsha said. "Stop it with the voices already, will you, all right? You know I don't like it."

And Elkin, suddenly very sad, kept his mouth shut the rest of the ride home.

CHAPTER SEVEN

FOR THREE DAYS, he'd been stewing about it. The goddamn Elkin party. Everything, it ruined everything, that little shindig. Max Rosenbloom was a mad manhole rocking with steam and ready to explode. It ruined even this: Max Rosenbloom's one day a month with his mistress, Shirley Cohen.

"In my own house. A fucking *schmendrick*, that's what I looked like," he was hissing to her. "What am I, a schmuck?"

Shirley Cohen said quietly, "You're a man with capacities, Max. Calm yourself. Have another drink."

Max Rosenbloom thought of Shirley as his mistress even though he hardly ever saw her and never talked to her otherwise. Always, though, he left her a little gift. Something from Tiffany's usually, a diamond this, a solid gold that, a necklace, a watch, a pendant, something. Shirley Cohen, as far as Max knew, was a substitute high school English teacher with a studio apartment on 81st and Second, a third-floor walk-up. The place was a box. A sprawling, canopied bed fit into it and, nearby, a small scruffy sofa. Not much else. Photos, all over the place, of Shirley and her parents at various stages of life and SHIRLEY spelled out in big theater-marquee letters in three places on the wall.

"If the plan was to piss me off, she did it just right," Max Rosenbloom said.

Shirley slipped off the bed, took her beer bottle and settled in on the sofa, naked. "That Vee," she said. "She enjoys you mad. Like a bull."

"She's had practice," Max Rosenbloom said.

He was still lying under the covers, tracing her change of location. He liked to watch Shirley move. She still had a pretty good body for 36, her ass was still up there, good legs, tits didn't matter. But the thing Max liked most about her was that she was so plain. Not pretty, not ugly, just a pleasing face and a decent body usually hidden under dull clothes and Max Rosenbloom didn't have to do anything, not anything, except be a nice guy. Gifts, a good dinner, some chitchat, he could relax. It wasn't like Vee, who had the right to expect something from him. And it wasn't like being with, say, Raquel Welch—or, say, Sari. That's where you had to be working all the time, knowing the woman was wondering, "Why am I with this clown and not someone else?" That's how Max Rosenbloom looked at it.

"Goddamn Elkin, he keeps digging at me," Max Rosenbloom said. "He's inside my mind."

He had to wipe the spit off his lip when he told Shirley how much he hated Elkin and mostly Elkin's son who'd started it all. That led Max Rosenbloom into telling Shirley how much he hated his own son, who he never heard from, the kid was no good from the word "go." How's this for a laugh? Max told her about taking his son out to help him learn to drive when they'd had the MG and they'd stopped at a corner where there was no left turn permitted and Max looked around for a cop and was a cop around? No. So he told the kid to make the turn. And would the kid make the turn? No, again. And Max said, "Jesus. Make the turn. What are you, a goody two-shoes? Schmuck." And the kid just sat gray and sullen and waited for the light to change.

"That sorta sounds like he is one," Shirley Cohen said, "if you don't mind my saying. He's one of those guys. Big on the law but breaks the unwritten rules, the real rules."

"He didn't get it from me," Max Rosenbloom said. Thank God for Shirley Cohen. He was starting to calm down. Max Rosenbloom was glad to see her, even now that she'd dyed her hair platinum instead of keeping it natural mousy. Like it'd been when he'd first met her on line in the liquor store around the corner from his office on East 40th. It was nice to have someone to talk to once in a while. Not like sometimes, when he was out of town on business and he found the top-dollar working girls, only sometimes. Once in a while. That was different.

"You know who else is just waiting to screw me?" Max Rosenbloom said and he told Shirley Cohen about Larry Passoff, being very careful about the details, making up a fake name.

"He's a chickenshit little prick who doesn't have the moxie to do business," Max said. "He can take the old neighborhood and shove it up his ass."

Max had been sending Boris out to see what Larry Passoff was up to because the son of a bitch was up to something, that's for sure. Crack of dawn and Boris would tail Larry Passoff, wait outside his place in the garment district and then go after his footsteps, see where he went and who he spoke to. And goddamn it if Boris hadn't rushed back to Max with the report that for two days running, the days Boris tailed him, Larry left his office, went to the corner of Sixth and 37th and closed himself into a phone booth.

"Who'd he call?" Max said.

Boris did a crude little wiggling of his shoulders.

"Did you get any part of the number?" Max said. "Did you look?"

Boris gave back a slow smile like his intestines ached.

"Schmuck!" Max shouted. Boris was certain now that his plans to ask for another date with Sari would have to be put back. Also his hopes of sitting down with Max and "talking American business."

Boris's pale, flat features began to tremble and he stammered out an apology. "You are a father to me," Boris said.

Max knew that a stammered apology especially in that stupid Russian accent wasn't going to get the deal done and if the deal wasn't done then he'd have to dance. He'd have to finagle another way to pay for Sari's move to Paris. And everything else.

He didn't exactly shoot his mouth off with Shirley Cohen, he didn't use any names, not "Larry Passoff," his old man had taught him better than that, he said "Benny Schwartz." Afterwards Max Rosenbloom felt much better. Then, when he was leaving her apartment and about to kiss her goodbye, Shirley Cohen said, "Oh, and I heard your daughter's name mentioned on the radio."

Max Rosenbloom drew back. "That was before."

"This morning," Shirley said. "Just a mention."

"What are you talking about?"

Shirley told him. It was what she thought she heard, anyway, on Elkin and Fox. Then she was saying, "Hey, c'mon Max, no kiss goodbye?" as Max Rosenbloom double-stepped down the stairs of her walk-up, his boat-sized wingtips slamming the boards as he ran.

He wasn't sure what to do when he got back down on the street so Max Rosenbloom called Boris. They headed on over to see Larry Passoff.

Everything that happened in the canyon of the garment district made Max Rosenbloom even angrier. He walked beside Boris at a clip and the air of the place was rage and grease and gas fumes. The trucks that backed up on the sidewalk. The inventory packed together and swinging from the moving, rattling racks as the Spanish kids pushed them along. He even got angry at the guys who were loading the truck, tossing boxes to one another, angry even though it was Max who bumped into them and got a call of "¡Chinga!" in return. Max was angry at the street itself, backed-up with double-parked jobbers and the outlet stores and the sidewalks where you were hemmed in, rushing and standing still while human electricity pushed everything toward money. Boris was trotting alongside, keeping pace but out of breath. He was wondering if now he might get lucky enough to show Max Rosenbloom what he was made of, the way they built Jews in the Soviet Union, not with *schmaltz* and *chazerai*, but with hunger and cold that would crack your bones.

By the time they got to Larry Passoff's dingy office, the carpet worn so thin you could see the threads, the paneling half off the walls, Max was ready to snap Larry Passoff's pencil neck in two.

"SCHMUCK!" Max shouted at Larry Passoff. "COCKSUCKER!"

"Jesus, Max, you don't knock, call? You come here personally? What? Lucy!" Larry Passoff shouted. "How did this man get in?"

Larry Passoff's secretary, Lucy Ostrow, was a stubby little woman in a flowered dress, the sleeves short enough so you could see numbers tattooed on the inside of her forearm. "Belsen," she would tell any curious gaze, "and don't ask me to explain because I was there and even I can't explain." She was also not going to risk her life for Larry Passoff even if she'd answer his phones and open his mail. You want to fire me? Fire me. Goodbye and good luck and hello new job.

"He got in," Lucy yelled back, "because he got in."

Boris shut the office door and stood with his heel against the bottom to keep it closed. Larry Passoff sat back in his cheap metal chair and put his hands behind his head to act like nothing was going wrong. This was just Max Rosenbloom from the old neighborhood, a loudmouth for sure, but a respecter of certain boundaries.

If you were a Jap, Max might pop up and kill you. He remembered when Max came home, how he talked, only a little bit, yes, but enough to know. If you hurt the Jews, watch out for Max. If you went after his family, Max would destroy yours to the seventh generation and hang the sliced-off ears around his neck. But Max wouldn't hurt Larry Passoff from Bay Parkway in Bensonhurst. They'd burned stores together. Max had even helped Larry's old man with his own store when he needed the insurance money. He'd even kept the guineas away from little, skinny, bar mitzvah *bocher* Larry during one of their fist-swinging Wop-Kike walks home.

No, Max Rosenbloom was OK, a little wild, very tough, but OK.

"YOU PENCIL-NECK FUCKING SCHMUCK," Max roared. "STAND UP! I'M GONNA BREAK YOUR SKEEVY LITTLE NECK!"

"What's this about, Max?" Larry Passoff shrugged. "We had such a nice lunch the other day."

"It's about I offered you a deal and then you drop a dime on me, that's what it's about."

"Drop a dime on who, Max? What are you talking about?"

Max told him. Boris nodded. Larry Passoff said, "You're imagining things. There's no reason for any dime-dropping because it's all on the up and up, you said so yourself."

"In spades," Max Rosenbloom said. "So don't make me send Boris up to Scarsdale."

Boris nodded again.

"You think you're gonna make a *putz* out of me, Larry?"

"Maxie, why so hot under the collar?"

Max Rosenbloom took a step forward. He picked up a scissors off Larry Passoff's desk, then meat-handed the point into the beat-up wood. The scissors stood straight, bayoneted into a groove. Larry's Adam's apple jiggled. Then Max Rosenbloom grabbed out the scissors and swiped Larry Passoff's two-dollar tie into his tightening fingers. Larry Passoff was jerked closer. The scissors opened, the scissors closed, Larry Passoff was thrown back into his chair and Max Rosenbloom was still holding the two-dollar tie, now cut into a pair of one-dollar ties.

"I'll tell you what," Larry Passoff said. He paused like he had to take one quick moment in the depths of thought. "If it makes you happy, I'm in. You've got a partner. How's that?"

"So what are you giving me such a hard time for?" Max Rosenbloom said.

Max and Boris went back down the filthy gray elevator in silence and they walked out of the garment district back to Fifth Avenue like they were cutting through the jungle with machetes. They were that far away, Max waited until then before he turned to Boris and said, "That's a lesson. Do that sometimes to get what you want."

He handed Boris the cut off tie. "Souvenir," Max Rosenbloom said. "Now drive me home."

Down in the garage, Boris opened the door of the Rolls for Max feeling that he had learned something, that he was grateful for being taught, that this Max Rosenbloom was his father, his spiritual father of America, and he would join the Rosenbloom family and make Max proud. Max couldn't wait to get the hell out of there and get the hell back home and clear up everything else. And, by the way, fuck Larry Passoff.

He never did trust that pencil neck. Not even in Bensonhurst. And he sunk back in the Rolls, watching the exit signs toward home. Thinking again of who he hated.

Topping the list—Max Rosenbloom boiled this over in his mind as he shook along the LIE in the Rolls, sniffing the leather Flower of New Car smell—most of all, the major schmuck in this whole adventure was Jake Elkin. At first he'd actually liked the kid, too, the little *pisher* had something to him. But now Jake was a schmuck of the first order.

This was the source of all trouble, in a phrase.

That's what Max Rosenbloom was thinking when they passed the huge billboard that read, "Elkin and Fox, the 10 Funniest Guys in Town!"

"Asshole!" Max Rosenbloom said.

At the wheel, Boris bit his lip and frowned. He promised himself he would do better, not sure of where he'd gone wrong.

Max was fuming, rolling it around in his head. Elkin. What's this with Sari on the radio? What does he think, he's gonna take over my life? And the schmuck's son. This idiot kid Elkin makes a fool of me? Laughing behind my back? Laughing at me? The steam rose higher as the Rolls turned off the LIE. A fool? You think I'm stupid? Do you have any fucking idea who the hell you're fucking with? Do you have any fucking idea where I've been?

By the time Boris turned into Max's driveway and parked next to the Jag, it was early evening and the sun was low.

Max pulled a $100 bill from his clip. "Stay here," he said, "Mrs. Rosenbloom will call a cab." And Boris, seeing the house, remembering the sight of Sari that first time fresh from the shower, said, "I must come in and…" Was that the Angel of Death who, just for a second, passed across Max Rosenbloom's face? "I will wait," Boris finished.

And inside the house, Sari stepped away from Max after kissing him hello. She knew better than to get in his way when she saw him like this. So did Vee. And when Max said, "What's his number, the Elkin kid?" Sari knew better than to do anything but blurt it out. Twice.

"You stay right here," Max said. To Vee, he said, "You, too."

Then he picked up the kitchen phone and started dialing the home of Jerry, Marsha and Jake Elkin. It was 7:15 in the evening. Sari knew because she looked at the kitchen clock.

Jake was sitting in the den with his head on one arm of the armchair and his legs dangling over the other. He was reading a book by Norman Mailer that raged on about the dead, lock-step mundane conformity of American life and included some good scenes of fighting and anal sex. That's when the phone rang.

It was 7:15 in the evening. Jake had no idea this was the time because he didn't wear a watch and there was no clock in the den. He could have guessed it was around 7:15, though, because his father had just wished him good night and gone upstairs to get ready for bed.

The house was quiet. The German maid in the book was being fucked in the ass but Jake had to break off from his reading because the phone had uncovered something very wrong hidden in the silence. The ringing phone was going to put it right. The ringing phone was all he could hear.

Jake picked it up.

"This is Mr. Rosenbloom," Max Rosenbloom said. It wasn't really "said," though, it was more a handsaw going through bone, an ice pick in the eardrum, a cave voice that charged out of the silence with lips stripped back and fangs glistening, deep, hungry, incensed. Jake opened his mouth to say "Hello" but…

"If you ever come near my daughter again," Max Rosenbloom said. "I'll break your fucking back."

Then he hung up.

The house was quiet again. Jake held the phone to his ear as the buzzing rushed in. Not that Jake could have cooked up an answer. If the line hadn't gone dead, what then? What would he have shot back? "Uh, wha? Huh? Why?" That's what he had to toss at Max Rosenbloom. The buzzing kept on in his ear. Jake listened to the buzzing for a moment and then he hung up and wiped off a little patch of sweat from where it had suddenly sprung, right at the base of his skull. It was wet and uncomfortable and his shock was shame enough. He wanted to keep the sweat from running down his neck.

Jake left his hand on top of the phone and stood there holding onto everything that he knew. He knew that he had stopped breathing. He knew that when he began breathing again, it was like all the muscles tore in his chest.

Then he knew that he was walking through the hallway of his house, that he was seeing the tastefully subdued wallpaper with the earth tone leaf print and that he could see his mother's feet on the ottoman where she was watching television. He knew that he was standing in front of her, trying not to block her view. She was wearing a light blue housecoat made of some kind of shiny material, he didn't know what.

But he knew he was saying, "Mom. Can I borrow the car for a little while?"

Marsha Elkin suspected this had something to do with girls and if it had to do with girls it had to do with Sari Rose-in-bloom. Marsha Elkin was going to stay out of it. So now she looked up at Jake like he was a kid about to slam his head into a wall just for laughs. But all she said was, "If it's meant to be, you'll find each other." The TV screen reclaimed her. "You don't need the car."

Jake said, "Shit!" and headed for the front door. He could hear his heart slapping against his ribs, he was breathing the way he'd breathed watching that horror movie "Village of the Damned." He was thinking that Max Rosenbloom was a schmuck but that he, Jake, could only move, move now, move forward. The metallic sound of a screen door rattling shut. Cool air, the late spring evening, it all began to work him over. His eyes went wide. He wasn't thinking. There was only "here," some sensed movement, and "there" where he was heading. There was his bicycle, leaning against the wall of the garage—there it was. Somewhere, bombs were falling. Here, the evening was quiet. Move, Jake said to himself. Move, move, move.

He jumped on his bike and began peddling toward Max Rosenbloom.

* * *

The nose of Sari Rose-in-bloom. The lips. Sari Rose-in-bloom. The curve of her hip. Sari Rose-in-bloom. The line of her smooth thigh. The arched muscle of her calf. The V between her legs. All this, so perfectly rendered, was soon to be on its way to Italy, to a workshop just outside Florence, where Bernardo Chinita's craftsmen would turn her into stone. Where each of these Sari Rose-in-bloom pieces would be reassembled and somehow animated and the mystery of Sari would stand in marble forever.

Chinita and his assistant, Javier, sacrificed that morning on their hands and knees on the unfinished wood slats of the studio, rolling the drawings into shipping tubes, pressing sketches flat in protective cardboard. The radio was on, they were listening to Elkin and Fox, good company for lonely work.

That was it. Elkin and Fox. Such wonderful voices. There was an entire world coming out of that little box. But when everything was packed up, Bernardo Chinita was even more lonely and he stepped back and looked at the long black shipping tubes and the huge flat brown packages and he understood that this was all he had left of Sari Rose-in-bloom. He would not see her again in life, he would not look upon her until the construction in marble was done. Chinita felt something go loose in the center of his chest. He walked along the line of packed Sari Rose-in-blooms because he knew now that it was done, finished, he could feel it, he was no longer inside of her, putting images on paper.

"I want her luminous," he said to Javier. "Use the copal medium, would you? We'll paint her from memory."

What always amazed Bernardo Chinita was how Javier kept himself so tiny and so lithe. He ate all the time and still a fawn. So now, Javier, in his paint-spattered jeans and stained white T-shirt, who was sitting on the floor rolling the last drawing, drew his feet underneath and leaped up straight, striding to the stove in one motion. Chinita watched him melt the resin, heat and mix in the oil and pour the amber-colored medium into a row of cups, awaiting their colors.

The copal, he knew, would give this Sari a look of the Old World and the brilliant New World, both at once, like the goddess herself. Bernardo Chinita was ready, he would paint Sari Rose-in-bloom as he wanted to keep her, forever, in his studio. A private Sari all for himself. He was holding her image in his painter's mind's eye when Elkin and Fox went into a live commercial for Hanes pantyhose, Ted Fox talking to Jerry Elkin's uptight, dowager lady Miss Emma Reel.

Chinita had only the smallest crook of a smile going but he noticed that Javier's little shoulders were shaking with more than mild amusement. And then suddenly Chinita thought he was losing his mind. He thought he heard the name Sari Rose-in-bloom coming from the radio. This was not possible. This was too much.

But he wasn't crazy. Ted Fox had said the name, Ted Fox had said Sari Rose-in-bloom and now he was saying it again. On the radio. So, yes, Sari Rose-in-bloom would become a mystery in stone. As Chinita told Javier, she would stand with Michelangelo's David (though somewhat smaller), the stance and expression, the body, the features, once turned to marble they would be flesh the way flesh yearned to exist. This Sari, he had told Javier, she would captivate until the Earth stood still, she was the Mona Lisa's smile. She was the moment beyond all explanation, there was no theory that would allow you to forget her and move on. But now? Now, this Sari was also a radio wave. And radio waves danced off into space and lived forever.

"Javier!" he shouted. "Why don't you fix us some tea!"

On the radio, Ted Fox was asking Miss Emma Reel whether Emma's friend Sari Rose-in-bloom wore pantyhose.

"I can't believe she lets her legs go naked," Ted Fox was laughing.

And Miss Emma Reel sounded somewhat testy when she replied in her high, grumpy, dowager British accent, "Can we not mention this Sari Rose-in-bloom again!" and now Bernardo Chinita was laughing and laughing and laughing.

"Did you hear, Javier?" he said.

Javier brought over two cups of tea.

"It is like a, what do you call, epiphany!" Javier said. "A strange moment of grace."

Bernardo Chinita was nodding quickly, "Somehow, hearing her name on this Elkin and Fox, I understand. With this Sari, we are at the crossing point of many waves. At the center. It is all one. Sari. We are on the side of the angels."

They raised their tea cups in a toast. To art. To Sari. To angels.

Three hours later, Javier collapsed on the floor by the sink and Bernardo Chinita was stumbling backwards, tripping over a canvas and a spray gun and collapsing at the far end of the studio near the big, hissing industrial radiator. Elkin and Fox had long ago said, "Let's make it morning!" and the packed Sari Rose-in-blooms had been shipped off to Europe. Bernardo and Javier had watched the ecstasy of Sari Rose-in-bloom disappear into parcels and they had committed her vibrations to memory and had heard her name turned to radio waves and they had laughed and loved and kept the Sari image before them.

So much so, that Javier's mind had also been seized by Sari. Meaning that Javier's mind had been on something else when he'd poured the copal medium. And when he made tea. So he'd mistakenly poured their tea water into the same cups he'd used for the copal. For that, Javier now lay unmoving, staring at the unfinished wooden floor and Bernardo Chinita lay on his back and watched the studio around him grow dark.

The radio was still on. Elkin and Fox were over but Bernardo Chinita put what was left of his life and energy into listening. Hoping he would hear Sari's name again. Hoping she would save him.

Just say "Sari Rose-in-bloom" and I will live.

The sound faded. Blackness swept in. He was thinking of Sari. Seeing her. Seeing his stunningly beautiful images of her. Then the radio played Frank Sinatra's new song "My Way" and Chinita began to dimly hum the music. The end was here. He was facing the final curtain. Chinita's hum grew faint. He'd loved. He'd laughed. He'd cried. He'd had his fill, his share of losing. Chinita forced a few more hums.

He decided that he would buy this new Sinatra album.

And that was the end of it.

CHAPTER EIGHT

MAX ROSENBLOOM WAS JUST ABOUT READY to cool down. The I'll-break-your-back call to Jake had quenched some of the acid in his gut because Max liked to talk tough and knew he'd make good on it. But he still wasn't sure about Larry Passoff. So that evening, Max was settled deep in his favorite leather chair down in his playroom, head resting back, sipping a Chivas, deciding how to fuck over Larry Passoff and make it stick. That's when he heard the sound.

It was a fall-down confusion clanking of metal clattering on stone. Like someone throwing down a bicycle. Then Max heard footsteps, running toward his house.

A dull groan, the kind his father used to make, escaped from Max Rosenbloom when he stood up. Just in time, because through the big playroom window, he could swear he saw Jake Elkin bolting across his lawn. And piled on its side in his driveway, Max saw the bicycle. After that, Max Rosenbloom heard his front door opening, then closing, then heard his daughter Sari Rose-in-bloom up in the foyer saying, "Don't fuck around with my father, he's a very tough guy."

And his wife Vee chiming in, "I'll call the police. And if Mr. Rosenbloom finds you here, you'll be glad I did."

Then Jake was shouting to the entire house, "MR. ROSENBLOOM! I'm calling you out!"

This, Max Rosenbloom was thinking, I don't need. Not tonight. I was just starting to feel good but my head still hurts and I got trouble. Go back to your old man and make funny voices.

"Mr. Rosenbloom!" Jake was calling. "I want to talk. Where are you?"

OK, Max Rosenbloom was thinking, the kid's got some guts, so good. "So, so, so," Max heard his own voice rumbling in his head saying other words like "moxie" and "OK, OK," and suddenly he had the strange wish to take this Jake Elkin and sit him down on his big Max Rosenbloom knee. And bounce him up and down. And softly sing the old kids' song "Pony Boy." Like he used to do with his own kid who no longer talked to him.

So now, Max Rosenbloom, feeling old, walked over his parquet tiles in the paneled hallway of his furnished basement near the playroom and when he turned the corner, he was facing off with this little guy at the top of the short stairs: perfect skin, hair grown almost to his shoulders, all decked out in jeans and a light-blue work shirt like a prisoner or someone who worked in the field. And OK, Max thought, this little schmuck has the *chutzpa* to call me on this and I'm gonna have to read him the riot act. The Truth, that's what he'll have to hear.

Jake saw the big Max Rosenbloom face float into view and for a moment it was like someone flushed his brain. He couldn't speak. Then he said, "We're gonna talk. And I don't care if you call the police."

"Police?" Max Rosenbloom, glad for a chance to smile. "I think I can handle this by myself." He pursed his lips. "Come down here."

Jake followed Max past the framed photo of the dead JFK, past the photo of beautiful Sari, the ungrateful son who never called, the old photo of Vee Vee when she was young and lithe and Sari-like, before she had Sari growing inside her. They went out the back entrance and stood in the driveway near the Jag and the Rolls.

"Go move your bicycle," Max Rosenbloom said.

The darkness was broken by the garage lights that made the cars look painted against the night. Max watched Jake trot over and lift the bike up. "Where should I put it?"

"Just get it out of the way. On the lawn," Max said. And as Jake set the bike on the lawn and trotted back, Max said, "Nice night."

Jake looked up. Moonlight and fast moving clouds. The breeze was sweet with the smell of grass, lawns freshly mowed. The sky seemed huge, a country sky over the soft swell of the road and the houses. That's when it occurred to Jake that he might die here or soon or on this night. It didn't seem logical. It didn't make any sense. Maybe he was just being dramatic. Except Max Rosenbloom was looking at him now, frowning a little, like he was very sad about something.

"This is some car, isn't it?" Max nodded at the tan Rolls. He started moving down the side of the car, fingering the moonlight that gleamed from the perfect paint, patting the roof like the car might start talking. Max Rosenbloom went full circle until he was at the front grill and then Max touched the silver hood ornament.

"Spirit of Ecstasy," Max said. "That's what it's called," running his thick fingers over this little statue of a beautiful woman poised leaning forward, arms or wings thrown back, ready to fly. "I always tell Sari it reminds me of her."

Max made another pass along the side of the car, his finger tracing the path, the fender, the window, the door.

"You ever drive a Rolls Royce?"

Jake shook his head.

"Let's take a ride," Max said. "I want you to drive me."

Jake was saying "No," and "C'mon, I don't want to," when Max opened the door and guided him behind the wheel. One immense Max Rosenbloom paw closed around Jake's upper arm and Jake tightened his muscle to show Max that here was a man who did push-ups, but by that time, they were already pulling out into the street.

"Mrs. Rosenbloom isn't allowed to drive it," Max was saying. "I don't let Sari drive it, either. And not my son."

The rush of new leather, real leather, took Jake in its Rolls Royce arms and he carefully set his hands on the veneered wood steering wheel wondering what damage he'd caused already. Like he'd never been in a car before. Maybe he hadn't. Maybe this was a real car and the rest were all cheap imitations, simulations that you sell to the peasants, maybe this was the way it was supposed to be. Everything with its own sheen. Everything made by a human hand that was skilled in craft and perfection. The creating hand that cared. Fine wood, real glass. Nothing seemed churned out by machine, nothing seemed to sneer, "Here, take this piece of shit and be thankful for it," no, this was a car that said, "You deserve this. And not only this. You deserve everything. Most of all? You deserve to live."

Jake thought he should take off his shoes to step on the gas, he didn't want to get anything dirty. Beside him, Max Rosenbloom drew in a deep, deep breath like he was inhaling jewels.

And what if some schmuck pulls out of his driveway and slams into us, right into the side? Jake was saying to himself. Whose fault would that be then? Then Max would have a right to kill him. That's what he was thinking when Max said, "You love my daughter?"

Jake clenched his jaw, the rush of heat rising to his cheeks. "Yes," he said.

"That's good," Max said. "I love her, too."

There was no talking for a little while after that. Jake was gripping the wheel so tightly that he was getting tiny shocks of pain between his fingers and he thought he'd pop a vein in his eye, that's how carefully he stared through the perfect windshield into the dark street ahead. The car seemed to lift above the white line of the road. On the hood, the Spirit of Ecstasy pulled the Rolls along with Jake steering. If the Spirit of Ecstasy reminded Max Rosenbloom of Sari, then she was Sari for Jake, too, she was pulling them both through the night in this emperor's chariot. Jake kept his gaze locked on the ornament.

Max twisted to the side. He was looking at Jake and shifting, breathing like he was uncomfortable. He started to say something and stopped. Jake gave him a quick glance and said, "Where should I drive?"

Max Rosenbloom let out a "whoosh" of air and finally he said, "During The War, I was in this outfit. We had a pretty tough time. I'm lucky to be here."

About 25 years before this day, Max Rosenbloom made the top of a man's head come off. And when the jungle dirt near his left boot began to flick and kick with bullets, he'd turned and fired his Thompson submachine gun into a Japanese sniper who was tied way up there in the palms. And Max fired for so long that the Japanese man, who was trying to kill Max Rosenbloom, broke in half and the head and stomach and shoulders tumbled down into the long grass in a rain of blood, of gray and pink jelly. The G.I. standing next to Max, who was killed the next day, said, "Jesus," and he blinked a couple of times and snorted. And Max told him strangely, "What else can happen?"

Jake could feel the heat from Max Rosenbloom's stare.

"This war now?" Max said. He shook his head. "Stay out of it. It's not worth it. Don't believe the crap they tell you. You're being lied to. Take care of yourself."

Jake said he would.

Max Rosenbloom was quiet again and then he said, "That's what I learned.

"Just keep driving," Max Rosenbloom said then.

The Rolls glided by the little stores on Middle Neck Road, the place for candy and the newspaper, the grocer, the small red-brick fire department. The steering was heavy. Jake thought this must be what it's like at the wheel of a ship. And there was a strange sensitivity to the car, Jake felt the shove and jangle of every bump, every hole in the asphalt. Something's wrong, he thought, I've broken the Rolls Royce. He pumped the brakes once and they grabbed just enough for Jake to know that he must have touched something, hit the wrong this or that, to ruin the world's greatest car.

When he turned, Jake took the car up a calm, dark street so that the Rolls Royce drifted by small, sedate houses, shingled and squat, each with a driveway that held a car that was just aching to pull out and smash this beauty. His eyes clicked off every exit path. Then he turned again, taking the Rolls by the white steeple of the high school and the empty parking lot of the public pool.

"It's funny," Max Rosenbloom said. "Things usually don't turn out the way people hope, and all the time they're so surprised. Your old man made a fool out of me. My wife is screaming about you. I'd really like to hate you, Jake. But I don't."

The school used the pool parking lot for the first lesson on how to drive, letting the future speeders, double-parkers and scofflaws get the feel of the wheel in a safe, secluded area.

"You learn to drive in this parking lot?" Max Rosenbloom said. When Jake nodded, Max said, "So did Sari."

The lot was dotted by streetlamps, big overhanging lilies of light that showed off the empty spaces.

"Turn there," Max Rosenbloom said.

Jake wondered whether this is what it felt like when they drove you somewhere to kill you. His lower lip trembled and went dry. He made the turn. When he passed near the cyclone fencing and into the empty lot, Jake said, "What now?"

"Just drive," Max Rosenbloom said. "Make circles."

The Rolls Royce drove in a wide circle around the lot.

"You know, I like you," Max Rosenbloom said. "So it's not that. I want you to understand me."

Jake concentrated on turning the wheel, turning it so that the car avoided a concrete divider.

"Mostly, it's Mrs. Rosenbloom. I don't exactly know why she's got it in for you, but she does."

Jake learned to drive from an instructor who'd suffered

rheumatic fever as a child and had lost all the hair on his head, his beard, eyebrows, everything. It was like being taught by a giant talking egg. Jake now concentrated on remembering that.

"She's my wife. I want the best for her. I want to give her the best. And if she's gonna hock me day and night about hating some high school kid, then I'm sorry, but you gotta go."

"What does Sari say," Jake wasn't sure he'd actually said it.

"I know Sari pretty well," Max Rosenbloom said. "Sari will get over it."

The Rolls made another circle. Max let his eyes run down over Jake, checking off the work shirt and the jeans and how Jake sat like he was at the handle of a .50-caliber machine gun, scanning the horizon. He looked at the kid and felt sorry for him.

"Here's the truth," Max Rosenbloom said. "I know how you feel. I know you're gonna be heartbroken. For a little while, anyway. But no matter what, even if Mrs. Rosenbloom loved you, even if you keep spending every afternoon in my house, you're not gonna end up with Sari."

Jake took his foot off the gas and the Rolls slowed down, almost stopping.

"You're gonna hurt for a while. But if you're smart, you'll hurt and move on."

The night came down on them hard and the car lumbered now in the parking lot, drifting, an abandoned boat. Jake shifted. Now, he was staring deeply into the muddy undersea, the brown eyes of Max Rosenbloom, trying to block out any more of the wounded face and trying not to think about the jungle and all those other stories he'd heard about Max. Jake needed a good answer, OK, he knew what to say, he was about to make a crack but...

"If I had to guess," Max Rosenbloom said, "I'd say that Sari is going to end up with a guy who's a little older, who's got a little power and a lot of money. That's the simple case. All right, I mean, if she keeps on having whatever it is that she has now? Then, I don't know what. If she keeps on being Sari, then Mrs. Rosenbloom thinks she'll be a princess. Maybe like Grace Kelly.

"Except not in show business," Max Rosenbloom said quickly.

Max took a pack of cigarettes from his breast pocket and offered one to Jake. They lit up and filled the Rolls with smoke. Max opened his window.

"The one thing I can promise you is…she's not gonna end up with a guy she met in high school."

"You don't know."

"I'm trying to be a nice guy," Max Rosenbloom said. "Believe me. I know what you think's gonna happen. But it ain't gonna, kid. That's just the way it is."

Jake opened his window and tossed the cigarette into the lot.

"I'll tell you something else. Even if Sari thinks she's gonna end up with you, she won't. She doesn't know the landscape. Not yet. But I promise you. She will."

Jake gave the Rolls Royce some gas and headed back toward the gate. "Thanks for letting me drive." Why the fuck had he said that? Jake shifted and thought of putting the Rolls into the metal criss-cross of the cyclone fence and watching as Max pitched forward, hopefully through the window. You have the guts for that? No, you schmuck. The bad thing was, he almost liked this Max Rosenbloom. Jake almost believed what he was saying about how Sari would end up. The other bad thing was that what Max said seemed to waft out of that place of real-knowing-but-who-wants-to-hear-about-it. But that's just the thing, don't be fooled, Jake told himself. He knew that Max Rosenbloom might be right, but even if he was right, Max Rosenbloom was wrong. As wrong, right now, as Max Rosenbloom had ever been in his entire schmuck, scumbag life. Jake was trying to figure out a way to say this when Max Rosenbloom said, "How's your old man?"

Jake said nothing. He felt he'd been killed.

"Funny guy," Max Rosenbloom said. "Funny, funny guy. I was pleased to meet him. I guess."

When the Rolls Royce pulled into the Max Rosenbloom

driveway, right alongside the Jag, Jake turned off the ignition, sat there, and then passed over the keys. Then Max thanked him and offered his hand. "I think we understand each other," Max Rosenbloom said. They shook on it.

Outside the car, Jake wasn't sure of what to do next. He wanted to go over and touch the Spirit of Ecstasy statue but he thought that would show Max too much of his longing. He wanted Max Rosenbloom to ask him inside and offer him a drink. He wanted to go say a dramatic goodbye to Sari even though he knew this was not goodbye and he was going to keep on seeing her. Forever. But now Max came around the side of the Rolls and dropped his hand on Jake's shoulder and began to guide Jake step by step toward the spindly metal salad of Jake's bicycle lying on its side on the lawn.

"How'd you like driving the Rolls, by the way," Max said.

"Great car."

"Yeah? I've always been a little disappointed," Max Rosenbloom stopped at the curb. "It looks great. And everybody stares at it. But it always feels like it rides sort of rough and the steering's a pain in the ass."

Jake picked up his bicycle and climbed aboard.

"Goodbye, Jake," Max Rosenbloom said then. "Remember what I said. Take care of yourself."

Max didn't wait around. He walked away back up the driveway as Jake bicycled off, every foot press on the pedals like a pump to his corrosive anger. And what was worse, he kept imagining himself on the bicycle, tossing newspapers on the front lawns of every home, Sari's house, too, a paperboy to Max Rosenbloom.

＊　＊　＊

"Hello, there, you king-sized schmuck!" Elkin shouted it out, driving alone in his Volvo, five a.m., passing the huge billboard of "Elkin and Fox, the 10 Funniest Guys In Town!" He'd made an appointment to see his manager, Marty Horowitz, and beg, plead or threaten (whatever worked) to get him, Elkin, out of his contract with Ted Fox. It was going to be a big day.

That morning, mostly the show went well. They got a call from Barbara Walters complimenting one of their routines and then one of the salesmen had come to the studio with the beautiful news that Coca-Cola had phoned and wanted Elkin and Fox for the voice-over in a new campaign. This had everyone dancing until they headed into the eight o'clock news.

That's when Ted Fox made another mention of Sari Rose-in-bloom. This time, Ted Fox asked Elkin on air whether he thought Sari had ever sailed on Holland America. They were doing a live spot for the passenger line. With Elkin feeling a strange sickness coming on, Ted Fox wouldn't let it go, now asking Elkin did he think that this Sari would like to sail with him, Ted Fox. Elkin quickly made it into a bit where his Dr. Huckleberry character began psychoanalyzing Ted Fox for this strange obsession. But then Ted Fox started singing a few bars of "Come Fly With Me," singing, "Come sail with me, come sail on the Holland America Line," and he ended it with, "C'mon Sari! Sail with me!" and, because their producer, Sgt. Al, was a pro, Sgt. Al already had the Sinatra record heading into Elkin's hands. Elkin got the record cued up and then they went into the eight o'clock news which was mostly about American warplanes secretly bombing Cambodia and Laos.

Sgt. Al said, "Ted, what's with this?" and Elkin said, "Al, let me take care of it," so Sgt. Al and his tattoos left the studio.

"You gotta stop," Elkin said.

"What?" Ted Fox smiled. "I'm happy. I'm in love. That's all."

Elkin repeated this story to his manager, Marty Horowitz, about two and a half hours later in Marty's soaring office at 50th and Madison. He told the story on his feet, moving across the tight khaki rug, sometimes picking up a magazine only to throw it back on the coffee table by the long sofa. The only thing he added to the story was a reference to "that schmuck" every time he said the name Ted Fox.

"OK, OK, I heard the routine, I heard all of them, I hear you every morning," Marty Horowitz said. "It works. It's funny. What's the problem?"

Elkin kept pacing around the office and Marty swung his little party-hotdog legs so that his feet were up on the desk. This guy, Marty Horowitz, he always looked to Elkin like he was a tight little trashcan Jew, a short, tough, stalking target of dark hair and putty-faced features. Hard to hit. Always in a black suit and a white shirt. When he walked around, Marty Horowitz swung his shoulders like he was in a boxing ring, that's what Elkin thought, but he also thought that if you wanted someone to manage you, you wanted someone who wasn't afraid to put his *tuches aufn tish* and go hard-line on all lines.

"You know what you're saying," Marty Horowitz said after Elkin finished a half hour's worth of complaining and explanation. "You're gonna bust up one of the most successful radio comedy teams ever. And all because of some little tootsie?"

"The tootsie is one step too far," Elkin said. "And how many possible fucking great deals has this fucking guy squashed? Schmuck. If I didn't have to carry this guy...."

"Carry him?" Marty Horowitz slammed his stumpy legs down on the floor again. "Ted's as good as it gets. Have you talked to Teddy about this?"

"Every fucking time I come here, Marty, and try to break the contract and go out on my own, you talk me out of it."

"And you go away happy," Marty Horowitz said. "So cool the fuck down."

"You think that if I went out on my own, I'd go down in fuck-ing flames." Elkin planted himself back down in the chair across from Marty Horowitz. "And that'd be a goddamn big bite out of your yearly stew, wouldn't it, *bubala.*"

"It's a lot more serious than that," Marty Horowitz said. "We gotta make sure we don't walk into a nice fat lawsuit for collusion."

"SO SUE ME! I STILL WANT OUT!"

Marty Horowitz clipped the end off a cigar and lit up. He blew a thick plume across the desk and Elkin said, "Jesus, you're making the room smell like my father. Put it away."

Marty Horowitz stubbed out the cigar. His eyebrows were now like two thick black roaches when he raised them and said, "This time you're not just whining."

"Get me out, Marty, I can't take it anymore."

"This must be some tootsie," Marty Horowitz said. "Can I meet her?"

"NO!" Elkin took off his glasses and slapped one palm over his face. He sat there like that breathing hard and rubbing. Marty Horowitz asked him if he was OK and Elkin said, "How soon do you think we can do this?"

"I'll figure a way," Marty Horowitz said. "But Elko, do me one favor, will'ya? Go home. Think about this for a day or two. Cool off. Get some rest. Then call me and give me the lowdown."

Elkin nodded with his face still in his hand. He felt like if he took the hand away, the face might fall off. Soon, though, he felt a little better and put his glasses back on and watched the thick features of Marty Horowitz return to focus.

He was at the office door when Marty Horowitz said, "One thing I want you to think about. Think about where you came from and where you are now. Because once we start this, there's no going back."

"I'll be in touch," Elkin said, and walked out.

Elkin started thinking about it as soon as he hit Madison Avenue. After thinking about it for three or four steps, he needed a drink. Actually, he needed the drink right after the show but he didn't want to show up at Horowitz's office with booze on his breath. He was beginning to scare himself. He needed to get away. Struggling to change his mood, Elkin did one of his little air jumps, spun around, came down and started striding through the midtown crowd swinging his arms back and forth in a comic walk. He didn't stop this until he heard someone on the sidewalk say, "Hey, there's

Jerry Elkin doing some kind of walk."

I'm out of my mind, Elkin wanted to say. But The Ridiculous will protect me.

Elkin picked up the pace. He said "shit" under his breath and clobbered the impulse to look behind him, suddenly worrying that Ted Fox was giving chase. Elkin didn't stop until he got to P.J. Clarke's up on Third and 55th. Good. Maybe the comfort of an old-style New York saloon would do the trick. Wooden stools, dinged-up bar, checkered tablecloths, the white tile floor looked like someone had taken a chisel to it. Out of breath, not feeling any better, Elkin stood at the bar and asked for a Gimlet.

"Hey, Mr. Elkin!" the bartender was that short guy, with a big, happy, open face who looked like he'd just crawled out of a coffin. For the life of him Elkin couldn't remember the guy's name. "Haven't seen you for a while, is Mr. Fox joining you?"

Elkin did a quick Coach Bruce Bruise voice and said, "Nah, the quarterback's run off with some dame."

The bartender laughed. Then he said, "Not the one he brought in here the other day. Jeezy-peezy, I thought there'd be a riot. What a dish!"

"What?" Elkin said quietly. The bartender came closer in a gesture that said, Big Secret.

"Tell ya, Mr. Elkin," the bartender said in hush. "Never seen anything like it. A real man-killer. Young, too, a kid. With a funny name, like a flower or…"

Elkin did the Gimlet in one swift pass and handed the glass back to the bartender. "Another if you would, my good man," he said in an English accent but he thought he might pass out. From the other end of the bar he heard, "Elko! Jerry!" and swung around to see the boxer Rocky Graziano coming toward him like he was coming out of his corner in the ring.

"Rocky!" Coach Bruce Bruise called out. This was the answer. Don't think about it. And how could you think about it when you weren't you, you were the Coach. Now, Elkin didn't have to think about anything except how much his shoulder hurt after Graziano gave him a welcoming right hook. The guy was a killer, great fighter, always looked sort of happy, Elkin thought, at least he did if you weren't in your shorts trying to hit him.

They shook hands. A real pump, up and down. Elkin had first met Graziano back in 1955 at the Friars Club after the middleweight left the ring and was doing his TV comedy show with Henny Youngman. It wasn't a very funny show but Elkin and Fox said it was great and put him on their own show after Rocky's was cancelled which was almost immediately. As Elkin would say.

"Teddy with you?" Graziano said. "Jeez, that guy's the end. He was in here the other day with a piece of tail that was..."

"Let me buy you one, Rock," Elkin said.

They drank. Graziano went into his story, again, about losing to Tony Zale in '46. They drank some more. Graziano went into his story about winning against Tony Zale in '47. They drank again. Then again. Some more after that. By this time, it was getting dark and Graziano was demonstrating combinations along the bar. Anyone who was standing there drinking made a small, polite move but definitely out of the way. Rocky didn't quite have all of his control going. Watching him, the cadaver bartender put on the expression of a man who was about to run his truck into a wall. Graziano's fists were swinging in short, sharp, practiced jabs, rights, uppercuts and Elkin caught the backdraft from a couple of shots. If he stepped away—the smart thing to do—he might trip. So Elkin did the big freeze. And Rocky got on his ring-gaze, shined it on Elkin as he went on to explain the next move and the next.

Like a dance routine, Elkin's entire day kicked and stepped and bowed in his head. The show in the morning, Ted Fox, Sari Rose-in-bloom, Marty Horowitz, boxing with Rocky Graziano. All the separate worlds colliding. It was all nuts. That's what he was thinking as Rocky took a little bit of a bad step on P.J. Clarke's white tiled floor and caught Elkin in the right shoulder again, this time with a solid left hook.

Elkin jerked sideways and stumbled. His Gimlet glass went out of his hand like it was on a spring and as it shattered somewhere else in the bar, the cadaver bartender said, "That's it, Rock, sorry, you gotta settle down."

"Look at him, the coach is fine!" Graziano was weaving a little. "Nothing hurts this guy. Do Mr. Nosh, go ahead!"

"Goodbye, everybody!" Mr. Nosh smiled and waved and he blew a kiss to Rocky as he tried to find his way to the door.

He hoped he didn't die on the way home. The car wasn't weaving but the white lane dividers of the Grand Central Parkway were moving around a little. He wasn't sure why he was on this road, anyway. Maybe I drive better with a couple of belts in me, Elkin thought. Yeah. He'd forgotten to buy gas for the Volvo. He wasn't sure there was enough to get home. And that fucking Jake! Gotta talk to him. Gotta say something. Gotta get him away from that tootsie, as Marty Horowitz called her...

...and away from the police siren that was now sounding behind him. The car was unmarked. A hand reached out of the driver's window and put a small red light on the roof.

"Uh-oh," Elkin said to himself. His heart started tap dancing. The sweat that broke along his forehead smelled like you could bottle it. And he pulled over to the grassy side of the Parkway, watching in the rearview as the shadow of the cop approached in the darkness.

The cop was looking over Elkin's license and Elkin was thinking that this wasn't some kid they put on traffic, this looked like a very tough detective or plainclothes guy who was trying to get home.

"You know how badly you were weaving?"

"I'm sorry," Elkin said.

The cop looked at the license again. "I thought I recognized you," he said. "I know who you are."

Elkin made his funny face up at the cop but he was having trouble keeping his eyes focused. "Do you want me to do Mr. Nosh?"

"I want you to get home without killing yourself," the cop said. "Or anybody else."

"Don't arrest me, please."

"No. I'm gonna do you a real big favor. Hand me your keys."

Elkin took the keys out of the ignition and passed them to the plainclothes guy. "There's a phone booth about a half mile up the road, just up there," the cop said, pointing. "Go call your wife." Then he turned around and threw Elkin's car keys so the little leather key tag arced up in the air against the light of the night sky and sailed away, disappeared somewhere in a darkened bush. "Tell her you need a lift home."

The cop started back to his own car. Elkin called out, "Thank you, Officer!"

And he sat there for a moment with the booze pulsing in his cheeks, his eyes sliding out of focus. Could have been bad. Very bad. That guy was OK. During The War, there was an early morning when the Japs came down on them in a quick and dirty bomb run over the base. Elkin was near enough to the blast of one of those whistling fuckers to be blown up, picked up and jacked up through the air so that when he landed, he tumbled into the field latrine with his left foot broken at the instep and most of his body covered in shit. Clinging, the stink made him sick. All that and he was shrieking, too, screaming in pain. And nobody wanted to go fish him out.

Today was almost that bad, Elkin thought. I'm in trouble. He tried to calm down.

OK. A half-mile walk I can do, Elkin cleared his throat. Start small. Head suddenly shoving through the open window of the car, he vomited down the side of the door into the gravel.

Then he began searching in his pockets to make sure he had the coins to make the call home.

CHAPTER NINE

GRADUATION. Six students refused to show up to protest the war. Twenty-three students wore peace signs on their gowns. Four students unfurled a long banner that read, "End the War NOW!" and four others held up a sign urging, "Resist The Draft, Don't Register!" One student hid a bicycle horn in his armpit and when handed his diploma gave it two quick pumps, ala Harpo Marx. This last, for Jake, seemed a fine summing up.

A world of war and No Sari. At graduation, Jake got one half of a quick look at her but Max and the Mrs. stepped across to wall her in just as Jake got off the beginning of a smile. No good. That split-second glimpse froze his lips in the expression of a snarling trout and Jake walked away hoping he'd left her better memories.

So, gone. Banned from her life. That was the official story. That's what Max Rosenbloom had ordered. So, OK, Jake said to himself. You want a piece of me? Let's go.

New guys came to take Sari out. Jake saw them.

He lay down hidden in an ivy patch across the street from the Rosenbloom house and watched the guys come to the front door and then leave with Sari smiling and laughing and talking beside them. She was, Jake thought, a terrific little actress.

Jake wasn't sure who owned the ivy patch which had a musty, compost smell, but it made for excellent cover. When he was right down there flat on his belly, he was sure nobody could see him in the darkness but he had a clear shot of Sari's front door.

The first guy to take her out was the blond beach boy executive type that Sari had told him about. The one her mother had invited over at Rockefeller Center. Even in a light gray business suit and with his sporty BMW, this guy had Nixon written all over him. Jake watched as the little Nixon went in and he watched as the little Nixon came out with his arm around Sari. When they drove off in the BMW, Jake thought about following but he couldn't figure out what he would do when he caught up to them. The best thing was to wait and let Max Rosenbloom think he'd won.

The next guy Jake saw was an older man that Jake could have sworn was Ted Fox. He saw that Vee Vee and Max gave him a big hi-ho greeting at the doorway and they were doing a lot of talk-and-touch, treating him like an old buddy, like he was gold. Jake was going to tell his father about this, his father had to know, he had to do something. This was absolutely crazy. The world couldn't be like this. But when he'd told his father that Max Rosenbloom had threatened to break his back and how he'd gone over to the house for a showdown, all Elkin had said was, "If he hits you, fall down and we'll sue him." Elkin couldn't think about Max Rosenbloom now because he had to think about Ted Fox.

And that was Ted Fox for sure who was now putting Sari in the T-bird and taking off with a last wave at the open door where Max and Vee Vee stood smiling and blowing kisses. This time Jake was seriously going to tail them but first he had to think about it and in the middle of his thinking, two hours later, the T-Bird was pulling back into the Rosenbloom driveway and Sari was jumping out and doing a little run-and-skip up her front walk with a last pirouette and wave back at Ted Fox. Like she'd had a wonderful, magical time.

This had to stop. He called her once but Vee answered. Jake bobbled the phone, nearly taking out his two front teeth, then banging the receiver on the table in his rush to hang up. Then he began riding his bicycle around the Rosenbloom Zone. No luck. Sari never came outside. Maybe the bike was too fast, maybe he'd missed her. So he started jogging, then walking, past the Rosenbloom home three times a day but with his gaze locked houseward he developed a stabbing crick in the neck that aped the symptoms of several horrible diseases. Jake had checked them all in the home medical encyclopedia.

And then once, when Jake was on the sidewalk after buying cigarettes at Frederick's Soda Fountain, he caught a quick shot of Sari in a black Caddie, riding next to that guy, her father's Russian business partner, she'd said. The two of them whisked by like they should be tossing pennies to the poor but Jake was certain, he could feel it. Oh, Sari knew he was right there, she just pretended not to see him so nobody'd ask any questions. Brilliant. That Sari! Jake could see exactly how the universe worked its wonders.

He went back to hiding in the ivy. But Jake was starting to suspect it was making him crazy. The dirt was cold and left dark patches on his knees and elbows. When he popped up from hiding, he congratulated himself for being a kind of Vietcong of Love, out to ambush the night, but moments later, he was sure he'd get arrested. When he lay there in the ivy and saw Sari come out with a Somebody Else, Jake felt like he'd been drilled in the chest. When he wasn't jealous he was lonely and when he wasn't angry he was lonelier.

In his room, he read, talked to himself, jerked off, finally lying on his bed in a stupor, unable to complete a thought. He became an archeologist of the future, trying to dig out the mysteries of what was to be. He began looking at his newspaper horoscope every day. When that didn't give him enough trustworthy information he bought the I Ching and started throwing pennies and reading the hexagrams. Will Sari come back to me? "There is a great bend in the river. A moving wind." What the fuck did that mean? Shakespeare was next, the big one-volume edition with the Rockwell Kent illustrations that his aunt had given him. Does Sari love me? He closed his eyes, flipped some pages and poked his finger on a line. "Hostess: Say, what thing? What thing?" Fuck Shakespeare, too.

Finally, Jake took down the thick, gold-embossed Old Testament that had been a wedding present to Jerry Elkin, the same Jerry Elkin who'd told his son he'd stopped believing in the Old Testament after guys who were 19 or 20 and who'd barely had time to sin, play grab-ass were blown up by Japanese bombs on Guam. Now, Jake flipped through this same Bible sweating for some word, some sign that Sari Rose-in-bloom was aching for him. Nothing. Everybody dies, it said, everything is vanity. Chance. Life is short. Oh, and by the way, don't mix milk with meat.

Hoping to forget himself, Jake went to a party at his pal Bob Siegel's house. Bob was the only person still friendly with Jake now that Jake did nothing that didn't involve Sari Rose-in-bloom. Bob lived about five blocks over from the Rosenbloom home in a sprawling ranch-style home bought with a G.I. loan by Mr. Siegel who was under indictment for fraud. Mr. and Mrs. Siegel were spending the weekend in the city. By the time Jake got to the party, the Siegel piano was down to two legs and lurching forward like a dying hippo, a naked girl was jumping up and down on the living room sofa and Jake could count one fucking-couple and one hand-job-couple in the far hallway. Everybody else was sitting on the living room floor looking at album covers.

Bob Siegel was alone in his room smoking a joint. His big Jew-fro Dylan-like hair was scrounged in by a headband and he was sitting on his bed, up against the wall, listening to the radio play "She's A Rainbow" by the Stones. Jake sat down next to him. Bob passed over the joint and when Jake emptied his lungs he said, "Sari gone, heart broken" in the tinny, monotone voice of the old cop-movie police-radio announcements. The Now-Hear-This voice.

"Must get her back," Bob said, also in Now-Hear-This. It was the only way they spoke to each other.

"May have to commit crime," Jake said. "Sneak in house. Take girl away."

"Do not commit crime," Bob said.

"Have no other plan," Jake said.

"Must find plan," Bob answered.

The conversation went on like this through the Beatles' "Get Back" and Elvis's cover of "Suspicion." Stop this fucking music, Jake was thinking, it's all about Sari Rose-in-bloom. Bob's girlfriend of two weeks, Mindy, walked in the room holding the front of her shirt closed. She settled in next to them on the bed and Jake passed her the joint. Mindy lived with her mother who was always drunk and who collected toy frogs and she'd been suspended from school for two weeks for cutting pictures out of library art books. She used the pictures to illustrate the journal she was writing, an autobiography.

Jake explained what was going on. "Switch dates," Mindy said. "I go with Jake. Bob picks up Sari. We meet and trade."

"Excellent plan," Bob said.

"Very excellent," Jake said. "10-4. Over."

Jake got up and went home.

Two nights later, Bob Siegel picked up Sari Rose-in-bloom and Jake picked up Susan, Bob's new girlfriend. They met out at the off-limits dead end that edged onto the grounds of the Gatsby House. That's where they were going to make the switch. The only one who didn't know this was going to happen was Sari Rose-in-bloom because, as Jake explained to Bob Siegel, "Must test love."

"Do not test," Bob Siegel said.

Jake smoked and walked back and forth near Jerry Elkin's Volvo while the new girlfriend, Susan, told him he wasn't very talkative and asked if something was wrong. Jake pointed up in the distance, beyond the stone gate, to the glimmer of lawn, to the white, piled pearls of the mansion that they could barely see for the grove of trees.

"That's the house that Fitzgerald used in *Great Gatsby*," Jake said.

"Yeah, I know," Susan said. "I was with you on the class trip. In tenth grade."

"Oh," Jake said. "Yeah." They were at the end of the small road that circled around past the gate. Jake now pointed his cigarette toward where they could barely see the shore because of the trees. "You can sneak through there to the water and see across to the other side," Jake said. "We can watch the light flicker. Like what's-his-name does in *The Great Gatsby*."

"Calm down," Susan said.

Jake flipped his cigarette so he could check out the blast of sparks when it hit in the darkness. "How the hell long does it take to get here?"

"They were probably killed in an accident," Susan said. "Did you ever think of that?"

Jake lit up another cigarette. "Maybe they got lost."

"How could they get lost, it's thirty seconds away."

"Maybe her father is hip to this, he's calling the cops."

"And maybe Bobby is parked someplace, balling her in the back seat," Susan said. "That's probably it. The boy's hung like a mule, he needs a third sock."

Jake blew smoke through his nose and then puffed out a perfect smoke ring with the rest of it. "I've been in gym class with the guy since we were twelve," he said. "So don't give me any *schlong* talk."

Susan was bobbing her head a lot now and she said, "Jake, this is the first time I've been out since my nose job, OK? Don't ruin it."

"You had a nose job? Let's see," Jake held her chin, turned her face. "Nice."

"There's a little scar but I don't think it'll be…"

Jake didn't hear the rest of it because up the drive he could see the approaching headlights like the eyes of a huge bug. Bob and his little white Karmann Ghia. The car zoomed past them and turned around and there was Sari through the window as the car headed back up the road, in the opposite direction, away.

"Funny and fuck you," Jake said to the car.

"Is he always like this?"

The Ghia disappeared around another turn and when it came back, this time it was moving so slowly that Jake, nervous, began to laugh.

He stopped laughing when he saw Sari jump out and start running toward him. She threw her arms around Jake and knocked him back against Elkin's Volvo and when she kissed him her right leg bent up in the air. Sari was crying and she whispered in Jake's ear, "What took you so long, Buster?" and then Jake couldn't take in very much except that Bob Siegel and Susan were gone and Jake was running through the trees holding the hand of Sari Rose-in-bloom who was laughing and ducking branches.

They got down to the dark shore where they could see the moon glisten off the Sound. On the far side there was a dock, and a green light, but it wasn't blinking, it just hung there. It was all shadows, even what they could see of the Gatsby House, just a big candy box shadow in the distance. Jake led Sari to a large rock near the water and they sat down with their backs against it so at least, if anyone came searching, they wouldn't be so easily seen.

"I think my mother knows," Sari Rose-in-bloom said. "She gave your friend Bob the third degree. We could've been there all night."

"Your mother's nuts," Jake said. He saw that little detonation go off in Sari's eyes and knew he was at the deep edge of a screw-up.

"She's my mother," Sari said. No more talking after that until she said, "She's having an affair with Paul Newman."

"The actor?" Jake said. "I thought she was fooling around with that Mafia guy."

"Now it's Paul Newman," Sari Rose-in-bloom said. "That's what she told me."

They shared a cigarette. "Maybe she's not the only one who's been out with a lot of guys."

Sari Rose-in-bloom cocked her head and spit smoke. "Not so many," she said. So Jake started ticking them off. He was expecting her to say something like, "Have you been spying on me?" but instead she said, "I like Ted Fox. He promised my father he'd act like a perfect gentleman and he has. He's a grown man."

"He's a hundred years old."

"A hundred and four," Sari said. "You forgot your friend Bob. I was out with him tonight."

"Jesus Christ!" Jake said. "And he's in love with you, too, now, isn't he?"

Sari smiled then she suddenly put on a clown face, bulged out her eyes at Jake and started laughing. "Bob doesn't like girls."

"Oh, so he's a fag? I've been in gym class with the guy since we were twelve and…"

"He told me he's into psychic adventure," Sari said. "Not girls. He said he'd call me after you and I broke up. He was stoned to the gills, too."

"What about that blond Nixon in the BMW."

"The one my mother set me up with? He died."

"What?" Jake said. "Died? How?"

With anyone else, anyone human, Jake thought, he'd be feeling like the two of them were just staring at each other but with Sari Rose-in-bloom that wasn't it. She allowed Jake to gaze upon her, made him take notice. There was a method behind it: she let Jake breathe in what it was he stood to lose. Because Sari knew that if right now, this moment, she just stood up and walked away, it would be Jake whose heart stopped, Jake who left for The Other Side.

"He fell in front of a subway car," Sari said. "Or maybe he jumped. After our date. They had a little thing about it in the papers."

Sari Rose-in-bloom stood up and said, "Jake," under her breath. Didn't exactly spew the name but Jake didn't like hearing it sound that way. She brushed off her ass and left him, walked closer to the water, hugging herself and looking out. Jake followed.

He circled his arms around her. She pressed back against him. He was aware that the air he was breathing might never be this sweet again and that this might be the only time in his misbegotten life that he felt such love and yearning and loneliness and expectation, that all of it beat in his chest and it hurt and he didn't want it to stop. Jake thought his entire body was starting to vibrate. He could barely say, "What are you thinking?" and when Sari said, "About all the things that have gone on here, right on this spot," Jake turned her around. They were face-to-face and breath close. "And I was thinking about the moonlight," Sari said.

Jake kissed her. Now he thought his entire body would vibrate and then explode. So Jake said, "I love you, Sari," and Sari said, "I really think I love you, too."

"You think? Why you *think*?" Jake said. "Why can't you just say it?"

"Because I'm telling you the truth."

Jake kissed her again, harder this time, and then he pulled her down on the grass. He was certain now. He was going to vibrate, explode, then reconstitute as someone better and he was going to fuck Sari Rose-in-bloom until the Earth stopped moving. No, no, he told himself, not like that, think "make love" to Sari Rose-in-bloom because he was certain that nobody could just fuck her, they'd turn to stone if they tried. Unless it had happened already. Who had "made love" to Sari already? Who'd fucked her? Ted Fox, I bet. That douche bag. I hate that schmuck Ted Fox, Jake was thinking, I hate him, how can my father work with that guy? Ted Fox fucked Sari and I'm gonna…

That was the last clear thought that passed through Jake's brain because now he seemed to be waking up in a world where he'd pushed up Sari Rose-in-bloom's T-shirt and crushed aside her bra and his mouth was on the small, sweet bud of her nipple. He was unbuckling her belt and her jeans, his fingers finding the light dusting of hair between her legs, then moving into her, feeling her wet and feeling her breath go hot and fast against his cheek. She said, "I can't. Then I won't be the mystery woman."

"But you'll be you," Jake said and wondered if that had any meaning at all. Probably not. He didn't care.

"A couple of years ago my mother took me to the doctor," Sari said then. "He broke me down there. So it wouldn't be painful and bleed. The first time."

"What?" Jake said. He was going to add, "Your mother's nuts" but now he knew better so he zoomed into, "That's horrible." And then he wondered if she was lying. Maybe it was a way to keep Jake from knowing that she'd already fucked Ted Fox. More evidence! That goddamn schmuck! He hated that fucking Ted Fox he was going to…

He stopped. He realized she was saying "yes." Jake wasn't sure any longer how Ted Fox figured into this, but here on the grass, under the brazen moon and near the bright water, near the Sound, near the Gatsby House, he was going to fuck Sari Rose-in-bloom. Maybe the ghostly Gatsby himself would come running out of his house and find these two Yids *schtupping* on his lawn. Even so. Even with Gatsby yanking at his ankles and shouting for the police, Jake was going to have her. Make love to Sari. For me, right now, Jake thought, this will be like coming home alive from World War Two.

"Have you done this ever?"

Jake told her "yes" and then he was kissing her and her jeans were pulling against her thighs. He'd been with four girls before. An older girl who'd made the first move, one of Bob Siegel's girlfriends although he never told Bob, one of Bob Siegel's cousins who was in visiting from Texas which he never told Bob about, either, and a hooker after he'd read *From Here to Eternity*. He knew this was different and that it was going to change the world. That's what had been pulsing through his brain since he had first laid eyes on her.

And then when he could still think, Jake was thinking that it was amazing how quickly things turned awkward and even more amazing how quickly the awkward turned ridiculous.

Jake's chest was against Sari, he was kicking his pants away from his ankles. And then he was inside her. He heard her grunt. When he moved inside her, she made another soft sound, a softer tone of what Jake heard from his dog when it was hit by a car. Jake arched, stared down into Sari Rose-in-bloom's eyes and he thought that never before in his entire life, maybe in anyone's life, had anybody seen such a look of disdain, a woman's face painted in a kind of hateful dignity at violation. Every time he moved inside her she grunted, or gritted her teeth or tightly shut her eyes and turned her face away. Jake reached down between them and then with his hand in the darkness before his face, he could just about see that his fingers came up bloody.

"I thought you said…"

"Finish it," Sari Rose-in-bloom said.

"You're gonna do this sometime," Jake said. "Now's as good a time as any."

He wasn't sorry he said it and he did what she told him to do. Everything went blunt inside him and in that moment he hated her. She was showing him he was a son of a bitch, a schmuck, that he had it in him to smash her and enjoy the smashing. And if you could smash Sari Rose-in-bloom and enjoy it? Jake thought. Then you were fucking insane. Mad. The whole world. Everyone. And at the same time, he thought: she has it coming.

After that, when it was over, Jake thought he could hear cloth moving, the crush of leaves and maybe twigs snapping but not her breath. They were standing back-to-back. He wanted to say something, something important, something they'd both remember, but for that, you had to know words and Jake was having trouble zipping his pants and staying on his feet. That was about all he could handle.

When they walked back through the trees to the Volvo, Jake was getting his bearings. It was like his pores had opened and he was sweating apologies. He told her he was sorry. He was sorry even when there was only the sound of crickets and the light traffic hum from far away. Sari kept her arms around herself, walking.

Jake still hated himself, he was his own Ted Fox. He started on more "sorries" while he was figuring (since he was going to be with Sari Rose-in-bloom forever) that maybe they would have sex again sometime. They'd have to work something out. He was sorry. He didn't mean to hurt her. He thought she said that her mother had…but he broke off and told her again that he loved her. Sari Rose-in-bloom kept quiet until the Volvo got near her home.

"Stop here, "she said." My mother will see the car."

They were still a block away. Sari sat upright looking straight ahead and then she said, "I don't love you. At least I think I don't. Not right now."

"But you might again later?"

She slammed the car door before Jake could stammer out another apology or say good night. He watched the light go on above her front door, saw Vee Vee appear in the doorway as she scouted the street for Bob Siegel's car. Then there was only the door and the light went out. Sari was inside.

They were saying something, Vee and Sari, it killed Jake that he didn't know what. The whole thing was killing him. Jake backed up and made a wide turn, started on a different route home so that he didn't have to pass by any snooping mothers at any fucking window. What was Sari going to say to her? And all the way back he was thinking to himself that this was not supposed to have happened that way, something was out of whack, it wasn't right. And of all the schmucks in the collection of big schmucks in the world, Jake Elkin said to himself, he was the biggest schmuck of all, King Schmuck of all time.

CHAPTER TEN

AT THE MEMORIAL for the late Bernardo Chinita, while Andy Warhol was giving a eulogy, Max Rosenbloom had a flash image of having sex with his daughter.

Oh, how could he not? Max sat slumped in his folding chair, butt cold and sore, arms crossed over his chest. And Warhol? You couldn't hear the guy. Even sitting here, right up front, it looked like the little man was only moving his lips. So Max studied the drawings of Sari, each and every part of her fantastic body, rendered so magnificently and with such glowing life that Max started to get antsy in his seat.

Sari was everywhere. The Chinita Saris, as the drawings had come to be known, decorated the walls and the podium and were propped up on the floor of Warhol's Factory at Broadway and Union Square. Max Rosenbloom was proud of her, but he was thinking, there were limits. Max tried to put Sari out of his mind. Max tried to read lips and concentrated on what Warhol appeared to be saying, something about how Bernardo Chinita had gone the way only a great artist could go, drinking copal medium while preparing a new canvas. Then Warhol showed off a special piece of his own, called "For Bernardo," which was a lithographed image of a soup can with Sari's picture on it, available for sale. Whatever that girl had, Max Rosenbloom hoped she kept it.

The place was packed. Vee Vee Rosenbloom nestled beside Max in the front row and Max was positive he could hear her humming. Very quietly, but humming under her breath. And every so often Vee would turn to stare at the people on the folding chairs, sometimes twisting around in the black dress that she wore like a huge storm cloud, Max thought, and then she would turn back, lean closer to Max and whisper something like, "Jasper Johns is here." Or tell him she had seen Roy Lichtenstein. Or George Segal.

"For Sari," Vee Vee would add. "Not Bernardo. They're here to see Sari."

Max Rosenbloom had to do a little "shshshshsh" and got back the inevitable "Don't shshshshsh me" and then he took Vee Vee's hand and patted the back of it and set her hand on his thigh. She pulled away.

"That's Sari," she said. Vee then nodded at another image. "That's Sari, too."

"Stop it," Max whispered. "What are you talking about?"

When he tried to take her hand again, Vee Vee stood up so that her chair clattered on the floor. Her large black dress made a rustling sound and she hustled off loudly, past the front row of mourners and down the aisle toward the door. Her exit came just as Vladamir Nabokov started to say from the podium how wonderful it was that soon the massive Chinita statue of this Sari goddess would be unveiled at the Metropolitan Museum of Art and all the world would...

He stopped as Vee walked out.

"How dare you! Someone tell me, who is this woman?" Nabokov stepped away from the podium.

Nobody spoke up until Max Rosenbloom called out, "She's the mother of the girl." Then Nabokov stared at Max Rosenbloom like Max was still working his way through "See spot run" and Nabokov paused, then whispered, "Chinita is the mother of the girl!"

Everyone applauded.

Max kept his mouth shut. He didn't want to but he didn't want to do anything that would make the memorial last any longer than it had to. On the other side of Max, Boris Jampolsky gave a soft nudge so that Max had to say quietly to him, "It's OK. Leave it alone." He didn't need to have Nabokov roughed up, what the hell good would that do? Max was a little worried about Boris. The crazy Russian was still cooking with gas, Max thought, still hot and just off the plane that morning from Atlanta where Boris had tried to reassure the guys with the warehouse that Max would still be shipping in the poisoned children's clothing. They wanted to know where and when and mostly they wanted to get paid. The deal was still on track, Max promised, which it most certainly wasn't. And it wasn't because of that schmuck Larry Passoff, but they didn't need to know that. So to show good faith, Boris had gone down and helped one of the guys with a different warehouse, helping him collect some insurance by creating a situation where insurance had to be paid.

"Go find my wife," Max Rosenbloom murmured to Boris. But when the Russian started to get to his feet, Max stopped him, motioning up at Nabokov who'd resumed speaking. "When he's through," Max said.

It was all trouble, just the kind of *tsuris* he didn't need. Max had a bad feeling about Larry Passoff, there was something very unkosher about how he was handling the whole deal. Larry had said he was in but every time Max called Larry Passoff to find out what progress had been made and how he was making out, Larry would say that someone was in the office or he was just leaving and couldn't talk and he'd call Max right back, right back he promised. But he never did. That was bad enough. But worse, if Max kept pushing, Larry would launch into some kind of code which Max finally translated as "Don't call the office, I'll call you from a pay phone."

Something was up. Back in the old neighborhood, where Larry's father just got by with his hockshop, Larry had helped his father out with a small time numbers game run from the back of the store but Max never figured the clown for any kind of an operator. "Pencil neck Larry," this guy was, the kid who needed protection from the dagos and the micks. The best thing to do would be to have Boris find out. Boris had a couple of buddies who were ex-Israeli something or others, Mossad or commandos or something who could find things out and weren't afraid to hear the bones crack. Max would do an off-hand to Boris who would do an off-hand to his buddies and there would be no breadcrumbs to follow if things got rough. Max Rosenbloom didn't like doing it but, hell, what choice did he have? It was schmucks like Larry Passoff who always put you in this kind of goddamn position. They couldn't play on the up and up, yes or no, in or out, it was always they had to think things through or take their time or they were too chickenshit just to say "Thanks a lot but no thanks." The whole thing stinks, Max thought, and he was getting angrier and angrier as he thought about it.

So, that was one problem. But the other? Jesus! This sudden volcano between Vee and Sari. It had started the other night when Sari came home from that date with that kid Bob Siegel. He'd seemed like a loveable enough schmuck, Sari wasn't going to end up with him, they'd go out and have fun, that's all, they were kids. But Vee had been certain that Bob Siegel was fronting for Jake Elkin and she and Sari had gotten into a pistol of a fight when Sari walked in, shrieking at each other until Max Rosenbloom had had to jam out his cigarette in the night table ashtray, then get out of bed and shout at Vee Vee to get the hell upstairs.

A door slammed, Sari heading into her own corner, and Vee steamed into the bedroom to start slapping through the closet full of dresses that didn't fit her. When Max tried to calm her down she'd pulled the pin on him. "SHE'S LYING! SHE'S LYING TO ME AND SHE'S LYING TO YOU!"

Max said he didn't think so, Sari wasn't like that.

"OH, YOU'RE SO SMART," Vee sneered.

Max said he'd already handled the situation.

"IN YOUR DREAMS!" Vee yelled. "IF YOU HAD THE BALLS YOU WERE BORN WITH YOU'D DO SOMETHING FOR REAL!" That's why Sari had refused to come here, to the Bernardo Chinita memorial that was now wrapping up. She didn't want to be seen around Vee, wouldn't grace her fat ass and, man, she'd told her so, really let Vee have it. Max had had to step in and shout, "Hey, that's your mother you're talking to!" And Sari would have been treated like royalty here, like a princess, hell, why stop there, like the goddess they were talking about. Max knew that at some level it was driving Vee crazy. She had to talk to somebody, a headshrinker, he'd get a name. He was starting to think it would be better once the girl was in Paris, out of the house. And what if Vee did it on purpose? What if Vee started in on Sari to make her mad, make her refuse to show up, steal the limelight from her. Max Rosenbloom shook that off. OK, Vee was having problems but they'd get through it.

But what a shame. Sari Rose-in-bloom was missing a room full of Sari Rose-in-blooms. The Chinita Saris. This he could not have dreamed up back in Bensonhurst. That Sari could have been here now, beside Max as he was introduced to Andy Warhol who asked whether Sari was real and if she was, offered to give her a tour of The Factory any time she wanted, just drop by. Max Rosenbloom said he would pass it on.

"You buy art, don't you?" Andy Warhol was saying, "I heard that somewhere, I think," but Max was already too far away to catch it and he felt that with Sari's image gracing the entire room, he didn't have to do anything else.

Outside, on Broadway, it was different. No Vee, no Boris. Max looked north and south and across the street but there was nothing but the buildings lining his side of the block, the park across the way and the metallic, lumbering sweep of traffic, people in a hurry. Then he saw her. She was a couple of doors away standing with Boris, linking arms with the Russian and speaking with another couple that Max didn't recognize. He walked closer. The couple pushed past Vee and Boris as if they'd been asked for a loan and Max now saw Vee pull Boris into the path of a different woman, this one in a bright red mini, who at first smiled at Vee, then took on a look of concern, and then also quickly got the hell down the block.

Max saw Vee spin around, still linked with Boris and she called to the lady in red, "Well, it's true! I'm Sari Rose-in-bloom's mother and this strapping boy is my Russian dressing."

"Oops," Vee laughed. "And this is my husband," as Max came up. Vee snatched her arm away from Boris and did an exaggerated comic giggle.

"Don't think it's true? Tell him, Khrushchev."

"Can't stop her," Boris was pale. "She keeps on doing."

Max Rosenbloom felt his gut go loose and he slumped his shoulders. Then he straightened his back because it wasn't going to be this way, and it wasn't because Max Rosenbloom said it wasn't.

"Kid, honey," Max said. "Vee. What are you doing?"

He did a quick finger wave to hail a cab. Vee didn't fight him. Boris held the door open and when they were inside, Vee turned to Max and said, "Max, I can't keep my lips sealed any longer. I've taken a lover."

Max shook his head. "No, you haven't."

"Bernardo Chinita," Vee said. "The great artist."

"He's dead," Max said.

"He is?" Vee said. "Well, then you'll never know."

As the cab drove away.

★　★　★

Elkin phoned his manager, Marty Horowitz, and told him that he'd thought about it and he meant everything he'd said during their meeting. Get me out of the contract.

All around him was home, his den, bookshelves, the

Book-of-the-Month Club selections, his phone, which was now in his hand. And his door, which was closed.

Marty Horowitz, on the other end, said if that's the way he felt, then that's the way it would be. Elkin said that's the way he felt and then he hung up and noticed a beautiful, old, dark blue volume of Edgar Allan Poe on the shelf, the book given to him decades before as a secret Bar Mitzvah present. A memory flickered and died: his copy of *The Great Gatsby*, which he'd carried through The War but never finished and which he'd thrown overboard into the Pacific with his Japanese skull. Elkin reached up and took the Poe book down and started flipping through the pages. A photo fell out. A sepia photo of him, Elkin, naked with a tits-and-ass naked Asian woman in a hotel bed, Elkin laughing and holding out his hand to stop the photographer who had obviously surprised the two of them.

Elkin had only the faintest memory of the photo's where-and-when. What was left in the dig, what he remembered: the picture had been taken in a Manila whorehouse and the girl had probably been a whore, but he couldn't recall that part of it and had no recollection of who took the shot or what was happening. It was gone forever.

He got on the phone and gave a callback to his manager, Marty Horowitz, and told him to wait, he'd been rash, he didn't want to stop working with Ted Fox, even if the guy was a schmuck who was losing his mind.

Marty Horowitz said not to worry, he'd figured this was going to happen.

Elkin hung up and thought about what Marty had said. He slipped the Poe book back on the shelf and sat down in the plush, upholstered chair with the flower print that he hated and said to himself, "How the hell does Marty Horowitz get off figuring this is going to happen?" His fingers dabbed at the edge of the Manila whorehouse photo.

"You know what, Marty," Elkin said when he got Marty Horowitz on the phone again. "Forget what I said."

"This time or the other time?"

"Any time," Elkin said. "I'm not going to have a dead dog like Ted Fox around my neck, dragging me down. Our contract? It's over. I want out."

He hung up.

The phone rang. Elkin picked it up and heard Marty Horowitz on the other end. "Jerry, don't be too concerned about this, but someone using your name just called me and said he wanted to break his contract with Ted Fox."

Elkin laughed. OK, OK, he said to his manager, Marty Horowitz, I get it. I'm making a schmuck out of myself. Send the son of a bitch some flowers. "It's Elkin and Fox 'til the end of the world."

Reaching up again, Elkin retrieved the volume of Edgar Allan Poe. The binding was almost rotted through but the lurid illustrations were bright and still frightening and he remembered how much he'd wanted the book but his father didn't think he should be reading it. Elkin read the faded inscription on the inside page, written in the almost perfect cursive style that had long since perished. "To Jerry. Just a little secret something extra. Love, Mom."

Elkin started to choke up. He remembered getting the letter on Guam telling him she'd died and how strange it had seemed when there were so many other people dying all around, so many planes that went up and never came back, planes that seemed to just disappear in the sky. She'd been terribly ill when he was shipped overseas. He remembered being at her bedside, saying goodbye, talking to her then about some of the news, the small items, about what was happening to the Jews of Europe. She had stopped him. "When you're this sick," she'd said, "you can only think about yourself."

Staring down at himself in sepia and in a whorehouse, he began tearing the photo from The War into pieces, tore it until it was piled in pieces too small to tear again. Then he got up, picked up the pile and went to the bathroom and flushed the pieces down the toilet.

Then Elkin called his manager, Marty Horowitz, again. "Yeah,

Marty," he said, now straining to fight off tears. "Oh, I don't know. I'm just sitting around here scratching my balls and I'm sort of thinking that right now, for me anyway, something's gotta change. Like maybe I really should take this seriously and wish Ted Fox goodbye and good luck."

"I understand and it's not a foolish idea," Marty Horowitz said. "And you're handling this exactly the way you should. Pondering it. Mulling it over. Thinking about it. And don't call me anymore."

Elkin called him back as soon as he heard the "click." He told Marty Horowitz that when he talked to his manager he, Elkin, expected to be taken seriously, that that was the least Marty Horowitz could do, and just because Elkin was a comedian didn't mean he didn't have some very serious concerns.

"How long have we known each other, *bubala?*" Marty Horowitz said. "You were a child when you walked into my office the first time. A *pisher* with a plea. Marty, you said, please. Watch over me and guide me. May the words of my mouth and the meditations of my heart be acceptable to you, Oh Marty, and help me make Elkin and Fox a household two names with an income in the upper brackets."

Elkin hadn't been prepared for that so he cleared his throat and said in his best Mr. Nosh Yiddish accent, "But now…it's over and done."

"You said, Marty, for the love of all that's holy. Please. Protect me from myself. And should I ever call you at home annoyingly in the early evening asking you to break my contract with Ted Fox, please forgive me. And hang up on me. Amen."

"Bye, Marty," Elkin said right before he heard the buzzing from the other end.

He snuck out of the den, poured himself a Scotch with one ice cube in the kitchen, then took it back to the den and shut the door. In the quiet of the room, he sipped and listened to the ice pop and click against the glass. Why was he like this? What was he so afraid of? And was it really so bad to continue on with Ted

Fox? He told himself that he was acting like a total schmuck. But why had he balled-and-chained himself with a family? That was it, they were holding him back. Just like Tex Fox. Like everyone. And that's when his wife, Marsha, came into the room and said that their son, Jake, was going to join the Army.

"Wait," Elkin said, spitting some of the Scotch back in his glass. "He joined? Or he said he was going to?"

The story came out. Jake had told his mother, Marsha, all about the night at the Gatsby House and what had happened with Sari Rose-in-bloom or most of it, anyway, and he was so distraught, Marsha said, that Jake had concluded by declaring that he couldn't take it anymore and that he was going into the Army, probably the paratroops or Green Berets.

"That stupid little shit," Elkin said. "Tell him I want to have a word with him tomorrow."

"Tomorrow? Maybe when you hear him yelling 'Geronimo!' over the house, then you'll talk to him."

"I need some time to think," Elkin said. "I have to think about Ted Fox."

Marsha left the room and a few minutes later, Jake walked in and propelled himself into the upholstered chair with the flower print Elkin hated that matched the chair he was sitting in.

Elkin breathed in like he was about to go 20 leagues under. "Your mother tells me you're going to join the Army."

Jake began his tale of Sari Rose-in-bloom, the threat from Max, sneaking around, the ivy patch, Ted Fox, the Gatsby House, everything until Elkin said, "Stop, I know this already. I'd like to run away with her, too, but you know what? She's just a girl."

Then Jake began another tale of Sari, this one about how she wasn't "just a girl" and how Jake would never, ever find someone that special again and he finished it up by telling Elkin that Sari wasn't just beautiful outside but she was beautiful inside, too, and that she had "a glowing light that everyone can see." So, Jake said, it didn't matter that he was very much against the war, he was still going in and he was going to lose himself or die which he was going to do now, anyway, because Sari was gone.

"I need another drink," Elkin said, thinking he should fill the glass before he threw it at his son. And when Elkin sat back down again in the chair that he hated, he started to tell Jake every bad thing that he could remember that had happened in The War. When the stories came around to the Japanese skull, Elkin couldn't finish because by that time he'd started to cry.

"You've got to look out for yourself, Jake. I've tried to tell you."

"That's what Mr. Rosenbloom said, too."

"He's right," Elkin said. "He's a schmuck but he's right."

Jake said he was lost without this Sari.

Elkin broke down again, racking sobs this time. He was able to get out the words, "Their promises aren't worth the blood they're written in," and Jake wasn't sure what he was talking about, the Army or the Rosenblooms or someone else. Or human expectation. Or some unstated cosmic promise, maybe. But that was it for a while. Jake thought of going over to hold Elkin but he was too frightened. He should go get his mother, that was it, that's what he was thinking when Elkin said, "Jake, don't let them waste your life."

Jake said, "Yeah, OK," like he'd entered into some kind of agreement and he left his father sniffling in the chair.

Elkin cleared his throat, ripped a tissue from the paper-box dispenser on the lamp table and blew his nose. How the hell am I gonna get to sleep now? His eyes hurt. Poor Jake. He hoped he wasn't going to do anything so stupid. And this girl, this Sari Rose-in-bloom. Elkin wished they'd come and take her for the Army, who the hell was worth this kind of trouble? Oh, shit, what's happening? The best thing to do now, he thought, was to call his manager, Marty Horowitz. He'd call Marty and tell him that this time, no fooling and no screwing around, this time he really wanted Marty to figure out a way to…

"Oh, fuck it," Elkin said.

He dialed Ted Fox. When the familiar voice came over the

phone saying, "My liege! How good of you to call," Elkin knew he was in the right place. He told Ted Fox how he just happened to be up and awake and in the voice of Coach Bruce Bruise he said he was in the mood for a little conversation.

For the first time that night, Jerry Elkin felt at home.

They were spectacular the next day, really sailing, top-notch if Elkin did say so himself, which he did to Ted Fox right after the "Let's make it morning!" sign-off. Their producer, Sgt. Al, told the two of them to "take a bow or even a bow-wow" and he started barking like a dog and the fake tough guy sports announcer, Steve Leo, came in and told them how he, Steve Leo, had cracked up everyone at yesterday's afternoon show by doing his complete sportscast without wearing pants. Elkin and Fox asked him to leave.

But the show? Who could ask for anything more, as the song said. Elkin couldn't put his finger on the why. Could've been the call the night before, maybe. Could've been that he'd just stopped wiggling back and forth on the Ted Fox question, at least for now, or maybe there was no reason. Dumb luck. The Radio Gods were smiling upon them again.

When the show was done, Elkin and Fox got a cab and headed over to the recording studio on 22nd and Seventh to do the Coke spots. And Elkin was glad of it this time, glad to be out with Ted Fox. He was glad he could spend the afternoon working. This was exactly what he was supposed to be doing. Working. This was mostly what he was glad about. He was glad for a good excuse to stay away from home.

And they treated Elkin and Fox the way Elkin and Fox should be treated, the two of them walking into the reception area of the recording place and "raising Cain," as Ted Fox said. Elkin talked in his Chip Chopper voice, then took off his hat and tried to hang it on a secretary's silken off-white breast while Ted Fox sang a few bars of "My Way" then lay down flat on his back across the other secretary's desk and placed her pencil holder cup on his stomach.

After that, Elkin and Fox danced together in the middle of the reception area as Elkin did his Miss Emma Reel voice shouting out joyously, "You dance divinely, Maestro!"

The director had to come out and yell, "Jesus Christ! What's going on out here!" and then shift into, "Hey, they're here! Elkin! Fox! Boys!"

The director, the copywriter, the engineer, two secretaries, everyone asked for autographs and went tripping over themselves to make "our two boys comfortable" which was what the director kept on shouting. Elkin did his Viennese Dr. Huckleberry voice and told the director to "call my nurse and come see me in the morning" because the director seemed to be slowly turning into a Munchkin, Dr. Huckleberry said, playing off the man's shortness, his scruffy beard and his suspenders. The sound engineer kept limping around and Elkin and Fox only laid off the jokes about him—calling him "George the Gimp"—after they found out he'd lost his right foot when his jeep hit a mine outside of Saigon. The copywriter sweated a lot and kept a pencil behind his ear and failed every time to get his copy into the hands of Elkin and Fox who went behind the glass of the recording booth and started yelling, "Where's the copy? How can we record a spot if no one shows us the copy?"

Elkin and Fox stood at the microphones and read the copy while the engineer played them the visuals. It wasn't much, just a Coke bottle taking off like a rocket ship and sailing through outer space. They watched, read, joined up in the Elkin and Fox universe where only Elkin and Fox were allowed to play, and then both of them in synch like Rockettes crumbled up the copy, tossed it back over their shoulders and launched into their own routine.

Elkin started in with the daffy but textured voice of a sudden, new character, Mr. Sweetbubbles, Coke's traveler in outer space. He was being interviewed in flight by Ted Fox. Mr. Sweetbubbles had been sent to see if somewhere out there in the universe there was a drink that was better than Coke but so far, no dice. Now he just wanted to come back to Earth but the guys on the ground were determined to search everywhere.

Standing in front of the mike, inventing Mr. Sweetbubbles there among the music stands and the wires and the off-white perforated soundproofed walls, Elkin lost the rest of the world and he was, at last, at peace. They did four takes. Then Elkin looked through the glass into the engineering booth and said in his Mr. Nosh voice, "So, *bubala*, what do you think?"

No answer. They couldn't hear anything on the other side of the glass but Elkin and Fox could see that the director looked like a fat, hairy, attacking bird, screaming at the copywriter who was wearing the scrunched face of a colicky infant and the sound engineer was trying to get them both to settle down.

"Far fucking out, boys," the director said through the intercom. "Hang on." He went back to screaming at the copywriter.

Elkin and Fox both started in with funny, clown motions, holding out their arms as in "What gives" until the director came back on the intercom. They saw the copywriter walk out of the booth.

"I just canned that *strunz*," the director said. "You guys are here two seconds, it's brilliant, that half-pint worked for a week and it's shit."

"DON'T FIRE HIM!" Elkin shouted into the mike as Ted Fox yelled, "BRING HIM BACK OR WE WALK!"

They kept this up while the director's face twitched and his flesh rolled and they added some shouts of "STRIKE!" and "PASS 'EM BY!" until Elkin and Fox saw the director rush out of the booth in silence. The sound engineer shrugged and said, "Schmuck," through the intercom motioning with his head.

Then the copywriter was standing in the sound booth again. He waved and mouthed "Thank you" and blew a few kisses in the Elkin and Fox direction. Elkin and Fox were still in their own Elkin and Fox universe, which signaled to them that they were on to something and should push it as far as they could, so Elkin and Fox got on the mikes at the same moment and began a chant of, "Give him a raise! Give him a raise!"

"More money for the kid!" Mr. Sweetbubbles said. "The raise or it's homeward bound!"

And Ted Fox ended up with, "The kid! He's a child of wonderfulness!"

The airlock door hissed open. The director was standing in the recording booth with his hands hooked in his suspenders bouncing his eyes from Elkin to Fox and from Fox back to Elkin. "Boys. A joke. Yes?"

"A joke he thinks," Mr. Nosh said.

"There are union issues," the director said.

Ted Fox hit the intercom button. "You're getting a raise, kid, you can take us out to dinner."

And Elkin leaned in for, "And kid. If you don't get that raise, call us at the studio."

They skipped out of the studio linked arm-in-arm singing "From This Moment On" as the director called out "Great work!" and the sound engineer whistled the song to accompany their music and the copywriter shouted "Thank you!" And once out in the light afternoon sun, hearing the squeal and honk and whoosh of the traffic, the two of them stood still for a moment, buzzed, high and ready to fly.

"We got the kid a raise," Ted Fox said, "but then we should have demanded that that bearded cocksucker quit."

"Right," Elkin said. "Well, fuck it, at least we did something."

It was Elkin who suggested the drink. Not only the drink but going to the Peacock Alley Bar at the Waldorf, even tagging on, "C'mon, it's on me," as Ted Fox said, "Lead the way, my liege!"

Later, when he was trying to piece everything together, Elkin remembered walking through the hotel lobby and thinking that it was like a big, popping explosion of gold and fine wood and ornate carvings that had frozen in the air. He recalled hearing "Elkin and Fox" spoken from two, maybe three, different areas, voices of recognition in a whisper chamber. And the bar. He remembered the long Deco bar with the glasslike sheen and how the bartender had told them that it had been a great show this morning and don't expect a tab.

Elkin remembered that it was still early afternoon and the bar wasn't very crowded but at some point he remembered Ted Fox telling him seriously that he was "crazy about that kid Sari." Even though, as Ted Fox said, "the deed has yet to be done" he was still going out to her house to see her from time to time and couldn't stay away.

Elkin remembered putting his arm around Ted Fox and telling him not to act like a schmuck and that it was one thing if Ted Fox was a pussy-sniffer in every bar in Manhattan but the girl was still a kid and it could lead to no good.

"And another thing," Elkin said. "My son loves her. And if you fuck her I want to take pictures of her naked."

"I will ring for your services," Ted Fox said.

Elkin also remembered that at one point they were talking to two women who were in from Chicago and staying at the hotel, two blonds with long hair, the same quick smiles, the same please-tell-me brown eyes and air of tourist excitement and what-could-possibly-happen-next. Doreen and Letty. Those were the names. They started asking Elkin and Fox where to eat and what shows to see after the bartender told them, "You want to know New York, these guys *are* New York." Up in their room, the girls said, they had seen a TV commercial that promised Elkin and Fox were the ten funniest guys in town.

What Elkin didn't remember, when he woke up at nine that evening in a Waldorf hotel room in bed with a woman who wore her blond hair long, Elkin didn't remember if this was Doreen or Letty. He also didn't remember exactly how he got there. For just a second, he thought he'd better ask Ted Fox who was asleep across from him in the other bed with the other blond.

That took maybe a second, then an A-bomb flash. *Wham!* In the rising cloud afterwards, all Elkin could think about was that he was gonna have to do some fancy dancing and how the hell had this happened, anyway? How? Ted Fox, Elkin thought. He didn't have to believe in Satan, he had Ted Fox to worship. How could he explain this to Marsha? Probably by lying. They'd been married more than 20 years and, OK, there'd been one or two nights out when he'd first made it big in the Big Time, when they'd first made the billboards and the print ads and the money and the offers had started rolling in, but that Let's-Not-Talk-About-It stuff was long ago. And who'd he been following then, too? Ted Fox. He had Ted Fox to blame. And, yeah, OK, maybe Jerry Elkin.

Elkin saw himself trying to explain as Marsha's screaming shot down each funny voice, until the only character voice he had left was the private voice, Mr. Begging Whine. Elkin saw himself throwing some things in a bag and heading off in a cab. OK. OK. He'd treat himself to a good hotel. Very expensive. Maybe Ted Fox could put him up. He'd figure out something. He was gonna survive.

He was gonna have to run for his life.

CHAPTER ELEVEN

MAX ROSENBLOOM AND JERRY ELKIN now had this in common: their wives were no longer talking to them. And when their wives did talk—which was not often—it was more like seeing lethal ice cubes shoot out of someone's mouth, not words.

But Vee Vee Rosenbloom was talking to Boris Jampolsky. She talked to him on the street outside the Chinita memorial and she talked to him when she phoned Boris at home, just to be sure the Russian knew what was what.

And that's why Boris was following Sari.

Two days after the memorial, he followed Sari on the LIRR into the city where she met Jake at an apartment building on the corner of Sixth Avenue and 59th Street, very rich looking. They stayed inside for many hours. Jake's friend Bob Siegel's father who had recently pleaded guilty to five counts of fraud owned an apartment in the building.

When Sari and Jake came out, Boris followed them to the top of the Empire State Building. To Boris, to Jake, too, to everyone who was oohing-and-ahing on the observation deck, the day was a searing, bright, cloudless blue but it was Sari Rose-in-bloom who looked rare, exotic and radiant. Maybe it was the backdrop of New York City laid out beneath her like a personal kingdom or maybe it was how the air was thin. She presided over it. All around, there was New York, not relaxing and spread out and stringy like some other cities but angry and full of *chutzpah*, close-in, stone and glass and neon grabbing you by the shirtfront and built like it planned to be around a long, long time, a lot longer than you.

Up on the Empire State, a man in a striped jacket and checkered pants broke away from his chunky wife and chunkier son and asked if he could take Sari's picture with the city all around behind her. Another man, this one with long hair and a cowboy poncho who was standing off to the side and pretending to use the telescope, called out to Sari, "It's no match, sweetheart. The city loses."

Sari turned to the man and smiled and brushed the last wisps of hair from her face where the wind had tousled it. That's when she noticed Boris. She shifted her gaze, whispered to Jake and walked over. The crowd stepped back to let her through.

"It's magnificent, yes?" she said to Boris. "Can you imagine everything that's happening down there all at once. All at the same time?"

Boris was beginning to breathe fast.

"Did my mother send you?"

"I love you, Miss Sari," Boris suddenly said. "I came to follow you and report back but the more I follow, the more I love."

Sari reached out and laid her fingers softly on Boris's cheek. "I can see why my father trusts you and loves you like a son, Boris," Sari said. "And in my own strange way, you're with me, too."

Boris wasn't sure exactly what she meant but he was ready to leap up and dance the Kalinka on the ledge of the Empire State, dipping and kicking as birds landed nearby and sang. Thrilled, he let the city take a whirl around him.

"You mustn't worry about me," Sari said. "Jake is a nice boy. Nothing bad will happen."

"Your Mama does not feel this way."

"She loves me and wants what's best," Sari said. "But I have my own life."

Boris turned to fix his gaze northeast, toward the spire of the Chrysler Building and farther, to the East River. A light cotton of mist had settled on the water. Boris felt suddenly at peace. He forgot about Jake. He watched a scow float by on the river and he wanted to tell Sari that right at this very moment, the world was the way the world was supposed to be.

"I will take you to the Tea Room for caviar," Boris said.

Sari said that would make her very happy. "But what would make me the happiest," she said, "is if you didn't tell my parents anything about me."

Boris gazed over to where Jake was standing. Maybe this Jake would somehow lean too far over the edge and go tumbling way, way, way down to the…

"Forget about him and look at me," Sari said. "Do you promise?"

He gave Jake one more look. Then Boris promised. "I will keep your secret," he said. "But for you. Not for him."

Sari touched his face again and Boris drew a deep, deep breath and tilted his head back to look up at the point of the building, the antenna. When he looked down again, Sari was gone.

The bad thing now? Mrs. Rosenbloom was talking to Boris but she was talking too much. She was calling three, four, five times a day to find out what Boris had found out. And Boris was lying to her and Mrs. Rosenbloom knew he was lying. He had to do something.

That's when his friends from Tel Aviv called with some very bad news.

So, Boris and Max Rosenbloom were now sitting at the darkened bar at Lüchow's on 14th because Max wanted to give Boris a sense of what he called "Old World German charm" with the heavy, gloomy carvings and the colored chandelier. And maybe eating a little wurst and Sauerbraten washed down with a wheaty Weihenstephan in a big glass that was shaped like a big boot (or maybe an amputated leg) would bring back just enough Hitler to get their blood up. Because listening to what Boris was saying made Max Rosenbloom want to pull the trigger.

The information all came from Boris's friends, the Israelis who were good at finding out things and who knew all the places you could hit and hurt. They also knew how to get into Larry Passoff's office at night and how to follow him through the garment district. Which they had done. They had walked behind him in Central Park, bugged the phone in his office, bugged the phone in his house in Scarsdale.

Let me tell you what is happening, Boris was saying. The story he told, as Max understood it: Larry Passoff apparently had gotten himself in some trouble a few months back. Things were not so great in his business. Something had to be done. In a moment of completely cool, calculated stupidity, Larry Passoff decided to stop paying Social Security taxes for the nine people in his company. This should have been difficult to detect, Larry Passoff thought, at least for long enough to get the business back on its feet, and when all was well, Larry Passoff would suddenly discover the error and pay Uncle Sam back all that he owed.

But, well, that didn't happen. Things—money things, anyway—kept getting worse. Not smart on Larry's part was that he sent the tax forms through the mail, which might have seemed like mail fraud if anyone wanted to get picky about it. Then, with the business still shaky, maybe he wrote a couple of checks that were not, strictly speaking, legal. Larry fudged, he shuffled, he took from Peter to pay Paul, then he took from Paul who finally dropped a dime on him.

One day, some men in suits showed up at Larry Passoff's office and flashed badges from the Federal Government and then used a bolt cutter to open Larry Passoff's safe. Out came many of his files and papers, which they placed in a locked brown briefcase.

"But the schmuck hasn't been arrested," Max Rosenbloom said. "I got a bad feeling."

"You will feel worse," Boris told him.

Worse, because Max Rosenbloom's name had figured into Larry Passoff's trouble. It had happened like this: when the men from the government had put the cuffs on Larry, they had put them on tight enough to pinch and make his palms go dead and his fingers tingle. Like slamming a cell door. That echo. Just in case Larry Passoff didn't get the message. Which Larry Passoff now got because he immediately started blubbering like a snot-nosed kid and saying to the government men that he was mostly a good guy who had never been in trouble and he was not some schmuck who did wrong and wasn't it possible that a deal could be made.

What do you know—it *was* possible. The government men told Larry Passoff that exactly the same thought had crossed their minds, too. They'd heard that there was a lot of mob action going on in the garment district, lots of stuff involving unions and payoffs and shipments of goods that shouldn't be shipped and money that was being laundered and all kinds of *chazerai*. Which had been Larry's word because Larry Passoff said he'd heard the same stories. But Larry was a little guy, Larry said, a nobody, a zero.

That's not good, the government men said. Not for you, Larry.

Larry tried pleading. If he hadn't been in handcuffs he'd have put his palms together and prayed. He kept talking, saying, please, sirs, agents, he didn't know any big shots, just knew a few guys who, well, who had a little touch of larceny in their heart. Nothing elaborate. No mob or gang or secret handshakes. Just guys from the old neighborhood and if the government men gave him some time, a couple of weeks, a few months, he would be able to help the Federal Government with just this kind of guy.

The government men shrugged which squeezed out more pleading.

A guy, say, like Max Rosenbloom, Larry said. Larry had heard that Max sometimes used fire to help businessmen in need collect insurance. Couldn't that be called arson? Or how about insurance fraud! And, wait! Now Max might be involved in something that involved poisoned children's clothing. Should I find out more?

"I knew that schmuck was no good," Max Rosenbloom said. He watched Boris drain the last wheat beer from his long, amputated-leg glass and then Max did the rest of his Scotch and lit a cigarette. He took the plastic stir stick from the bar and snapped it in half.

"How much do they know?" Max Rosenbloom said.

Boris shrugged. Max turned away from him, disgusted. "What can I do for you?" Boris said.

"You can use a little *sechel*, you know what I mean?" Max said. "After you do it, I'd like if I didn't wind up sitting in your lap in the electric chair."

Boris wasn't listening. He went blank with fear and said, "My friends, they are ready to help."

"Help what? I didn't say anything."

Boris nodded. How could he be so stupid? Sari Rose-in-bloom didn't get her brains from nowhere and this Max, his boss, he wasn't going to say anything that could get back to the wrong people.

"Sir, I will help in any way I can."

Max Rosenbloom was jabbing one fingernail into the wood of the bar. "What are you trying to get me to say? Tell me something, Boris. How do I know you're legit? Maybe these friends of yours are just some made-up cockamamie bullshit or maybe you're in with that schmuck Larry Passoff, too, and I'm gonna wind up in cuffs."

"No, sir. Not possible," Boris said and what Boris wanted more than anything else right now was to burst out with the rest of it, with "Not possible because you are the father of woman I love." And also, because Max Rosenbloom was showing him the way. Boris now wanted to talk in that lowdown, busted growl just like Max Rosenbloom, dress like Max in expensive suits, move like him with that lumbering, heavy-stepping gait. From Max Rosenbloom, Boris was thinking, he had learned the most important, basic principle of American business: never tell anyone what you're really up to.

"I can be trusted," Boris said. "I will make you proud."

"That's gonna take some doing," Max Rosenbloom said.

Boris suddenly got to his feet. He placed his fist over his heart. "I will do things," he said. "I will protect you from all enemies foreign and domestic."

Now, it was Max Rosenbloom's turn to do some nodding. And while he was doing it he was saying, "That's enough, Boris, you'd better leave it right where it is, don't say anything else."

"You can trust me," Boris said. "I want you to be proud."

Max said, "Enough, OK? Enough."

"I know other things."

Max fumbled for a cigarette, patted his pockets for a match. Boris beat him to it, holding out a lighter for Max's cigarette, Max cupping his hand.

"It's about your daughter, Sari," Boris felt his lips quivering, everything was going dark. "I made a promise to her. But I will break it. For you."

He told Max Rosenbloom everything.

After that, Max jammed his cigarette into the ashtray so hard that it snapped in half. Boris leaned forward with his elbows on the heavy wooden bar, shaking his head. In the mirror across from him, he wanted to see a man sunk in some kind of deeply profound misery but all he saw was a big-mouthed, flat-faced Russian Jew who couldn't keep a promise to the woman he loved. Max saw Boris staring and patted him on the back.

"You did good," Max said. Then: "Goddamn it," Max Rosenbloom said. "This is all I need. My wife is gonna have fucking apoplexy."

The next afternoon he phoned Jerry Elkin at home.

Elkin was glad to get the hell out of the house even if it meant meeting Max Rosenbloom. A distinct chill was still in the air. Three days ago, what with his getting home at 11 p.m. and smelling like he'd been sampling perfume, the night on the town with Ted Fox—that's when the no-talking had started. Elkin had done a laughing rendition about the Coke spot and how great they were, Elkin and Fox, while Marsha sat there without blinking. Afterwards, Elkin said, he'd gone out with Ted Fox and some sponsors and then he explained it all again, trying to keep the story straight, and that was when Marsha had gotten up and glided off to bed, leaving Elkin on the sofa, hearing nothing but his own inner hum.

They hadn't spoken again until today. Marsha had shouted from the kitchen, "JERRY, IT'S FOR YOU!" She'd held the phone out to him like it was rotting meat that could still attack and then into his ear had come that voice of tossed stone and open wounds.

"I'll settle this," he told her as he left the house. Given the delicate situation, Elkin put that at the top of the charts for a snazzy goodbye.

Driving further out on the Island, he stoked up his rage. This time it wasn't that schmuck Ted Fox who got it as he passed the other sign, the second sign, for "Elkin and Fox, the 10 Funniest Guys in Town!," it was Max Rosenbloom.

So, you're really a tough guy, Elkin said out loud in the Volvo, OK. I don't give a crap. Another small-time creep, a third-rate hood. The music business was crawling with them. They were not much different than this schmuck Max Rosenbloom. Always trying to get Elkin and Fox to do them favors or plug this or that, play their records, pay someone off, let some broad they were trying to make come into the studio. Drugs, girls, money, these clowns drifted through the studio and wanted to trade. No thanks, was the answer they got. And a couple of times, Elkin and Fox picked up the paper a few days later and there they were, the guys they'd met, a story about how they'd been found face down in an alley somewhere.

"Fuck 'em, they can't keep me from laughing," Elkin said this out loud before he got out of the car. He'd written the same line to his father from the Pacific during The War. "Ridiculous," he said now as he headed for the restaurant. He said it over again three times, pronouncing the word, "Re-dickel-us." It was what there was left to believe in, a good name for his own personal religion,

The Ridiculous. Elkin said it again. If they wanted a show, he'd give them one. They can't keep me from laughing.

Elkin was still talking to himself when he sauntered into the bar of Manero's Steakhouse. He caught sight of Max Rosenbloom right away, there he was raising a meaty hand and signaling, a big, bald bull at the bar with a Scotch and a cigarette and a Florida tan. Elkin made his way closer, suddenly sensing that his eyes had dried out behind his glasses and that soon he wouldn't be able to see. Another phony-baloney joint, Elkin told himself, a bar that wanted to be for cowboys and rubes with splintered wood everywhere and red-and-white checkered tablecloths and that goddamn sign up near the booze bottles, the one that showed an American flag and a soldier kicking a donkey. It read, "Put your heart in America or get your ass out."

"Why'd you pick this place?" Elkin sat down next to Max and told the bartender, "I'll have what he's having."

"Jerry Elkin?" the bartender said. "Elkin and Fox?"

"Where!? WHERE!?" Elkin comically searched the room.

"And this must be…no," the bartender said. "Ted's got hair."

The bartender was wearing a western shirt that pulled tight across his chest. Elkin was about to say, "Don't pop those snaps, Hopalong," but by then the guy was shoving a pad and pen in front of Elkin, grinning and asking for an autograph. Elkin felt bad about the Hopalong crack even though he hadn't said it. He wrote, "Let's make it morning! Jerry Elkin" and finished with, "This isn't a bill, is it?" grateful for the bartender's laugh. Elkin wanted to laugh, too, right in Max Rosenbloom's face and then he wanted to spit on Max's shiny shoes. The drink appeared on the bar and the bartender vanished, a guy who knew when to take off.

"I chose it because it's out of the way," Max Rosenbloom said then. "And no one would recognize us." He wasn't smiling. "Also, it's very unusual."

Elkin nodded. Max wasn't exactly stupid, Elkin thought, but he also wasn't going to be a source of laughs and high times. "Unusual," Elkin said. "That's an unusual thing to say." He took another gander at the flag-soldier-ass sign and decided he'd never come back.

"We've got a couple of things to talk about," Max Rosenbloom said.

"Then let's talk," Elkin said.

Max Rosenbloom blew smoke through his thick nostrils while Elkin watched, wondering if this was supposed to create some kind of effect or maybe give them both cancer.

"And if you don't mind," Elkin said, "let's keep it brief."

"Sure. OK," Max Rosenbloom said. "To you, I know, I'm a schmuck. But I got some serious concerns."

"You threatened to break my kid's back."

"I told him to stop seeing my daughter. My wife says he's still at it. Sneaking around. I think she's right."

Elkin let it ride. The best thing about this, he thought, was that it got him out of range from Marsha after a couple of horrible evenings.

"I'm not gonna waste anyone's time," Max said. "So this is it: I don't want your boy seeing my daughter. And by the way, it's not me."

"It's not you what?"

"Mrs. Rosenbloom is very upset. Your boy's a good kid. But for whatever reason, and even I'm not sure why, she wants him to stay away. If the situation was reversed and it was your wife, you'd do the same."

"You think so? At some point, you start solving your own problems."

"OK, that's you. For me?" Max Rosenbloom said. "She's still my little girl and Mrs. Rosenbloom is still my wife. And I want to buy them things and treat them right. That's most of what it's all about, don't you think?"

"I'm more worried about my partner," Elkin said. "As far as your little girl is concerned."

Max Rosenbloom snapped a plastic stirrer in two as if to say, stir stick first and then your fucking neck. "Mr. Fox is OK by me," he said.

"Your daughter's making Mr. Fox a loony bird, if you want to know. So, here's what. I'll keep my kid away from her, if you keep her away from my partner."

"Mr. Fox is a class act."

"He is that, I'll grant you. And he's married with two kids. And also, he gets more ass than a double-decker bus."

"We have his word, not that it's any of your goddamn business." Max Rosenbloom took a deep breath. "Maybe we should order some food. You want a burger or something?"

"My kid's eighteen years old," Elkin said. "His biggest problem is staying out of the fucking war and figuring out what to do with his life. I really don't have much say in it."

"I hear you," Max Rosenbloom said. "Still. There are ways."

That voice. I gotta use it on my show in the morning. New character: Max Schmuck, tough guy. Elkin was aching to mimic Max Rosenbloom, wanted to do a Max voice, make Max talk to himself. If belching sewers could talk. And this guy, always like he was ready to hit, Elkin said to himself. Charlie-fat-chance. I know these guys. A lot of hot air.

"Ted Fox thinks he's in love with your daughter."

"I'll make this easy," Max Rosenbloom slowly put his hand inside his sports jacket and brought out a checkbook. Then a silver Montblanc. He leaned in when he started writing, a little kid taking a test, hiding his answers with one palm so you couldn't cheat off him. There was something flowing about it, like this was an everyday routine in Max's world. When he finished, Max Rosenbloom let the check-now-leaving-its-booklet sound hang in the talking air of the bar and he presented the blue check to Elkin by handing it in low.

"I think I spelled your name right. I've seen it on that big sign." Max Rosenbloom said. "That's for ten thousand dollars."

Elkin's hands came down off the bar so fast that he banged a knuckle. "I'm supposed to take that and do what?"

"Pay for the kid's college. Send him to Europe. Keep it for yourself. Do whatever you want. Just keep him away from Sari."

The check was now settling like it had wings of its own, Elkin saw it landing in front of him on the rough wood, right near his Scotch. It was just for a moment, but before he stopped himself, Elkin was worried that this check for ten grand would lose its way, get wet and ruined, an innocent who horribly finds his path to the water circle made by a Scotch glass and destroys himself. Elkin's eyes focused on the poor little check and they stayed focused right there. Where it said, "Pay to the order of Jerry Elkin." Where it said, "Ten thousand dollars."

"I know you're a big deal," Max Rosenbloom said. "But that's a lot of money."

Elkin knew he'd begin stuttering if he tried to speak. "Ridiculous," he silently invoked his belief. An act of The Ridiculous and this schmuck didn't know it. What he probably knew, though, was that if you put a $10,000 check in front of Jerry Elkin, made out to Jerry Elkin, offered to Jerry Elkin, then Jerry Elkin would want to pick it up.

Elkin gave Max his best soft laugh as in: you and me, we know the score. Both of us, Max Rosenbloom and Jerry Elkin. The hand on Max's shoulder and Elkin's wry smile radioed that message to Max, that's what Elkin hoped. Money, fear, desire and insanity were in the saddle. When you know the score, that's the score you know. And then? You had to dance. You didn't fight it. And why not? Because if you did, whoa boy, watch out. Then, for your whole life, you bitched and moaned until you rolled over and you died. You died in hiding. Elkin nodded and cleared his throat and finally, he said, "That is, as you say, a lot of money. You are, indeed, right. My liege."

Elkin picked up the $10,000 check. He folded it in half, careful to do it neatly. Then he reached in and put the check into his inside jacket pocket.

"Thanks," Max Rosenbloom said. "I know you'll make everything OK. And I hope, whatever you do, you'll have a good time with it."

"You shouldn't be, but you're a likable guy," Elkin said. "I like you, Max."

"That's good to hear, Jerry. I like you, too."

"Thanks, Max. And this unfortunate incident with my son and your daughter. I think you're doing something legit. Basically. You're being a stand-up guy, Max."

"We'll drink to it, Jerry," Max and Elkin toasted. They finished their drinks. When Max offered, "One for the road?" Elkin shook his head "no" and let Coach Bruce Bruise say, "I'd better be on my way."

Max laughed. He even gave Elkin a good-pal shoulder jab. He even called for the tab. Elkin made a move to grab it but, come on, Max was a tower, a fortress, and he snapped the bill away, then reached way, way up there, holding the plastic tab case above his head so that Elkin would have to jump up like a dog to grab it.

"You're a man among men," Elkin said. "I thank you."

He watched Max sign and saw that he gave the bartender a tip that cried out "No cheap Jews here."

"Ready?" Max said. "Shall we ride?"

"One thing, "Elkin said. "Ted Fox." And he reached in and took the check out of his jacket. "I share everything with my partner." He tore the check in half. "And I know it's a pain in the ass, but you'd want my wife to get some of this, too, I know, Max, you're a nice guy." Elkin tore the check again. "Also, Mr. Nosh." Again. "And Chip Chopper and Dr. Huckleberry. They won't work if they don't get a taste."

The check was now a small stack of torn paper, barely worthy of Elkin's hand. So, he put the pieces in his Scotch glass and watched as the melting ice took its soiled toll, making the blue check paper go dark.

"Don't worry," Elkin said. "Nobody has to know about this. But next time, think about what you're doing."

In the parking lot outside, Elkin wanted to jump in the air and click his heels or pull some other Vaudeville stunt that would be a private pat-on-the-back for a great performance. This evened things up for his transgression with Doreen or Letty, for his dithering over Ted Fox. For everything. He wanted to call Ted Fox to tell him what had just happened, but the only thing was, Ted Fox would say, "You tore up WHAT?" siding with Max and hoping to clear the competition. Elkin was talking to himself as Mr. Nosh as he climbed into the car. "A top notch primo, *bubala*." Elkin felt great.

Back in the bar, Max Rosenbloom was moving slowly for the pay phone in the booth, all the way in the back of this fake Western saloon. A black-and-white walk, more Tom Mix than John Wayne, a heavy walk through deep forest on a lightning-lit night. Everything, everyone else was forgotten except: Jerry Elkin. He was going to call Boris. He was thinking of that huge sign that would now read, "Elkin and Fox are the 9 Funniest Guys in Town." Max Rosenbloom wasn't in a rage, exactly, he wouldn't have described it that way. It was more that he was trying to keep himself from telling Boris outright that Jerry Elkin could use a fucking bullet in the eye. No, he wasn't stupid, Max Rosenbloom, he wouldn't say that. He hadn't killed anybody since The War. A fire, a little rough stuff, OK. But he wasn't a schmuck. He wasn't a bad guy.

So with this Elkin? Maybe something would burn down that looked like an accident or somebody would get a clonk on the noggin that looked like a mugging. And as Boris picked up the phone, Max Rosenbloom was saying to himself that this Elkin, he was definitely way out of line.

He should not have done what he definitely did.

CHAPTER TWELVE

AFTER THAT, THINGS REALLY FELL APART.
Back from the meeting, back from being made to look—again!—like a fool by Jerry Elkin, Max Rosenbloom found Vee Vee at home in a stomping, floor-pounding rage. Even before he was inside the house, when he was coming up the walk, Max could hear crashing. Wrenching. The eerie vice twist of destruction. Vee was trying to destroy the place.

Max Rosenbloom was thinking: You know what's the purpose of something bad? Something bad is there only so bad can get worse. "Bad" is just a tiny little seed. A little something to start with. He cocked back his head and looked up. Not a cloud in the sky and the breeze couldn't be more perfect. Max Rosenbloom opened his front door and stepped inside.

Upstairs, the bedroom looked like somebody had tromped through in a violent ticker-tape parade. The room was a mess. Max Rosenbloom could see it from downstairs. Every piece of clothing owned by Vee, all the colorful little peasant blouses and hostess pajamas and miniskirts, the Diors and the Yves St. Laurents and the Mary Quants, all of them too small in a tiny size eight, all of them were tossed across the floor or were hanging off the side of the bed or the arm of a chair or bunched in a corner. Some of them were torn, a fray of ripped thread showed at the seams, the glint of a popped button on the floor. It was like a Technicolor cartoon had exploded. Vee had kicked them and pulled at them and ripped them after she wrenched them out of the closet. Vee was bent on ruin. Only an idiot would get in her way.

Taking the little staircase two steps at a time, losing his breath, Max heard the ruckus get louder. Through his open bedroom door, he saw a flock of metal and wooden hangers fly by and his ears picked up the tin sound of clattering and thudding, then the light thump of clothing bunched and crushed and hitting the floor. Also that heavy, growling sound. Vee was grunting. A muffled drift of colored cloth flew by the doorway and wrinkled in a twist around the bedpost before it dropped. The house was going to collapse from the inside, beginning with this room. Max noticed that Sari's door was shut.

"Honey, I'm home!" Max Rosenbloom yelled. He gave it another two or three minutes hoping the terror would pass. Then Vee was standing in the doorway in her oversized yellow muumuu cinched at the waist by a wide brown leather belt that made her look worse. Whatever makeup had survived her tears and tirade was now tracing wet black lines down her cheeks.

"I'm going to kill her, Max," Vee Rosenbloom said. "Get her out of here or I swear, she's a dead little bitch."

Max Rosenbloom used his fingers to wipe the dripping black lines off Vee Vee's face. He kissed her forehead, suddenly certain she was utterly insane and suddenly loving her for it. He held her by the shoulders, then he nudged her back into the bedroom and sat Vee down on the bed.

"My father didn't bring me up to live like this."

Max sat himself down next to her. "Let's hear it."

"You don't know anything, do you? You're as stupid as everybody else."

He stopped loving her for it. Max Rosenbloom was remembering what Vee had been like before she was like this but the way she was talking now? It stretched the whole marriage across his lungs like a tightening strap. He could barely speak. "I've been trying."

"Oh, yes, oh, you've been trying. What did that little Jew prick Jerry Elkin say?"

"He said a lot of things. Then he took my check and tore it up."

"WHAT?" Vee was off the bed like the springs had launched her, she was going eyeball to blue eyeball with Max Rosenbloom. "OH, NO. WE CAN'T HAVE THAT."

"Easy does it," Max said. "I'm working on it."

"Boris told me what's what. You're lucky I don't ask him to really get rough."

"Fuck Boris," Max said quietly.

Vee was searching through the piles of scattered clothes, searching for God knows what, her ungainly body barely able to strain forward for the effort and the sight of her was making Max sad.

"The girl's a liar and a whore," Vee said. "She lies to me and she whores with the Elkin boy."

"It's not like that these days, Vee," Max Rosenbloom said.

"You don't know. You're not a woman. For a woman it's always like that."

"Vee," Max didn't know what else to say. "It's enough. People are getting hurt."

Vee stopped searching. She picked up one of her small size belts and threw it across the room so that the buckle thudded against the wall and left a scar. She found another belt marked small and threw this one, too. The price tags were still attached.

Then she became a blaze facing Max Rosenbloom and said, "What about me, Max? I ask her things and either she lies or she keeps her goddamn mouth shut. Why does she get to do that?"

"I'll talk to her."

"You'll stay right where you are, mister. Right there on your big, fat ass."

Max Rosenbloom took another tight breath but now he was ready to let it bust loose. Because, goddamn it, how much do you have to take before you stand up and make it stop. In the entire time they'd known each other, Max Rosenbloom had never once hit Vee, not once, and he knew plenty of lousy bastards who used their mitts. But not Max, you don't do that. His father would climb out of the grave and come back to beat the living daylights out of him—forget the punch-ups in the alleys, the dead Japs, The War and everything else besides. He was ready to start yelling, though, that he could do. But right as he stood up to start going at it, Vee Vee spun on her heel and hustled out the bedroom door.

Max Rosenbloom said, "Oh, shit," and dropped back on the bed.

There were only a few steps separating their bedroom from Sari Rose-in-bloom's door. If Max had gone to follow, he would have seen Vee taking off the wide leather belt that had circled her muumuu and seen her double it over and hold it hidden behind her back. All that before she opened Sari's door and walked in without so much as a knock, a word or even a shout to let-me-in.

Sari Rose-in-bloom was curled up on her bed with her thumb near her lips. She sat up quick and ready when the door slammed open and the knob hit the wall.

"Mother," Sari said. "This is my room."

And that was true and that was another thing, Vee was saying to herself. This little girl has this whole big room to herself without a hitch and who the hell was it who made it grand? Who did the decorating? Who measured and shopped and thought and thought and thought about what would make it look like a princess should live there with the pink walls and the white frilled piping and the pink bedspreads and the little stuffed animal pillows? It was Vee

Vee Rosenbloom, that's who. And now, Vee thought, the end of it is what? The payoff? I'm getting the fucking shaft.

"I'll ask you again," Vee said. "Are you sleeping with that boy?"

"And I'm going to tell you the same. It's none of your business."

"Once more. Are you fucking him?"

"This is today, Mother. Not when you grew up."

"Are you fucking that boy, Sari?"

So Sari Rose-in-bloom shouted, "ALL RIGHT, GODDAMN IT, YES."

Vee swung around fast. Her whole weight was carrying it, the snap of the wide, leather belt in her right hand, hidden behind her back, now suddenly sweeping it in a hard, swift arcing crack of leather. It caught Sari on the side of the neck. A gunshot, that's what it sounded like. The shock, too. Sari screamed. She fell over on her side. Then the pain set in.

Max Rosenbloom got to the room as Vee Vee was raising the belt to hit the girl again. The bellowing, guttural, "GODDAMN IT, VEE!" filled the room, breaking every other sound in the house, the girl's screams, Vee's growling, the clicking of the metal buckle as Max grabbed the belt out of Vee's hand. He pushed Vee to the side and sat down next to Sari on the bed. She was shuddering and holding her neck. A deep scarlet streak was pulsing, rising to the surface of her flesh.

Max put his hand on Sari's head and then he turned to Vee. "Are you fucking crazy? Get in the goddamn bedroom before I kick your ass."

Vee waited the honor time, the you-can't-talk-to-me-like-that time but she was gone after that, back in her own room, slamming the door. Max heard the walls rattle.

"I'll get you some ice," he said to Sari Rose-in-bloom.

Max picked up Vee's big leather belt and carried it down to the kitchen. He tried to stay sober but the rage was making him dizzy as a drunk. Before he opened the icebox, he rolled the leather belt in a tight little coil and jammed it into the kitchen garbage bag under the sink. Then he said to himself, "Fucking crazy. She's had it," and when he took the plastic ice tray out and bent it, a touch of anger simmered through his big fingers, maybe a touch he didn't know about. The tray snapped in half and the ice cubes skidded across the kitchen floor.

And Boris?

Just that very morning, he had been so very happy about his sit-down with Max and now? How quickly things change, Boris Jampolsky said to himself. He took his small black notebook from the upended crate next to his cot and wrote this on the lined paper: "Things change quickly." That bit of wisdom took its place among all the lessons he'd learned from Max Rosenbloom on American business.

Also, what he'd learned from Elkin and Fox. Just that very morning, adding to Boris's happiness, Elkin and Fox had done their hilarious comedy moment where Ted Fox tried to speak to Mr. Nosh while Mr. Nosh ate his breakfast bagel and cream cheese on the air, talking with his mouth full of food. Boris loved this. When he was alone, he sometimes filled his mouth with food and spoke, practicing his English, laughing so hard that he nearly choked. He wanted to do it for Sari sometime, that mouthful-talk-joke, when they were alone together at last.

But now? Now he was remembering, "Don't tell me, I don't want to know about it, it's your business not mine," Max Rosenbloom had said on the phone. And what did he want Boris to do exactly? Boris Jampolsky didn't want to know except that if he was truthful, he knew already. It wasn't every day he heard Max Rosenbloom sound that way, a mad mountain steaming to blow its stack, and now it had Boris sitting on the crumpled green Army blanket on his unmade cot in his one-room Coney Island apartment, telling himself to think, think, think.

Again, Max was talking to him in that strange American business code. Or maybe it was just a special Max Rosenbloom code that Boris was supposed to decipher without a guide. Something about Mr. Jerry Elkin and Jake Elkin, too. "I don't want to see them," Max Rosenbloom shouted. To Boris it was like listening to a large bear. Then Max was rasping something about Mr. Larry Passoff, but still doing "It's your problem, I don't want to know" and with all that, Boris was trying to keep an eye on Sari, beloved Sari, who danced in his heart every minute of the day.

Boris got up and threw back the plastic curtain that hid his sink, his small battered refrigerator and the hot plate. He needed time to think. Leaning forward, sitting on his cot and waiting for the water to boil on the hot plate, Boris thumbed through the little notebook. "I'm not a criminal, there's nothing they can prove.— Max Rosenbloom" He'd written that two days ago. "Let's make it morning!—Elkin and Fox." He'd written that after Max had first introduced him to Elkin and Fox on the radio. Boris stood up and made tea. Then he sat back down on the cot and reached underneath to get the old cigar box where he kept his piece.

His friends, the ex-Israeli commandos, had told him where to get the weapon. A .32 with adhesive tape wrapped around the butt and five rounds with the tips flattened and a small "X" cut in the lead. Max Rosenbloom had suggested that he "pick up his tools" and that's when Boris had called his friends about the weapon. His friends said there were no serial numbers on the piece and he could do what he had to do and then ditch it and no one would be the wiser. Boris told them how great that sounded and then walked away thinking that the only thing about it that wasn't so great was that he had never shot anybody and wasn't so happy about doing it now.

He sipped his Russian Caravan tea and tried to think. This was how he got most of his ideas. Boris let the steam and smell of the tea drift across his nose and he closed his eyes. Think, he had to think. But the more he tried to think, the more his mind was filled with what he'd heard on the radio that morning, Mr. Nosh, Chip Chopper and his favorite, Dr. Huckleberry, with the funny accent.

What he was thinking was that Mr. Jerry Elkin of Elkin and Fox was his favorite funnyman and he couldn't bring himself to shoot him, Max Rosenbloom or no.

To kill Jerry Elkin? That would also be killing Mr. Nosh and the whole wonderful crew. No, Mr. Nosh had done no wrong. And a world without the hilarious Dr. Huckleberry? Dr. Huckleberry gone because of Boris Jampolsky? Max Rosenbloom could not mean him to do such a terrible thing, Boris was thinking, he knew Max too well.

Then it would have to be the Elkin boy, Jake. This would please Max Rosenbloom and especially Mrs. Rosenbloom and, best of all, it would mean one fewer man sniffing around Sari Rose-in-bloom who had come to live in his brain every minute.

What am I thinking? Boris thought. He saw himself walking up to the Elkin boy and firing the .32 into the back of the long, wavy, dark hair and he saw blood and brains and eyeballs and pieces of skull flying everywhere and he thought: how will Mr. Nosh be so wonderfully funny after that? Or Dr. Huckleberry? Where would the laughs go? There would be no difference in hurting Jerry Elkin or hurting his son, Jake, the end would be the same. No more smiling and laughing as he shaved and drank his coffee and drove his car in the morning.

No, it was impossible. Max Rosenbloom would be angry with him for a while but he knew Max and Max was like a father to him and Max Rosenbloom would never hurt Boris. Oh, more than that, Boris thought. When time passed, Max would thank him for it. He would grab Boris by the shoulders and look into his eyes and say, "Thank you, Boris, for knowing that I was like a mad bull and not thinking like a good man." Maybe he would even break down and cry.

So what was left? Boris was looking at the compact snub-nosed piece of black-blue steel in his hand and he was hoping that his Israeli friends had told him the truth and that if he pointed this and squeezed the trigger, then afterwards he could just toss it in the river and that would be the end of it. No police would show up at the door of his little apartment. Because the only thing left to do was to take the piece and go talk to Mr. Larry Passoff, that schmuck, as Max Rosenbloom always said. This Passoff was the key to it. He was the one who threatened to bring down Max Rosenbloom. He was the one who was talking to the authorities about Max Rosenbloom. And why? To save his own ass, that's why. No, Boris thought, to serve Max Rosenbloom he would go have a word and maybe much more than a word with Larry Passoff.

And once he was gone, this Larry, then Max Rosenbloom would be safe from harm and Max would be able to go through with his idea to sell the poisoned children's clothes and that would mean money, enough money for Max Rosenbloom to send Sari Rose-in-bloom to Paris.

Boris would weep when Sari was gone but he would visit her in the City of Lights and soon she would fall in love with Boris because it was Boris who made her life in Paris possible as he would make many, many other adventures possible.

All that was left was to make this schmuck Mr. Larry Passoff disappear.

*   *   *

Elkin heard the burglar downstairs at 2:30 a.m., about two hours before he was supposed to get up for work, Elkin though, until he remembered that it was Saturday. What he'd actually heard was a strained whisper, saying "Jesus Christ! What happened?" He sat up in bed almost glad there was possible trouble.

Elkin couldn't sleep, anyway. He'd been rolling around, tossing, trying to get used to the bed in the guest room. Where he'd slept since pulling that Ted Fox the other night. And thinking about that little incident led him directly to Max Rosenbloom, The Schmendrick King, and Elkin started going over and over how he'd given him the one-two after the crass, sleazy bid to buy Jake off his daughter.

Elkin had been laughing to himself, too, because thinking about Max, he began thinking of what he privately referred to as his "comic persona," the character that he generally played. Nicest guy in the world. Great guy. The Greatest Guy. The guy you'd want to have around. And the guy who could be taken to the cleaners by anybody and anywho. By Mr. Nosh, Chip Chopper, Coach Bruce Bruise, any of his many creations who dropped into the studio, into the "theater of the mind" as he privately held it, slamming the sound-effects door and then going into the act. And when it was just him, Jerry Elkin, going voice-on-voice with Ted Fox, then Elkin did the exact same thing. Fox was the debonair smart guy with a lot of class and speed. Elkin was always being taken in some way, nice guy who was up for grabs.

But that's the "comic persona," Elkin was thinking. That's not the guy who gave Max Rosenbloom a little show business this afternoon, no it was most definitely not, and it's not the guy who's now getting out from under the covers, going into his own bedroom, very quietly, and pulling out the baseball bat from underneath the bed.

The baseball bat was there for a night just like this. Elkin always remembered what they'd taught him during hand-to-hand training in the Philippines: "The first lesson of unarmed combat is never be unarmed." Mr. Nosh wouldn't grab a bat. Chip Chopper wouldn't, either, and certainly not Miss Emma Reel. What about the Coach? OK, the Coach might. Elkin always joked during The War that he didn't mind them teaching him all this stuff because he knew that when the time came, he wouldn't use it anyway, he'd be too chicken. But privately, even though it fit right in with his idea of The Ridiculous, right near his "comic persona" he kept the other persona, the one who could handle himself, who could teach Jake a few "old Army tricks," the persona who was now in a shirt and chinos, about to creep out of the bedroom with his weapon of choice.

"Put down the bat and go back to your own room," Marsha said as Elkin headed toward the door.

"There's a burglar downstairs," Elkin said.

"It's Jake and his girlfriend."

"OK. Then I'll hit *them*," Elkin said. "Now that I'm up, somebody's getting hit."

Marsha yawned and rolled over so Elkin started heading downstairs, don't try to stop him. Quiet was the law in the house after eight o'clock, the Elkin bedtime. He laid down the unbreakable law. It was now 2:40 in the morning. Didn't Jake know that? How'd you like it if I woke you up? Elkin was going to drive the point home, "How about I wake you up when I get up, how'd that be? I'll do it every day next week."

He kept the bat because Marsha wasn't right about everything and he half-hoped she was wrong this time so he could swing on somebody, really get the *thwock* of wood on bone, hit the guy who was stupid enough to steal from Jerry Elkin of Elkin and Fox. He was feeling mean. Jake should know by now: when you work the early morning shift, you never get used to it. You yearn for sleep. Thirst for sleep. Sure, money, too, and that babe who just walked by. And for Ted Fox to quit. But sleep, sleep, sleep. You can never get enough, you can never get it back.

The stairs creaked. Not every one of them but Elkin's footsteps set off a little Boris Karloff sound about every third step down when he shifted his weight. And after each creak, Elkin stopped and listened. His breathing seemed suddenly like a locomotive, the creaking stairs cut into his brain, likewise the voices of Jake and the beautiful Sari Rose-in-bloom. Elkin quickly peeked around the corner. They were sitting in the darkened living room with only one dim light on, the tiny light with the bulb shaped like a flame that Marsha had bought at United House Wrecking in Connecticut. He'd thought it was sort of like a chintzy *goyisha* Christmas light then, but in this one quick peek he saw that it made everything incredibly romantic and…he never should have bought that goddamn light! And now he heard Sari saying something, maybe something about her mother but he couldn't quite catch it, only a phrase, a word.

He was thinking there were certain pictures he could take, but then….

Sari's voice. Something else about the Rosenbloom woman. And Elkin thought she was crying and he heard Jake saying something but couldn't catch that, either. Jake seemed to be comforting her. Elkin wanted to rush to Sari Rose-in-bloom and push Jake aside. "That's not how you comfort a woman," he was going to yell at Jake. "This is how you comfort a woman," and he would show him, by God. Elkin had done his share of comforting. And if he wasn't going to take pictures of Sari Rose-in-bloom naked, then at least he could feel the warm, caring superiority play of the Older Man. Elkin listened for a while and thought that whatever it was, the girl's mother was nuts, and then Elkin wondered how the hell he was going to get back upstairs without anyone hearing him.

When he shifted around on the stairs, the wood started sounding like an old four-master just hit by a whale. Elkin stopped. Grimaced. Heard Jake and Sari go silent but as soon as they started up the hushed conversation again, Elkin took another step.

As his foot lifted, Elkin noticed that the light beige carpet on the stairs was just a tad worn and also, he heard Jake ask Sari to marry him.

The question seemed to suck all the sound from the house and everywhere else on the block up to the city line. Elkin stood there with his foot raised, afraid to make a move until he heard Jake ride forth with his proposal of wedlock which had now turned into a plea that was tipping over into a whine.

"We'll go to Maryland," Jake's voice was throaty. "We can get married there fast. I don't want you in that house any more. Your mother's out of her fucking mind."

And Elkin was about to shout, "NO!" and rush to the kid's rescue. Join the Army, get married, run away to the circus, this poor Jake didn't know what to do next or which end was up. And the worst thing was, Elkin knew there wasn't a goddamn thing he could do about it except offer the debris of his own mistakes.

Except shout "NO!" and try to tell him about The Ridiculous and how fast things can go south.

But that's not what happened. Because the wonderful Sari Rose-in-bloom said, "No, Jake, we're too young, I don't want to do that" and this time she was speaking more loudly and then Jake said something that was mumbled and the fantastic Sari Rose-in-bloom answered, "Jake, please, don't" and after that Jake whispered some more half swallowed words, and the miraculous Sari said, "I should leave," and then she was rushing out of the living room toward the front door.

Elkin set his foot down. Run, he was going to run up the stairs before Sari saw him. Like an air raid siren went off in his head. Jake called out, "Sari!" who said, "Oh, hello, Mr. Elkin" as she bolted, not bothering to close the Elkin door. Sari headed for the Jaguar parked in front of the house as Jake rushed past Elkin, growled "What are you doing here?" and then shouted "Sari!" again and was out of the door and in the driveway.

Elkin was now at the open door, watching Jake, who was holding Sari by the arms near the Jaguar. They were talking, maybe arguing. Elkin watched them kiss. He watched Sari get in the Jaguar and drive off and he studied Jake's face as Jake followed the slate walkway back to the front door. Elkin couldn't read him, though, it was like the kid had a cloud cover of young trouble over him.

And now he wanted to tell the kid, he wanted to warn him, he wanted all the knowledge that he, Elkin, had absorbed in the world from the death of his parents through The War and his marriage to Marsha and into show business, even what he'd learned when he was the comic emcee of strip shows back in the 40s, even from all the times he'd gone on stage or behind a microphone and failed, laid an egg, even what he'd learned from working all these years with Ted Fox, how "being in a team is like being in a marriage" Elkin would say, and Elkin wanted all of that knowledge to gently be pressed into Jake's pores so that the kid wouldn't get hurt. So Elkin said, "I hope she said 'no,' you dumb bastard. I hope you didn't change her fucking mind. Get married. Jesus Christ. You fucking schmuck."

OK. That wasn't exactly what he meant to say. Elkin wasn't certain why it had come out like that and he was going to try again except that Jake, who looked like he was crying, pushed past him and said, "I'm going to sleep." Elkin heard the kid's door slam like a slap for an ending. And Elkin thought, Then again, maybe that's exactly what I've learned. Maybe I said exactly what I meant to say in the exact way I meant to say it.

As he turned and started to lift himself back up the stairs, he was thinking about Ted Fox, he was thinking he was trapped, he was thinking about Jake and wondering whose fault is it, where did he get this from? How did Jake so soon become his own minefield, his every action a Rube Goldberg booby-trap machine, a catastrophe of his own making? How? Where?

Don't answer that, Mr. Nosh said.

Elkin went to bed.

CHAPTER THIRTEEN

AND JAKE?
Well, he could feel it. Sari was sending him very special Rose-in-bloom signals—he wasn't stupid—a code in tune with the universe that only he could decipher. He got hip to it that night when his idiot father had come downstairs. The "no" on marriage? That simply meant "definitely soon." The no time in bed or the times on low heat or that one time she'd cried and they'd just lain there, see, he understood there was a kind of secret rapture in what others might read as his own decline. Hang in there, kid, he told himself, you ain't even started yet. The sheer, dizzying, ball-tightening excitement of being terribly wrong. Read the signs, oh yeah. Nothing got by him. If anybody comes out of this alive, Jake told himself, it's going to be me.

Everything was laid out there right before his cossy eyes. Take the scarlet mark, for example. A scar, a welt, a wart? Hell, no. It only served to enhance Sari's radiance, make the heat of her beauty glow white. The wound drew Sari into herself even more deeply so that now she was more confidently Sari Rose-in-bloom than ever. People paid to see other people believe in themselves, shit, people died for it. Sari's own Sari belief was now sucked deep into the nucleolus, breathing through the membranes of her cells. You would be certain she had some secret that, once revealed, would answer everything. She flowed with it, too. The worst had been done, she could suffer nothing more. Sari burned brighter now and Jake could feel her go distant, she didn't speak as freely, she didn't laugh at his jokes. Almost always, Sari seemed like she was waiting, passing the time until something finally rode to its finish.

And three days later, the red mark was still there. Jake now understood that the mark was the symbol of a special Heroism of Love, a physical sign of all that he and Sari had been through together. And it was another omen. They would be together until the world stopped spinning. The mark was another "yes" from the cosmos, like when Jake was driving with Sari and correctly guessed that the traffic light would change or when he tuned in the radio and it immediately played a song they were singing. He told all this to Sari who said, "It's not true, Jake."

"There's drama around that bruise," Jake said then. "And I respect it."

He would have to fight. No position, no title, no wealth, no private plane, he had nothing to battle all those gloried predictions of Sari's Jake-less future. So, against this strange, new Sari Rose-in-bloom, Jake threw the only thing he had—he threw the country, the United States of America, the crumbling U.S. of A. He threw the tanks in the street and the cops with their beatings, he threw the tear gas and the smoke over the riot cities, he threw the wounds of every uncertain change, he threw the avalanche of lies and bullshit that came from power and the paper and the radio and TV and from himself, he threw the war and the visions of destruction and the knowing that somehow, in some way, they all would have to face up to all of it. He threw the weight of it, he inflicted it on her.

That's all Jake talked about. He told Sari Rose-in-bloom that they were living through history, they would never forget it, they would be shaped by it and so they should go as deep into it as they could go, immerse themselves in it.

And Sari Rose-in-bloom said, "But we are immersed in it, Jake. It's impossible not to be."

He took Sari to Washington Square Park, to a demonstration against the war. Here, he told her, here is our coming of age, here is our America.

But the mark was coming of age in America, too. In Washington Square, a man dressed in a kabuki Uncle Sam costume told Sari Rose-in-bloom she was magnificent and, with Jake standing right there beside her, the kabuki Uncle Sam ran his finger down the dark length of the red mark. A black man in black leather, black beret, black beard and black sunglasses took Sari's hand, kissed it like a viscount, and his eyes went watery when he saw the welt. Later, locked in with several thousand other people listening to someone in a work shirt and long curly hair shout, "OUT NOW!" through a megaphone from the top of the Loeb Student Center and all of them raising their fists in the air and chanting, Sari Rose-in-bloom felt someone's other fist reach into her knitted shoulder bag and take her wallet.

Sari spun around to face off with the munchkin next to her, a little wiry guy with a beard and granny glasses, and she said, "Give it back." When the guy said, "Give back what?" Jake joined in with "Hey," but couldn't think of anything else to follow it. The thousands of protesters kept shouting, "OUT NOW!" as Sari told the guy, "My wallet. Give it back." The little granny glasses guy eyeballed Sari, then pursed his lips, made the tip of his nose move and finally he reached inside his shirt and handed over a brown leather billfold.

"And ain't 'cause I'm scared of you, baby," he said. "It's 'cause I never seen no one like you. Even in the sunshine you've got this light shining...." Then he stopped and indicated his own neck and said, "Birthmark?"

"In a manner of speaking," Sari Rose-in-bloom said.

The little thief was jostling and pushing and making his way through the crowd, and Jake could have sworn that the guy's eyes were starting to flow, too.

A whiff of the mood in the park, Jake breathed it in, angry, restless and ripe, tinged with marijuana and cigarettes. This is the way the world will be forever, Jake was thinking. He was trying to mingle with it. He was trying to joke with Sari Rose-in-bloom, saying they'd won, they were together, even if Sari wore this rising red gift from her mother. They were the wily guerrilla fighters, the Revolutionaries of Love triumphing against the more powerful but clunky Max and Vee and Elkin and their...

"I have to tell you something," Sari Rose-in-bloom said.

They began pushing through the crowd, through the stink of it, the sweat, pot, incense, cigarettes. They pushed past the mounted cops and the riot police and the circle of people dancing barefoot. Past the shirtless flute player in beads by the fountain, the long-haired man sitting under the tree in the Army field jacket with the 1st Air Cav insignia. The kabuki Uncle Sam rushed past them, chased by somebody dressed in black Vietcong pajamas wearing a big comic Asian mask and carrying an oversized rubber club, beating the Kabuki Uncle Sam over the head. The kabuki Uncle Sam waved to Sari who flashed him a peace sign. A cop sitting on the moving tide of his unsteady horse pointed at Sari Rose-in-bloom and she made the V-for-peace sign for him, too, and the mounted cop stopped smiling and pointed to Sari's neck. That's when Jake said to her, "Is there anybody who's not in love with you?"

"Maybe you," Sari said.

Jake halted so awkwardly that a twinge of pain shot through his ankle. "What about the Gatsby House," he said. "What about how we...what about the fact that we...you can't forget that...just maybe you remember that we've been..."

Then Sari said quickly, "Jake, I'm going to Paris."

The "What?" and "When?" were wrenched out of Jake's mouth by some natural force beyond Jake's grasp but he got himself back in tow enough to say, "Goddamn it."

"My father is sending me."

"You're going with your lunatic mother? Oh, that's a great idea!"

"I'm going alone," Sari said.

"Holy shit! You can't do that!" Jake was almost shouting.

"One of my father's business friends has a flat."

"Well, when are you going?" Jake said. "I'll come over, too."

"Tomorrow," Sari said. "For a month."

It was fascinating how the grass and stones formed patterns on the asphalt as Jake looked down and walked in circles. Better off with head bent forward, he was thinking, because very soon he was going to throw up.

"All right, all right," after he threw up he was going to go breathless and have a heart attack, "we can handle this. Give me a couple of days and I'll get over there, we'll be together. Hey! You know? It's great! This is gonna be great! We'll be in Paris together, we'll have a great time!"

Sari Rose-in-bloom was going to be very busy, she said, interviewing at schools, the Sorbonne, maybe even doing some business for her father. Max Rosenbloom didn't say exactly what business. He'd confided in Sari sadly, saying that he might not be able to pay for years of school in Paris, maybe, we'll see, it's possible, but then again…he was finagling a big deal that still might go south. Still, it couldn't hurt for her to go over and scout out the territory.

"So I won't be gone long," Sari said. "It's just so I can get some distance."

"So you can fuck French guys!" Jake yelled at her. The kabuki Uncle Sam and the Asian-masked Vietcong ran back past them again, the Vietcong still hammering the kabuki Uncle Sam with his rubber club. They both waved at Sari this time as Jake screamed at them, "Eat shit and die!"

"Everyone needs to back away, that's what my father says. Until things calm down."

"Who the fuck's not calm?" Jake said. "They should send your nutcase mother away, not you. They should lock her up."

"I'm going, Jake," Sari Rose-in-bloom said. "I've never been to Paris. I'll be back, you'll see."

"You're ruining everything," Jake said. "Everything could be so terrific."

"Jake, we knew this was coming."

What Jake wanted most was to run. He wanted to hit Sari, harder than her mother had hit her, and then he wanted to take off through the park, legs churning, until the police got the bright idea to chase him. He had an image of the horseback cop riding him down, swinging his long club this way and that as he'd seen at the Friars Club riot and he saw himself stumbling under the beating club and then the hard, rampaging hooves and he thought that would be a painful way to die. He'd be screaming through his last alive moments and Sari Rose-in-bloom would be shouting how sorry she would be for the rest of her life and what a mistake she'd made. Or better yet: the recruiting station in Times Square. Jake would run from the George Washington Arch all the way up Fifth Avenue and then over to Times Square and he would run in and join the Marines, a sure way to be shipped where the fighting was worst. Jake would write Sari a lot of mournful but profound letters and she would read them and be sorry, even more sorry than if he were trampled by horses.

"OK, then," Jake said. "I guess. Well. So." He took a breath. "Have a nice trip."

Sari Rose-in-bloom's eyes welled up and she started to cry.

"What?" Jake said. "What did I say?"

"Aren't you going to miss me, Jake?" Sari didn't even wipe her cheek, she just started walking away. Toward the kabuki Uncle Sam who was still getting clobbered, toward the George Washington Arch, toward the crowd and protest signs and chants. Jake was damned if he was going to follow. That's what he told himself. There was a matter of honor to be upheld. He wasn't going to be led by the nose and go after some broad.

By the time he changed his mind, knowing that his life was

ruined, Jake called out to her, "I *am* gonna miss you!" and then he yelled it again. Sari Rose-in-bloom took a few more steps before she stopped and turned back to Jake. She smiled, then she waved to him. Then she flashed him a V, a peace sign. Then the crowd closed around her, also shouting for peace, and Jake knew that in the morning, he'd be in the ivy patch, watching Sari Rose-in-bloom leave for Paris.

Standing between the Garibaldi statue and the nonworking stone fountain, hidden by a young guy in a fringed vest who was playing the guitar and singing in a voice like a dying dog, there was Boris Jampolsky. He had followed Sari to Washington Square.

Max Rosenbloom had told Boris that there'd been some trouble at home. Sari was going away, Max had said. So Boris wanted to spend as much time with her as he could, but now, when he saw the blood mark on Sari Rose-in-bloom's neck, he shuddered at the evidence that someone had tried to destroy her. And not just someone. Her mama. Max had told him. An accident, he'd said, a loss of temper and Boris wanted to cry but he understood. In Russia, people were often hitting each other.

But such magic! Beyond beauty! Beyond words! The girl who was beyond the power of words was now branded with a physical blow that was, Boris thought, also beyond the power of words, come to think of it. Boris had made up his mind, sitting alone sipping his Russian Caravan tea beside his hot plate and his .32 caliber revolver. Now, watching Sari, wounded, here in the same world as the kabuki Uncle Sam and the Asian-masked Vietcong, the bad singer-guitar player and the mounted cops with their long, scalp-splitting batons, Boris knew that he had made the right decision. Someone had to set the world right and that difficult demand would come with a single name on it: Boris Jampolsky.

There was only one man to blame. That putz. The coward who'd made such trouble for his friend and very soon father-in-law Max Rosenbloom. So much trouble that the exquisite Sari had been damaged and everything had fallen apart. The boy, Jake, was no problem. He was a pathetic schmuck, anyway, Boris thought, and Max was right about him: Sari Rose-in-bloom would never end up with this Jake. Sari was going away and once she entered the world, the real world beyond the make-believe world of America, the shock of her radiant, unspeakable Sari bloom would be taken for the coin that it was. And Boris Jampolsky was a man of this real world. The type of man who acted, whose life was a life of deeds and who would make his deeds parade past Sari Rose-in-bloom as she looked on, judged, considered and, Boris felt sure, fell in love.

Sari Rose-in-bloom waved, flashed a V for peace and goodbye… and Boris Jampolsky, hidden in the crowd by a statue and a guitar player, unseen by Sari, waved goodbye to Sari and said quietly to himself, "Goodbye only for now." He flashed his own V sign of peace and then headed off to kill Larry Passoff.

Boris's friends, the Israelis who weren't afraid to hurt anyone, had done some legwork. Larry Passoff was alone in his office between 1 p.m. and 2 p.m. if he didn't have lunch out. If he was going to eat someplace besides his desk, he would have to walk through the circus of the garment district. Not too far from the front entrance to his building on West 37th, there was a narrow gap between the buildings with a rusty staircase that led down to an alleyway and the service entrance. The metal gate at the top of the stairs was usually left open. Boris could easily come up behind Passoff and quietly, gently shove him down the stairs then gallop down after Passoff's tumbling body and squeeze the trigger. With the shouting and honking, the engines and brakes, the pushcarts and the crowds, the general stink of humanity, Boris was thinking, nobody would give him any notice. So, either way, in his office or in the alley, Larry Passoff was going off to wander with Moses.

Boris went inside a shop across 37th that sold cheap trinkets at bulk, watched through the spattered window and waited to see if Larry Passoff came out of his building. A desk lunch today, that would be best, Boris didn't want to shoot this guy after knocking him down the stairs. He wasn't a schmuck, Boris, he was a man, a good person. Passoff was an old skinny *yenta* who was running his mouth off too much to the wrong people and Boris reminded himself that this had put Max Rosenbloom in trouble which meant that the wonderful Sari was dancing on the edge, too.

But knock this old fart down the stairs and then shoot him? Boris didn't want to be searching Larry Passoff's rolling, wild eyes while the old, spotted hands fluttered to grab where his head hit the rail or where his ankle got bruised. Better that Larry Passoff was reading the *Daily News* and eating a corned beef sandwich and those were his last moments before he was escorted into the World to Come.

Boris checked his watch one more time and then started across the street. Inside, waiting for the elevator, he was hoping that Passoff ate his sandwich and then brought some street hooker up to the office for a lunch hour blow job so that his last moments in the garment district would at least be memorable, not that he would need to remember. Boris regarded his own thinking with pride and would parade it before Sari Rose-in-bloom as proof of his merit as a man. Max Rosenbloom would hear of it as well. This was not the blunted deed of some Moscow Jew thug, it was the considered action of a thinking, feeling, experienced man. The squeal of pulleys and the jerk of chains. The elevator came to a jittery stop on the third floor and Boris stepped off, now holding the .32 hidden down by his thigh.

Larry Passoff Ltd. was at the end of the hall. Thick black letters across pebbled glass, Boris zeroed in on the "Larry Passoff" name as he moved closer. He noticed that once he got off the elevator, time ticked down and his ears opened like antennae for how each footfall crushed each individual grain of dust on the chipped, stained white tiled floor. There was a pain like a small infection above his right eye and a muscle cramp underneath his left arm. Boris began to wonder if the small red bump he'd noticed on his jaw this morning while shaving was possibly cancer. Then he was through the door and at Larry Passoff's entrance room, empty except for the secretary's dented metal desk sitting on the uneven floor.

"*You'rebackearly,*" Larry Passoff's voice came through the open door of his office. The words were wet and bent and pushed together and Larry Passoff had to call out "*Everythingallright?*" before Boris picked up on the fact that Larry Passoff was eating and that his mouth was full of something. So Boris took more steps across the worn and rotted green carpet and raised the .32 to aim as he turned for Larry Passoff's open door.

Where Larry Passoff was now standing. Holding a sandwich and rubbing mustard off his mouth with a napkin and chewing with a kind of succulent delight. Boris could smell corned beef and maybe chopped liver, which made it difficult to keep the .32 pointed between Larry Passoff's eyes, now widening and showing the white as his lips closed around the sandwich.

"*HOLYSHIT!*" Larry Passoff bit down hard then his mouth moved fast, like his lips had turned to spider legs. "*BORISARE-YOUFUCKINGCRAZY!?*" Larry Passoff wiped his mouth again but he kept on chewing.

Boris saw the tiniest mole and two gray hairs between Larry Passoff's eyes but even as he aimed the .32 for a brain shot it was that moving, chewing mouth that he couldn't stop watching and it was the deep meat aroma of corned beef and chopped liver that now seemed to be coating the inside of Boris's nostrils, making Boris famished. Hungry for deli. His mouth was beginning to water. But even more. He was thinking of this morning. Of the hilarious Elkin and Fox. That routine, how they did the bagel eating on the air and…

Larry Passoff leaned back against the doorjamb. Chewing faster now, he swallowed like he was stamping on the food to get it down his constricted throat and he said, "*Putthegunawaywhydon'tyou,*" and after another swallow Larry Passoff said, "Boris. Please. What are you doing?"

"I'm sorry, Larry Passoff," Boris said. His finger was ice against the trigger. Boris could smell his own sweat. Death was coming, Boris could already follow the bullet with his own eyes.

"Boris, I've got another half of corned beef in the other room. Pickles, too. Come. We'll eat. We'll talk. You'll tell me why you're gonna shoot me. Wouldn't that be better?"

Boris wanted Larry Passoff to vomit, to break down and beg for his life, any sane man would have done it. But Larry Passoff just stood there staring at Boris. A little spit up, a tear, a "please don't," anything that would make Boris hate Larry Passoff. But all he could think about was that funny-sounding food voice when Larry Passoff's mouth was full of corned beef. And on the radio this morning, Ted Fox had mentioned Sari Rose-in-bloom. "I love you, doll baby!" Ted Fox had said. Then Jerry Elkin had yelled, "STOPITALREADY!" with his mouth full of food, like he was really annoyed. How funny! And then they'd played a record, "Love's Been Good To Me," with the wonderful Chairman of the Board, Frank Sinatra.

So, Boris Jampolsky lowered the .32 and stood like a pillar of salt in the middle of the room. Larry Passoff said, "Good for you, Boris, I didn't think you were a schmuck who'd do a thing like that."

Slowly, awkwardly, Boris sank down on the floor with the .32 in his lap.

"Let me get the sandwich, you're probably hungry after pointing a gun."

Larry Passoff disappeared into his office and when he came back he was holding half a mustard-soaked corned beef sandwich and a pickle on a sheet of wax paper.

Boris was still sitting on the floor. But now, he held the .32 pointed up against his own forehead.

"Now you're being a schmuck again," Larry Passoff said quietly. "Here. I'll trade. A gun for a sandwich."

Boris didn't move. His brain, maybe shrinking from the bullet it knew was coming, was playing the same old Elkin and Fox routine, again and again, Jerry Elkin doing the funny food voice and telling Ted Fox to stop mentioning Sari.

He flipped the .32 over and handed the weapon butt first to

Larry Passoff. Larry gave Boris the half of corned beef and pickle.

"There's more mustard in the other room if you want it," Larry Passoff said. "I'll tell you, they pack those things so thick you could eat it for a week. Even if you'd shot both of us we'd still be eating."

An old man's laugh, then a groan and Larry Passoff was now in an unforgiving twist sitting on the floor next to Boris, watching the Russian chew and wipe mustard off his lips. He made a few jokes about how he hoped he'd be able to stand up again and then he was asking, "So, this business with the gun. This was Maxie's idea?"

Boris was so glad to be alive and eating this fantastic corned beef that he started telling Larry Passoff everything. Well, not really everything. Only about Max Rosenbloom and his angry phone call, about Sari Rose-in-bloom and how he loved her, about Jerry Elkin and Elkin and Fox. He skipped a few details: things like spying, snitching, Max making noise about how Boris should take care of it. And because he skipped all of that, soon both Boris and Larry Passoff were laughing. Boris was sorry he had gone to Larry Passoff's office with a gun. He was sorry he even possessed the gun. Boris Jampolsky had pointed a loaded weapon at Larry Passoff and then at himself and his intention both times had been to kill. But had he pulled the trigger? No. He was not a schmuck. The schmuck Boris had evaporated and Boris was now excited to see who this new Boris would turn out to be.

"Here, let me have just one more little taste," Larry Passoff picked a sliver of corned beef off Boris's sandwich and then he said, "Sari. I've known her since she was born. A magical little girl."

Boris began telling Larry Passoff how much he loved Sari Rose-in-bloom. No, he said, this wasn't love, he laughed at love, this was some kind of force from the heavens that graced Sari and no one before or since.

"A special little girl," Larry Passoff said. "But I can promise you, she won't go off with a killer or a schmuck."

Boris swallowed the last of his corned beef.

"Some cheap pistolero won't win her heart."

"I will go to her and beg," Boris said.

"Not good enough," Larry Passoff patted Boris on the dark material of his knee. "You'll have to do more. You'll have to work for it."

"I will plead with Mr. Max Rosenbloom," Boris said. "I will beg him to forgive."

"What do you think, Boris, this is the Old Country?" Larry Passoff said. "No commissar's gonna lend you a helping hand. You're not in the *shtetl* with a bowl of warm soup. I don't care what's going on out there in the streets between the long hairs and the cops and this crazy fucking war. I don't care, this is still America. You make it by yourself or you don't make it at all."

"I love America," Boris said.

"You think I'm talking about money? I'm not," Larry Passoff said. "If you want to make this right, you're gonna have to stand up, Boris. You want that little girl to come to you? You're gonna have to be brave enough to show her you know the meaning of justice. Show her you're not some two-bit hood."

"Show me, Larry Passoff," Boris said.

Larry Passoff nodded, patted Boris's knee again and said, "Now, you're talking, kid." With another old man groan he struggled to his feet. "I got some people you need to see. Believe me, it's the only way."

Boris was still telling Larry Passoff that he would see them, he would see any people Larry Passoff told him to see, he was thanking Larry Passoff for helping him and telling Larry Passoff how Sari Rose-in-bloom was the woman all men dream about, as Larry Passoff went into the office, picked up the phone and called his contact at the FBI.

CHAPTER FOURTEEN

ELKIN CALLED HIS MANAGER, Marty Horowitz, asking for an appointment to talk about splitting with Ted Fox but Marty said he'd be busy for the next couple of years and to call back in maybe a decade. So on this still-dark early morning, with the New York summer humid and easy and the air just beginning to go bad, Elkin drove past the billboard touting "Elkin and Fox, the 10 Funniest Guys In Town!" and shouted, "Fuck you, Marty Horowitz! And THEN fuck Ted Fox!" He was losing his mind and he knew it.

There was something else pushing him, too, another definite piece of proof that if he didn't get right with the universe the rubber room was near. It was when Elkin had seen the photos of the Chinita Saris in *The New York Times*. Nerves tickled his fingers and made Elkin dog-ear the paper as he read. The words wouldn't sound in his brain, he'd had to read the story four times. But it was the photos of the drawings that had rankled him. Impossible. How had this *alter cocker* Chinita grow the guts, the hit-the-beach balls to get Sari

Rose-in-bloom naked! And not him, Jerry Elkin! That this Sari Rose-in-bloom had hopped from being the girl he'd dreamed about in his own simple, little house, bought with a G.I. loan, that she'd "meta-morphed" as Miss Emma Reel would say into the work of art staring back at him? Jerry Elkin was an artist, too! How come he had to side with his own squealing, yellow streak? Would it have been so tough to just step forward and say to his kid, "Jake, I'm going to photo-graph your girlfriend who's not really your girlfriend naked." It was all getting away from Elkin, it was all leaving him behind.

And now, four weeks since the girl left for Paris and Jake went into his room and had yet to come out... Well, that wasn't so bad. What really was bad, though, was that two days after the girl had flown the coop, Ted Fox had taken a ride out to see Sari Rose-in-bloom and in his hot pocket he'd been holding surprise tickets to an upcoming Buffy Sainte Marie concert at Wolman Skating Rink. The Vee Vee Rosenbloom who'd met him at the door was a Vee Ted Fox had never seen before, a Vee of small, bumblebee eyes shrunken by constant tears, a face sliced with new rivulets and a Vee who was sinking even deeper into her own flesh. She told Ted Fox everything that had happened. Paris, Sari, Jake, the belt and the mark. She said that he would have to go to the concert alone. Unless he wanted company. In which case Vee would be happy to take Sari's place.

"You're a doll and that's a wonderful, generous offer," is how Ted Fox had answered, "but this is obviously for kids," and he'd kissed her cheek and quickly walked back to his car.

Ted Fox had been a mess to work with ever since. His timing was off, his mind drifted, he looked at Elkin during their routines like Elkin had broken out of the zoo and picked the lock on the studio. Oh, sure, he rallied now and then, Elkin expected no less, Ted Fox was nothing if not a pro, so for a few days it would seem like they were the old Elkin and Fox and the jokes and routines fired with perfect pitch, the music was exactly what the city wanted to hear. And their feel for the audience! Elkin always thought it was like playing for a great ball team, the way he and Ted Fox could get them out of bed in the morning, then tone down just a touch when they were shaving and making breakfast, then ramp it up again until morning drive was over and then glide to the finish and hand it off to the midday man.

But now, even though they sometimes had great shows, Elkin was walking into the studio like he was patrolling through the sniper-polluted jungle. At any moment there could be personal disaster. In the middle of a routine coming off a commercial, Ted Fox would forget what they were hawking and which characters were hawking it. He'd miss his cues. And he'd taken to reading a French tourist phrase book in the studio, so that out of the blue Ted Fox would begin saying on the air, in badly accented French, something like "Where is the Louvre, please?" or "Do you sell newspapers?" or "Would you call me a taxi?" and then he'd finish with "That's for you, *ma chérie* Sari!" Elkin wanted to call an ambulance.

And then there was also the Ted Fox marriage. Marsha described the union as, "Well, at least he always goes home," which was not strictly true. In the version told by Ted Fox and interpreted by a half-listening Jerry Elkin, Ted and Elizabeth had established a kind of liquid truce, the terms of which were that as long as the charm was winking and the drama was turned up, as long as the money kept rolling in and the drinks kept coming and as long as everything was silently agreed to be all right, then everything was, indeed, just hunky-dory.

"We understand each other," Ted Fox said.

Elkin kept his mouth shut.

On this morning at 5:30 a.m. as he picked his way through the newsroom to the studio, Elkin got a "Where you working next, Elko?" from fake tough guy sports announcer Steve Leo, who was jabbing into his typewriter with boxy fingers. That was the first indicator of trouble. Elkin was fighting to get himself up for the show, tap-dancing through the newsroom and shouting out, "Good morning, children!" in the voice of Miss Emma Reel, but he was secretly dreading whatever misery he was going to find in the probable disaster area of Studio B. You could hope, that's true, for what good it would do you, Elkin said to himself. He hoped this would be one of their good days.

Charlie-fat-chance.

Then their producer, Sgt. Al, came striding through the newsroom toward Elkin so desperately that his coffee slopped over the rim of his cup while he was pointing to the little coffee room behind him, saying, "Go back. Gotta talk before air time." And that's when Elkin realized he was maybe going to have to start telling himself once again, This is real and it's happening to me.

"He got a letter." Sgt. Al poured Elkin a coffee as Elkin concentrated on the blood-spewing World War Two Devil's head tattoo that rippled on Al's forearm.

"Who got a letter?"

"Who," Sgt. Al said. "Ted Fox. A bad one, too."

"The IRS," Elkin said.

"Worse."

"Shit! I knew it," Elkin said. "What did she say?"

"He won't tell me. He just sits there and reads it. That's all he wants to do."

Elkin thought that the smartest move now would be to quickly spin around and turn away from Sgt. Al, then run out of the coffee room, down the hallway and out of the radio station, jump in his car and drive to California. But who had the guts to do that?

"Just be warned," Sgt. Al said.

Elkin stepped into Studio B. The studio was masked in that special radio station quiet, a room protected from noise by sheet after sheet of soundproofing on the walls and on the ceiling and under the rug. By a double door with an airlock. As he walked into the studio this morning, Elkin flinched from the yellow cast of the lights and he thought the whole place reminded him of the movie "I Want To Live!" with Susan Hayward about a woman who gets sent to the gas chamber. That's what this was, a gas chamber, a place to gas in as in "talk" and a place to smell poisonous fumes and die. And Elkin wanted to live.

Ted Fox sat hunched forward on the metal stool near the turntable. His fingers tapped at the edges of what looked like a letter and he was moving his lips as he read, a man working his way through an ancient lost language and desperately trying to understand.

"So, you got a letter," Elkin said.

"Oh, hi there, my liege," Ted Fox said sadly.

"Why don't you put it away and we'll talk about it after the show."

Ted Fox nodded. "OK," he said. "But I was thinking of reading it on the air."

"After the show, just between us, is much better, " Elkin said.

Ted Fox nodded once again. Elkin glanced up at the big clock with the big numbers that ruled everything they did for the four hours of performance. It was ten minutes to six a.m. "Ted," he said quietly. "It's almost air time. Tell you what. Why don't we give them a how-do-you-do and maybe, just for you, we'll start off with 'Today I Sing The Blues.' Aretha Franklin."

"Then go into the airline spot," Sgt. Al was back in the studio, sorting through LPs.

"We'll bring in Chip Chopper and he'll be too sad to do the traffic and you'll cheer him up, how's that?"

Ted Fox shrugged and said "OK" so softly that Elkin could barely hear him.

Finally, Elkin said, "Can I see the letter, Ted?"

"OK," Ted Fox said again.

Elkin read the letter. It was on pink stationery with a slight waft of some spicy perfume, not bad, either, and the blue handwriting was graceful with a certain poetic flair. The letter started off, "Dear Ted Fox," and then went through several lines of describing Paris, how wonderful it all was. The feeling of sudden freedom in this wide, wide world was "like riding on a giant wave," Sari wrote. She couldn't believe all the changes that were happening to her so quickly! She felt like she had stepped out into a "beautiful universe of endless possibilities!" And there followed some lines about how she was spending her time day to day. Talking to the people at the Sorbonne about a possible spot as a student. Talking to another school in Reims, too. There was plenty of action, lots going on, still evidence of the big riots from the year before and the students maybe ready to riot again because the young people were so very excited about the Situationist International rebuilding the world and all. It was something to see! And she was also doing a little bit of work for her father, going out to dinner with clients and, well, just being Sari Rose-in-bloom. They seemed so taken with her, she wrote, and they all wanted to be seen with her "at all the best places.

"But here's the most surprising part of it all," Sari wrote. "I'm only telling you because you're a man of the world, as you've told me many, many (many) times and I know you won't be shocked. But I've met someone. And I'm going to be married."

Elkin cleared his throat and looked up. Ted Fox was sitting there, watching the rug very closely. It was five minutes before air time.

The introduction, Sari wrote, had come through Max Rosenbloom's friend, the man who was letting her stay at his beautiful apartment, just off Boulevard Saint-Germain. Her fiancé's name was Dr. Henri Louis Lévi, very handsome, a medical doctor, 28, and the son of one of the wealthiest Jewish families in France, a fortune made in lumber and furniture manufacturing. They would be returning to New York in about two weeks and they would be married soon after that and Ted Fox, who had been such a friend, Ted Fox would very certainly be invited to the wedding. "I'll be very, very angry if you don't attend," Sari wrote. Then she signed her name, Sari Rose-in-bloom (Lévi, soon).

"She went to Paris to find a Jewish doctor?" Elkin said. He started to chuckle.

Ted Fox bolted off the stool and straightened himself. "It's just a joke, isn't it. Everything to you is funny, Jerry. Everything's a big fucking laugh."

"We better hope so if we want to get paid," Elkin said.

"Do you see me laughing? I've been shot in the heart, Jerry, why can't you understand?"

That made Elkin laugh even harder. He gave the letter back to Ted Fox, pushing away any thoughts of how this little bit of cheer from across the Atlantic was going to play at home with Jake. "We'll talk about it later, like I said," Elkin said.

Sgt. Al said, "Two minutes to air," and Elkin got a swift gander at the clock, and then a swifter gander at Ted Fox, and then suddenly fell back on sheer Clown Instinct. He swung around to Ted Fox with his face like a big happy boy balloon, the same exaggerated smile that was posted on the billboard. Then he did a quick tap dance, a pirouette, put a finger on his head and spun around like a top, then a double side arm pump and a march in place. After that, he pinched Ted Fox on the cheek. It was tough work. But Clown Instinct, that was the life raft. It told Elkin that if the body was doing funny, then soon the spirit would be funny, too.

By some form of comic grace, Ted Fox began to snap out of it.

The news came on. The first story: Ted Kennedy. The Massachusetts Senator had been given a two-month suspended sentence after driving off a bridge with a girl who was not his wife and who happened to get killed. Now the question was whether he should resign from office.

"Hunh. Hmmm," Elkin said to Sgt. Al. "Go get 'I Happen To Like New York.'"

Sgt. Al made the "don't do it" motion with his hand but Elkin waved him off and Sgt. Al ran out and down the hall to the record library. Elkin didn't know why, but looking at the King of Glum, Ted Fox, it just seemed right.

A couple of minutes later Sgt. Al came back with the cut by Judy Garland, who'd recently died in London. She'd been brought back to New York City for a star-studded memorial service before being shipped up to Fernwood. The news finished up with new details on how U.S. B-52's had been secretly dropping thousands of pounds of bombs on Cambodia and Laos, followed by a story about rioting between the Catholics and Protestants in Northern Ireland.

Then the engineer opened the mike and Elkin and Fox did an energetic, "Elkin and Fox! Let's make it morning!" and they played the song where Judy Garland sings about how she wants to go to New York and not to Heaven or Hell when she dies.

"Mistake," Elkin said. "You were right. Not handsome, but right."

"I'm surprised she lasted this long," Sgt. Al said.

Elkin nodded. No snowballing, he told himself, don't get thrown. Even if Ted Fox had his smile turned upside down and all laughs were under threat. Snap to, Mister. Work.

As the record ended, they went into the airline spot with a sad Chip Chopper and a sympathetic Ted Fox, who handled the routine without a hitch.

Elkin kept working.

No bird of prey, the show this morning, this fucker was a dove. Elkin and Fox got on the soft white wings and flew through those four hours like they were following directions from the sign that said On Air. Somewhere in his backbrain, Elkin knew that Chip Chopper and Mr. Nosh and Coach Bruce Bruise and Dr. Huckleberry, all of them, were giving Elkin and Fox a big Standing O because they were laughing, they were being warmly ridiculous and you didn't have to look for too long outside to see that the rest of the world was going to hell. And the thing of it was, they didn't especially feel funny this morning. Not Ted Fox, that's for sure. And Elkin was down, too. There was a big sign that read "Worry About This" painted on the inside of his skull and beneath it were the names of Jake Elkin and Ted Fox, of course, and his wife, Marsha, and then a lengthening list in print that got smaller and smaller: the mortgage, a mandala of diseases, Vietnam, Nixon, atomic war....

And with all those gears and springs flying apart, and everybody else ducking, Elkin and Fox were laughing because they knew that, in some way, it was all completely unbelievable and ridiculous. And for four hours every weekday, their listeners could laugh, too. Just turn the dial and tune in.

End of show. And maybe they stepped out of the window in the sales department because that's how quickly they exited the station and got out onto the street.

Ted Fox gave a fluttering hitchhiker thumb signal which pointed right at the Miramar Bar across the pavement and Elkin said, "Here's a piece of unasked-for advice," which was a good time to become the Viennese Dr. Huckleberry. "With the letter from this girl, lay off the sauce until you get home."

"We'll just have one and we'll call it a day," Ted Fox said. "I won't even laugh if you have coffee, my liege."

"Here's an idea. Let's go home!" Elkin did his little ballet pirouette then ended by pulling his sports jacket up over his head like a hood. "I'm not sure what they are, but I have a lot of things to do."

"Right as you always are," Ted Fox said. "It's through the tunnel and over the bridge to grandmother's house we go."

"I don't know what you're talking about," Elkin said, straightening his jacket.

"Let's talk some business," Ted Fox said.

So they sat at the bar at the Miramar. Who else was in the place at 10:30 a.m.? Fake tough guy sports announcer Steve Leo. He'd obviously wormed out for a quick nip, something that management had put down in the never-do-that column. Steve Leo paddled a quick heel-and-toe out of there when Elkin and Fox showed up, but not before he got off a "They play together, they drink together, what won't these two madcaps do next!"

"I hate that guy," Ted Fox said when Steve Leo had vanished.

"Maybe a bus will hit him," Elkin said. "Maybe a bus with our ad on the side."

Ted Fox ordered them both Scotch. The Miramar was empty now except for Elkin and Fox who could read the sorrow in the empty red bar stools, the scattering of empty tables, all of it glaring back at them with no applause in the pebbled mirror behind the bar. The place was dark, it was carved out of black ice and didn't like the morning. "I want you to talk to Marty," Ted Fox said. "Set up a meeting. I'm ready to fly."

Elkin was afraid he'd blacked out and missed a major part of the conversation. He tasted the Scotch and started rubbing at the water circle on the bar with his fingers.

"Let's do it. All of it. I'm serious," Ted Fox said. "Movies. A TV special. We'll go out to the coast and sniff around, see what's what. We should go up for more commercials, too, I mean, why not? A couple more like Mr. Sweetbubbles and we could retire. Hey! And how about maybe we start thinking about a Broadway show?" Ted Fox put on his gorgeous smile and patted at his hair. "I know what you're gonna say. This isn't the Ted Fox that you've come to know and love and, Jer, you might be right but jeezy-peezy. I think this is going to be a better Ted Fox, you wait and see."

Elkin started counting his teeth with his tongue. Then he made a soft sucking sound and said, "This wouldn't have anything to do with the girl, would it? With the letter?"

"You're worried I'm trying to impress her or make her sorry she left me. Absolutely not."

"Goddamn it, Ted," Elkin said. "She didn't leave you. From the letter, you're just a version of her father with hair. Some older guy she thinks is listening to her and not staring at her tits, poor kid."

"You don't know Sari," Ted Fox said. There was a funny kind of light streaming off the ice cubes in his glass and Ted Fox got that man-with-a-mission expression, like his brain had been invaded by the King of Profundity. "She gets you with your face to the ground. Sniffing after her scent. But the thing is, she knows you're both in on the joke."

"Ted, there's no future in it."

"I don't want her in the future. I want her now. With Sari it's always Now."

"Ted, you've got to get some help," Elkin said. "Something's popped in your noggin."

The shining ice cubes did their clink-clink-clink as Ted Fox threw back the last of his Scotch and signaled for another.

"Have we not been great, my liege?" Ted Fox said then. "There's nobody to match you, Jerry. This has been one great goddamn ride."

Elkin didn't like the way that sounded with its little tinkling tones of too many sleeping pills mixed in a sea of booze or some rope play that was going to solve everything. He was thinking of Judy Garland. Elkin began singing, "I Happen To Like New York."

"OK," Elkin said after the first few lines, "all right. Ted, listen to me. I want you to leave your belt and shoelaces on the bar and also any sharp objects you're carrying."

Ted Fox started to laugh.

"Also your money," Dr. Huckleberry said. "And your house and car."

"And this is for my own good?" Ted Fox laughed harder. "I'll probably kill myself tripping over my pants."

Elkin nodded at the bartender for another drink, figuring this was going to be a Ted Fox afternoon. "About doing other things," Elkin said. "TV and movies and a ticker tape parade. Which ones were you serious about?"

"All in due time," Ted Fox said. "We'll get there."

"I'm going to set up a meeting with Marty."

"If Marty picks up the tab, I'll be there," Ted Fox said. "But I want to tell you. We got a good thing going here, Elko. And it might not be so smart to go someplace else. Like someplace where we can fucking fail."

"I don't plan on failing," Elkin said.

"Yeah, kid, funny thing. There's something about planning and failing that's got nothing to do with each other. And, Jerry, if we try something and we land on our fannies, it's going to be right out there, it'll be pretty tough to miss."

Elkin cleared his throat so it sounded like a radiator, even the bartender turned around. "You failed with the girl, what about that?"

"I haven't failed yet," Ted Fox said and his hand reached for some invisible pulley in the air as he made sure that drink number three was on its way. "If you're with that girl, Jer, I'm telling you. It's like nothing else in the world can ever go wrong again."

"Uh huh," Elkin said. "Tell me something. Did you bang her?"

Ted Fox was discovering something miraculous in the ice, that was his expression as he stared into his glass. "That's beneath you, Jer," he said. "I'm trying to say something but there's no words. No words." He looked up. "And don't ask me that question again."

They had another drink together and Elkin said he really had to go. As he walked out of the Miramar Bar, Ted Fox yelled after him, "Call my wife and tell her I'll be late, my liege!" and Elkin said he'd call her but that he was running out of lies.

This was the ridiculous that was not The Ridiculous, Elkin was thinking, because Ted Fox was doing it for a purpose. A stupid purpose to be sure, but a purpose nonetheless. Ted Fox was in the great, blind chase, poor schmuck. The chase that was just about chasing. He'd taken the bait of the Great Whirl. And how would it end? Elkin spoke to himself in the voice of Chip Chopper. It could wind up how? Try: badly. There was no other way.

It was like in The War, Elkin thought, when everyone just assumed they'd eventually get killed. You settled into it. Over the next few days, as Elkin sat in the den in the chair that he hated and tried to get his manager, Marty Horowitz, on the phone, he thought about how the worst would happen. When he was having dinner with Marsha, every bite of food and every word out of her mouth seemed carried to him on the magic carpet of "the worst." Elkin was always a little goo-goo eyed and distracted. He had "the worst" running through his synapses when he drove to the station in the morning and shouted at the billboard that read, "Elkin and

Fox, the 10 Funniest Guys in Town!" and he was waiting for the worst when he lay down in bed to go to sleep at eight p.m. listening to his heart rattle and the ringing that he was sure was developing in his left ear.

Then one evening in his den, while Elkin was nursing a Scotch and trying to get his manager, Marty Horowitz, on the phone, his son Jake came to see him with his face split into a smile that was an advertisement for expensive dentistry. Jake wouldn't let Elkin get out word one. The kid was practically dancing. In his hand, Elkin noticed a piece of pink stationary with a familiar spicy perfume and all Jake could say was how he was "soaring" because Sari Rose-in-bloom had written. He was "over the top and outta sight" and he was finally happy.

The letter told Jake all the same details that Ted Fox's letter had told him, except for one minor omission. "I have some incredible things to tell you, Jake," the letter read. "We'll talk all about it when I get home." There was no mention of Dr. Lévi.

Jake was jittering like he'd swallowed a wind-up toy. "So, I was right about her and me all along."

Elkin began to say, "That's your interpretation?" but Jake didn't want to hear any other voices, nothing but his own and the voice on paper of Sari Rose-in-bloom. He was out of there fast, leaving Elkin to sip his Scotch alone. After he'd listened to the ice cracking for a while, Elkin could hear the sound of grunting push-ups and shadowboxed Karate blows coming up from the basement where Jake was working out. Elkin listened, then rolled into the future. The Love Darkness was on its way. The girl would come home and let Jake know what's what. Then there'd be a hollowed out Jake, heart and guts gone and the rest of him draped in The Worst. Poor schmuck. The kid's really asking for it, Elkin said to himself.

Elkin wondered what Ted Fox was doing right now and what Max and Vee Vee Rosenbloom were doing, too, and he even wondered what Sari Rose-in-bloom was doing right at this very moment in Paris. A boozy instant of harmony crept in, the entire world in gear and churning.

Ted Fox was now driving past Sari's house every other afternoon to check if she'd come home yet and once he told Elkin that he thought he saw Jake sitting in an ivy patch across the street. "Probably not," Ted Fox said. "That would be crazy."

Then, finally, after two weeks had passed, Elkin and Fox did a show that made the asphalt on Times Square melt, it was so funny. It was so well timed. It was so filled with humor's love and venom.

The only thing was, throughout the entire four hours of the show, Ted Fox kept snapping his fingers and humming whenever a record was playing or during the news or recorded spots. Elkin held off as long as he could stand it and then about an hour before they signed off, Elkin said, "OK, I'll be the stupid one and ask. What's with the finger snapping?"

"Sari's back," Ted Fox did a little twist of the hips. "I drove past her house and saw her in the window last night."

"Wow," Elkin said. "To live through World War Two and have Sari Rose-in-bloom come back, all in one lifetime. You're blessed."

"Oh, by the way," Ted Fox did a quick tap dance, "that *was* Jake in the ivy patch."

But finger snapping and humming? They were gone the next morning, that's for sure. Happiness had shipped out to a theater of war somewhere far away and unpronounceable because Ted Fox was back to the slump and dump, the gloom coming off him was tingeing the recycled air black with tragedy. It was that quick. They did the show all right, no awards or cheers, but they got through it. And after they smiled into the mike, "Let's make it morning!" Elkin said, "What's up with you, Muldoon? Yesterday life was a conga line and all you could talk about was how Sari is back."

"Sure she's back," Ted Fox said. "But I met the guy she's going to marry."

"Golly winkles, Ted Fox!" Elkin said as Chip Chopper using one of Chip's favorite expressions. "What a calamitous misfortune!"

Ted Fox shook his head, said, "Fuck you, Jerry" and walked out of the studio.

That evening, still early, while Elkin was sitting in the chair he hated unable to get his manager, Marty Horowitz, to come to the phone, he got the call he thought was Marty and listened to the voice on the other end of the line tell him that Ted Fox was dead.

CHAPTER FIFTEEN

THE CALL CAME FROM FAKE TOUGH GUY sports announcer Steve Leo. He called Elkin "Elko" all the way through and he was doing a low-keyed, I-got-something-serious-for-you tone and sounded grim and dry. At first, Elkin thought this was some kind of insane prank from a stupid, drunken schmuck and his reaction was, "What! Oh, fuck you!" but Steve Leo kept on saying, "No, no, listen, Elko, listen to me," and went on with the story.

Everyone else was afraid to make the call, Steve Leo said. "So I volunteered."

Elkin's hand was still holding the phone down on the receiver when the phrase that zinged through his mind was, "The king is dead, long live the king." His head dropped forward so that his chin was on his breastbone. Then, without wanting to do it, Elkin began to pound his feet on the floor, fast and then faster and beat his fists into his thighs. All the time he was doing this, hitting himself, he was thinking, "He's dead he's dead he's dead!" with a glee that was going 200 miles an hour and showed no signs of pulling over for a stop. Elkin felt bad about it afterwards and anyway, it didn't last for long.

The police put together that Ted Fox, right after the show, after he walked out on Elkin's jokes and the voice of Chip Chopper, had done a serenade of his favorite bars. It was musical they way he'd done it, tickling the keys, place by place and drink by drink, beginning with the Miramar across the street and working his way north to The Four Seasons and P.J.'s and the St. Regis and The Oak Room and Bemelmans and Elaine's. Elkin liked to think that at each place where Ted Fox had been drinking, they'd celebrated him, even though the schmuck had been committing fucking suicide, Elkin hoped that every time Ted Fox lifted the tinkling-ice glass at the bar there were calls of "Ted Fox of Elkin and Fox! He's here!" and that Ted Fox was surrounded, in each and every fucking bar he stopped in, that he was mobbed by people who knew what this man could do behind a microphone. That's what Elkin hoped after he was glad and sorry he was glad. Elkin knew that on the radio each show was alive when you started and dead when you finished, going out over the airwaves and disappearing like an angel in the atmosphere and Elkin hoped that they sent Ted Fox out with cheers and applause and told him how funny he was and how great he sounded and how good he made them feel. That's what Elkin hoped. Because in the years to come, Elkin knew, soon, sooner than anyone expected, there wouldn't be any more radio, people would be doing something else, maybe listening to something wired into their brains, who the fuck knew, and they wouldn't know or care what it took to be Ted Fox and to do what Ted Fox could do, they wouldn't know anymore than people would give a lot of thought to the guys he helped bury on Guam after the battle, during The War. So Elkin hoped. Not that Ted Fox would be remembered, that's way too much to ask, not even that Elkin be remembered, who cares about that once you're gone, no, what he hoped was that Ted Fox had been treated like goddamn talent in every bar in town. And he hoped he went quick. He told his son Jake over and over, "That's what I learned in The War, when it's your turn to go, go quick," because he remembered what the screams sounded like when it took a long time. Elkin hoped that Ted Fox got a Ted Fox farewell even if no one knew it was farewell and he hoped that when the drunken schmuck Ted Fox drove his car into a barrier near the exit for Sari Rose-in-bloom's house on the LIE, Exit 33, he hoped that Ted Fox went quick.

Then, a couple of days later, there was the funeral. Marsha convinced Elkin he had to go. Elkin refused to speak at the service, he couldn't, and when they carried Ted Fox out in a heavy brown casket, out of the Frank E. Campbell Funeral Chapel on Madison Avenue, everyone there, all the mourners, stood up and applauded. Except for Ted Fox's family. And except for Elkin. Who stood up and shouted an agonized, "WHAT THE HELL ARE YOU APPLAUDING FOR? THE POOR SON OF A BITCH IS DEAD!" Marsha had to calm him down.

The station told Elkin that he was going to take two weeks off until they figured out what to do. Elkin's manager, Marty Horowitz, called and soon Elkin was sitting in Marty's office watching Marty put his little feet up on the desk while he told Elkin, "The best thing to do is…"

"I'm going solo, Marty," Elkin said.

"…we're gonna find you another partner. The best thing, we're gonna find a guy named Ned Rocks or Fred Knox or maybe Ed Cox. Then you can be Elkin and Rocks or Knox or Cox and in a couple of months, nobody will know the difference."

Elkin walked out of Marty's office as Marty was saying, "I'll start making some calls today."

Max Rosenbloom called and in his thick head-crushing voice he said, "I know we didn't get off so well on the right foot but I want to tell you how sorry I am. I know it must be tough." Then he told Elkin that Ted Fox was supposed to come to Sari's wedding but things being the way they were, he hoped that Elkin would come to the wedding instead, even though he hadn't been invited before and even though Vee Vee didn't like him. And Elkin, who'd swallowed two Valium a half hour before, said he would be there.

Then Sari Rose-in-bloom called. Elkin was "Mr. Elkin" all the way through and Sari told him what a great man Ted Fox had been and how much she had learned from him and how much her soon-to-be husband Dr. Henri Lévi had enjoyed meeting him. He'd been very impressed with, as Dr. Lévi called him, "the important American radio man." Sari said Elkin really had to hear Dr. Lévi's accent, maybe it would be good to use for a new character. She hoped that Mr. Elkin would come to the wedding. She knew that Ted Fox would want him to. Elkin, who was now on his third Scotch, said, "*That'sverysweetofyou*" and hung up, hearing himself, thinking of how many times he and Ted Fox had done that old eat-on-the-air routine and how people always loved it.

What was he going to do now? Elkin wanted to ask Marsha what to do but she would just stare at the TV and say it didn't really matter, like, he would find something, don't worry so much. And Jake. Poor Jake. Sari hadn't gotten around to calling Jake yet, but Jake in the ivy patch had seen Sari and Dr. Henri Lévi come out of the Rosenbloom house and it was as if he'd witnessed Sari being escorted away by some elegant, palace-rich French monarch who had not only avoided getting his head cut off but who also happened to be Jewish. Jake had told Elkin he was sorry about Ted Fox and that he was "thinking of a plan" for Sari and then Jake had locked himself in his room and wouldn't come out. Or that's where Elkin thought Jake was living. He hadn't seen the boy for a couple of days.

So he was going to be off the air for a while. And when he went on again, he would either be Elkin and Knox or Rocks or Cox or he'd be Jerry Elkin alone, which made each disc of his spine begin to spin. He could hear Ted Fox worry about failure. He could hear his manager, Marty Horowitz, and Marsha and he could…he could….

The Monday after the Ted Fox funeral, Elkin got up at the usual time, 4:30 a.m. Marsha was still sleeping and he was quiet as he left the house. The Volvo took to the LIE as if no one had told it that Ted Fox was dead and it drove Elkin for the exact same trip at the exact same time that Elkin had driven, every workday before dawn since 1954. And when he reached the giant billboard, the one that said "Elkin and Fox, the 10 Funniest Guys in Town!" Jerry Elkin pulled the Volvo over to the side of the expressway and got out of the car. He stepped over the metal divider into the high grass on the other side and walked toward the billboard. Elkin was remembering how it was in The War when they went out on patrol, how the grass was tall and sharp and how sometimes they found the dead in the grass, the ones who were forgotten, like when he took the Japanese skull off that poor Jap corpse and kept it for himself until he saw the Golden Gate and knew he was alive for sure. So now, standing like some little schmuck in the tall grass under the huge billboard, beneath the giant faces of Elkin and Fox making big clown smiles, Elkin picked up a craggy stone the size of a hand grenade and he threw it at the billboard, so hard that his shoulder ached. The stone hit Ted Fox just below the right eye. It made a dim thud and bounced away. It left a tiny black scar that Elkin could barely see.

Then he found another stone and threw it. This time he hit the grinning Elkin face and the stone fell straight down and his own likeness had a triangle tear on the bald forehead. So Elkin threw another stone. And another. He started chanting, "You son of a bitch, you fucking stupid son of a bitch schmuck, you son of a bitch, you schmuck" with each stone he threw. And he threw plenty. Enough to make the billboard look like it was peppered with machine gun fire, little black marks and tears bruising the faces of Elkin and Fox, who once had been the ten funniest guys in town. Yesterday. Long ago. Elkin kept throwing the stones until a police car pulled up and then he stopped and walked over, leaned into the squad car and started explaining to the police what he was doing and why.

The cop said he recognized him, asked for a quick Mr. Nosh and then escorted Jerry Elkin home.

★ ★ ★

When Max Rosenbloom answered the door that morning he said, "*Entrez, s'il vous plaît*," and let Jake inside, Max sweeping his hand in a wide, gracious bow. Then he introduced Jake to Dr. Henri Lévi, soon to be Sari's husband.

"I just want to speak to Sari," Jake said.

"I'll go up and get her," Max said. "Henri, this kid's the son of the other half of that radio team, the one with Ted Fox."

Dr. Lévi said "Ah!" and "Fantastic!" and began to speak about how funny those two radio men were and how they had nothing like that in France.

Max Rosenbloom watched them from the top of the stairs. He saw how Jake listened to Dr. Lévi's accent and how he ran his gaze up from the perfect leather boots that were hip but not too hip, along the fresh seam of the dark trousers that were trousers and not pants, to the light gray shirt that fell impeccably over the flat belly and then went up to the red patterned silk scarf tied around the doctor's neck. Max thought that Dr. Lévi looked a little like he'd walked off the screen of a foreign film, elegant and worldly even at 28, rich and comfortable with the world. I'd marry him myself, Max Rosenbloom was thinking. The money will help, so in that way at least he'll take good care of her. And he was thinking about the deal with the poisoned children's clothes and that schmuck Larry Passoff. She won't need the money now, Max Rosenbloom thought. I can let it go. And thank God Larry Passoff had pulled his brains out of his *tuchus* and decided to keep his mouth shut. And who to thank besides God that Boris had had the good sense to report back to Max instead of taking care of Larry after Larry confessed. Boris was a good guy, he was going to go places. And Sari? She was still a kid but she knew a thing or two and this was a good marriage even if it's only the first of two or three.

Then Max Rosenbloom was back downstairs in the foyer saying, "She's on her way," and he filled Jake in on Dr. Lévi's glowing life story. Jake tried to look like he was listening. All he could think about was that this asshole was fucking Sari Rose-in-bloom and that the French had surrendered in World War Two. Jake was jockeying to figure a way to work this shameful fact into the conversation when he heard the words "concentration camp" from Max and when Jake asked for a repeat, Max Rosenbloom said, "Dr. Lévi's parents were in a concentration camp. That's where Dr. Lévi was born."

"What?"

"Incredible story. He's been there and back, I'll tell you that."

"I'll bet," Jake wasn't sure he had heard right and he steadied himself with the idea that the fucking Nazis were ruining even this, his last shot with Sari Rose-in-bloom.

Max Rosenbloom gave Jake his favorite smile. He actually felt sorry for the kid. Well, he'd tried to warn him, tell him what's what, he'd done the schmuck a favor. Some people never listen and walk around blind. And the wedding? Jake might as well know. Max Rosenbloom was free with his plans. The rabbi was coming to the house tomorrow evening and they'd have a very quiet ceremony with just a few friends and family, just to make sure there would be no trouble. Then the next day there was going to be one helluva bang-up party at the Carlyle Hotel. That's where all of Sari's friends and Max's friends and Vee's friends would dance and talk and take pictures of Sari feeding cake to Dr. Lévi and afterward the happy couple would leave for Paris.

"I can't invite you to be there, Jake," Max Rosenbloom said. "Obviously. You probably wouldn't want to show up anyway. So why don't you say your goodbyes now."

"That's why I'm here," Jake said.

Then he saw Sari Rose-in-bloom. She came out of her bedroom dressed in a new sheer, light yellow, cotton minidress that seemed to cling to every curve of her body. Max Rosenbloom could hear Jake catch his breath. This was the Sari of the art piece, with gold now poured over her breasts, her nipples, her hips, ending in the sheer tan of her perfect legs. Dr. Lévi went to the stairs and held out his hand, saying, "No man in the world is happier or more lucky." Sari reached for him, smiled, took his hand and allowed herself to be led down the stairs as if she was being introduced to the royal court.

Vee came out of the room a moment later. She set herself at the top of the stairs. If it was possible, she looked to Jake like she'd become even larger, her body encased in a new, bright blue muumuu like a battle flag, her blue eyes with a rapier gleam, her blond hair pulled back to make her expression of triumph and rage even more noticeable.

"I'll let you say goodbye," Vee said. "And I hope you die before you ever come back to this house again."

"Vee, please," Max Rosenbloom said. "He's only a kid."

"The mama, she protects her little bird," Dr. Lévi said. "But now, I will protect, you can be sure of this assertion."

"I want to speak to Sari alone," Jake said.

Vee shouted, "NO! MAX, NO!" and when Max made a two-handed shrug and surrender sign as in it-doesn't-matter Vee made like a whirling tornado, spinning back to her room and slamming the door. Dr. Lévi said, "I will assist her!" and took the stairs two at a time. Max Rosenbloom got his fingers into the muscle of Jake's shoulder and said, "Don't make it long." He motioned at the front door with his chin.

Max Rosenbloom watched them through the little round window in his front door. Jake and Sari were outside now, standing, talking on the slate path. Max watched their mouths moving. The kid would remember all this, that's for sure. For the rest of his life he'd be thinking about her. Long after Sari could barely recall Jake's face. After all of Sari's adventures and marriages and children and her life in chateaus and castles, Jake Elkin would be a piece of lint in her mind.

Sari was walking Jake to his Volvo parked at the curb. Jake had his arm around her waist. They were still talking. When they got to the car, Max Rosenbloom tried to see if Jake was crying, Sari, too, but all eyes were dry. And she was gorgeous, this girl that he'd helped bring into the world. Not only that. The world was full of good-looking broads. Max Rosenbloom hoped that whatever wordless ecstasy Sari possessed, those rays of the essential female that seemed to power Sari Rose-in-bloom, he hoped she'd keep that as long as she wanted. He hoped that Sari…

They were getting into Jake's car. Max Rosenbloom stiffened. He turned to search the room for Vee and then his hand went to the doorknob. "Hold on," he said out loud. Max Rosenbloom's big, wrecking ball paw tore at the dull metal knob as he got the door open, the screen door, too, which rattled when he shoved it open, and he shouldered his way outside and stood on the brick stoop. Run after them you dumb son of a bitch, he could hear himself saying, get in the fucking car and go, go, go! He'd run to the Jag. Because by the time Max was out in the morning light, he got a clear earful of the squeal of tires and he could see Sari's face staring back at him as Jake drove the car up the block and made the turn, out of sight.

That was it. They'd made a run for it.

The phone call from Sari came about an hour and a half later.

Vee was in their room when the phone rang. Dr. Lévi had sedated her and now sat by the bedside guarding her sleeping body. Max Rosenbloom was at the kitchen table nursing a vodka, watching the smoke trail from his cigarette swirl around the overhanging light. When Max picked up the phone his voice was swamp thick and treacherous and Sari's voice on the other end of the line was telling Max not to worry, that everything would be all right, that she would be back tomorrow, that she wasn't crazy and that she knew what was best.

Max listened. When she was finished speaking he said, "Goodbye, Sari," like he meant it. And hung up on her.

By 6 p.m. the next evening, the Rosenbloom house was filled, the thick rug of the living room supporting the rabbi who was to perform the ceremony that wouldn't happen, Dr. Lévi the groom who wouldn't be, and the Rosenbloom friends Ben E. Fahr, the

Underwear Tsar, Stu Edelstein who'd made a mint off putting cellophane between cheese slices, and the guy who'd made billions from manufacturing staples for matchbooks. Vee Vee Rosenbloom was upstairs behind her closed bedroom door. Sari's brother who hadn't been home in a year had come in just for the ceremony but he still refused to speak with Max. He was in his own bedroom with the door closed.

Jerry Elkin wasn't coming but Max Rosenbloom wasn't thinking about Elkin. There were worse things to muddle the head so he let go of the phone call from Marsha saying they had to "take back their yes and make it no" because Jerry was too upset about Ted Fox. And he'd been on Valium when he had talked with Max. And he was on Valium now, too. "In fact," Marsha said, "me, too. A half."

"So's my wife, " Max said. "A whole one." He told her goodbye.

Max Rosenbloom sat in the chair in his living room that made him feel like a French aristocrat and diddled with the pieces of his antique chess set. The pieces were carved out of elephant tusk, very expensive, but Max Rosenbloom knew how to deal. He'd picked it up from a client in India who'd needed some help with his factory. A gift for a job well done. But now Max was thinking when it came right down to it, even though he'd walked out of the jungle alive from The War, at the one important moment that had been dropped in his lap, he'd failed. The moment he'd needed to grab had been yesterday. When he'd watched Jake drive off with his daughter. He'd failed. It was over. He was a schmuck.

"She'll be here, she's just a little late," Max told them all again. "She's beautiful. She takes her time."

"A wait that's worth waiting!" Dr. Lévi called out. Someone said, "Here here!" as Dr. Lévi put one hand to his mouth, closed his eyes and sat back on the couch, silently crying.

Schmuck, Max Rosenbloom said to himself. Max Rosenbloom knew something about guts. A certain style anyway. He hadn't had the guts to cancel the ceremony or to tell everyone that it was likely the marriage was off. To say those words and face Vee would be like running through an atomic cloud on a dare. "Sari will be back in time," he'd told her. So he'd chickened out. Vee probably knew anyway, knew exactly what was happening, she had radar for that kind of thing. So Max Rosenbloom let it ride and hoped that Sari would come back before he had to send these annoyed people home, probably laughing at him.

Max looked around. They all knew that something was wrong. The place had the funeral feel, all murmurs and polite conversation and strained little laughs. It was like being in a museum. Or maybe in a tomb.

"Everything OK?" said Ben E. Fahr, the Underwear Tsar. He appeared next to Max Rosenbloom with a low, trust-me whisper coming through a shaggy, gray goatee.

"She'll be here," Max said.

The Underwear Tsar winked, lifted his glass to Max and walked over to speak to the rabbi who was talking to the Cellophane King.

Max Rosenbloom just sat. He missed Sari. He forgave her everything. He didn't care. He just wanted her home and he wanted her to be happy. He thought about how when he had come home from The War what he'd wanted most was a wife and a daughter to spoil and how he'd had to argue with his old man for a piece of the business. Max Rosenbloom would sometimes tell Sari that she was a fairy tale he'd dreamed in a dangerous jungle long before he knew what she looked like or knew her name. The dream had turned out better than he could have ever hoped. Max Rosenbloom could just see her now, he could see her walking right through that door.

There was the sound of the doorbell ringing and front door opening.

And then like lava, Sari swirled into the room on fire. A little bit behind her came Jake.

Max Rosenbloom was on his feet. The bedroom door swung opened and Vee was now standing in the doorway, a carved idol with glassy eyes. Dr. Lévi stood up, too, and so did Ben E. Fahr, the Underwear Tsar. The rest of the guests were already on their feet. Nobody said anything until the rabbi said, "There she is! The blushing bride! *L'chiam!*"

"Shut up," Max Rosenbloom said.

That's when Jake Elkin stepped forward in front of Sari Rose-in-bloom, smiled at Vee, nodded to Max, took a moment to look around the room and said, "As they say in the sitcoms. Mom. Dad. We're married!"

Vee screamed. She whirled again, back into the bedroom. Dr. Lévi dropped his glass on the rug and said something in French that no one could understand. The rabbi kept repeating, "What is going on, someone tell me," and the rest of the guests were shuffling, gawking around, coughing and clearing their throats while the guy who made staples was saying, "Is this the wedding?" and the Cellophane King calling out, "What about the French guy?" as Max Rosenbloom moved forward slowly.

He stood in front of Sari and Jake and said nothing. Then he put his arms around Sari Rose-in-bloom and hugged her for a long time, giving her a kiss on the forehead before he let go. "*Mazel tov,*" he said. "If this is what you want." He wouldn't look at Jake.

"I take care of myself, Daddy, you know that," Sari Rose-in-bloom said. She told him how Jake Elkin had gone to Elkton, Maryland four days ago and gotten a marriage license and then yesterday they'd driven back to Elkton and had a quick, quiet ceremony, no questions asked.

Max Rosenbloom nodded his head all the way through this and Sari was watching his nostrils flare. She held his gaze. She was looking at him in a way Max had never seen before. And then she held up a piece of folded paper and said, "If you don't believe me, here's the license."

Sari Rose-in-bloom had the paper between her fingers for what seemed like a long time before Max took it from her and read it. "Everything's on the up-and-up, Mr. Rosenbloom," Jake said. "Max. I didn't do anything wrong."

Max Rosenbloom examined the slip of paper and gradually he

became happy. His big head went back to that certain nod again, the one that looked like he was taking aim at something.

"I can read," Max Rosenbloom said. "I see where Sari signed. It says right here: Sari. Rose. In. Bloom."

"That's her name," Jake said.

Max crumpled the marriage license in his hand. "Not legally," he said. "Not spelled like that."

"Give me the fucking license," Jake said.

"RABBI!" Max Rosenbloom belted out the call across the room. "You've got some work to do!" And quietly Max said to Jake, "I'm going upstairs to call my lawyer. We'll get it all straightened out. But this paper? Kid, it ain't worth the shit it's printed on."

"I'll sue you," Jake was beginning to stutter. "Tell him, Sari."

The edges of Jake's vision blurred now and he could only see how one of Sari Rose-in-bloom's eyebrows had raised like it was some kind of Banner of Truth. And how her lips, those magnificent lips, were pursed in an expression that anyone else would have read as pity. She shrugged. Jake thought he heard laughter. He saw that Sari had moved away from him and was slipping her arm through the arm of Dr. Lévi. That much registered in Jake's blurry world, but that was all. Because just as Jake Elkin was about to say something, Vee Vee Rosenbloom came out of her bedroom and began coming down the stairs with a wide, wild grin on her face. Her eyes were fierce now but staring at something that no one else could see. And she had taken off the muumuu and she was naked.

"Mama! This is not the way!" Dr. Lévi shouted. He rushed toward her. Sari Rose-in-bloom stepped backwards and Ben E. Fahr, the Underwear Tsar, had to grab her, hold her up, keep her from falling. "VEE!" Max got two steps closer to her but Vee Vee Rosenbloom was already at the door, "IT'S A MISTAKE!" Max was shouting. "LET ME TELL YOU!"

But Vee had turned into an immense, incredible, white flesh force, large bellied, thick and breasted like a statue, and she moved in a way that told you she had seen plenty, she'd seen more than enough of the world and she was announcing an exit that could not be questioned.

Vee Vee Rosenbloom was out the front door, walking naked across the front lawn. Jake saw the splay of dimples on her thighs. When she spun around to face the house he turned away. A glimpse of the pale hair across her cunt was too much. Jake went down on one knee, he could have been proposing. He stayed there. Dr. Lévi and Sari Rose-in-bloom hurried outside after Vee and it was Max who called for an ambulance.

CHAPTER SIXTEEN

THE BILLBOARD WAS GONE two weeks later and nothing was in its place so Elkin drove past a huge, empty blank space that was stuck up there alongside the LIE. He kept his mouth shut as the car passed by. Elkin thought he could still see the dings and the holes he'd put in the backboard but he wasn't sure. It was a little after five a.m. and still dark, still cool.

The station had promised they'd put up another billboard in the same place. This one would plug Jerry Elkin and his new one-man show that was starting in less than an hour. Elkin wondered whether the station hadn't yet put up another billboard because they were waiting to see if he got on the air alone and fell on his face. Jerry Elkin, Mr. Tune Out. Let's wait and see. Don't put up a billboard. That's what they were thinking. Probably. Trying to save themselves a cheap buck wherever they could. Elkin gritted his teeth, the bunch of schmucks. He hated them. All of them. They couldn't just back him up a little and put up a Jerry Elkin billboard.

So he could yell at himself every morning on the way in to work.

Elkin sang, did a quick "whoop-whoop-whoop" then a Mr. Nosh then Miss Emma Reel, warming up. His throat caught a little bit and he said out loud, "OK, so you're nervous but you're excited, too" and then he said out loud, "Listen to this schmuck, talking to himself" and then he considered turning the car around and driving back home and hiding under the bed. "Never fear, my liege!" he said out loud. So now, passing the shopping center, the cheap motels and the army of red brick apartments, sticking to the speed limit on the LIE, in through the Midtown Tunnel and over to the radio station, Elkin started talking to himself in the voice of Ted Fox. We shall never hear his likes again, Elkin thought. Ah, mystery of life.

In through the newsroom, Elkin gave out a big, "Let's make it morning!" in his own voice and the news guys who were tippy-tapping at their typewriters looked up and said, "Hey, Elko! He's back!" or called to him, "Break a leg this a.m. Elk!" or "We've made it morning already, leave us alone!" and they all laughed, Elkin along with them.

Then he headed over to the desk of fake tough guy sports announcer Steve Leo and waved away the smoke and said, "Hey, thanks for the call," and Steve Leo nodded without taking the cigarette out of his mouth and said, "Don't make me do that again." The ash fell off his cigarette and landed on his typewriter keys.

Elkin stood for a moment at the door of Studio B. Well, he was in it now, this is what he'd always wanted. Elkin was thinking of the talk he'd had with his son Jake, right after the stupid schmuck move Jake had pulled with that ridiculous Maryland marriage and after Jake had come home and locked himself in the bathroom after the girl had really gotten married.

When he'd finally convinced Jake to open the door, Elkin had sat him down on the toilet and sat across from him on the edge of the tub. Elkin never liked to talk seriously because it never failed to make him angry. So when Jake said, "Why would she do a thing like that?" Elkin gave him the two-handed I-don't-know gesture and said, "One of two reasons. Either you were such a pain in the ass that she thought it was the only way she could get rid of you… or she's a genuine schmuck. Just like her old man."

"She's not that," Jake said. "I know her."

"Look," Elkin said, pulling at his double chin, which was now near complete. "Just don't do what I've done."

"What have you done?"

"I don't know," Elkin said. "Just don't do it."

Then Elkin said, "Look, kid, I'm just a comedian. I don't know very much so here's what I know. Don't try to top a topper. If they're beating you that much on laughs, let it go. Also, you want to surprise them and not do the obvious to make 'em laugh, but, you know, sometimes you just gotta give them the joke they expect. Do it by feel. And also, and you can lock yourself back up in the bathroom after this, you want the audience to laugh with you…but you also gotta let them laugh at you." He stood up from the tub. "If you don't, then you've never really grabbed hold of the absurd." Elkin gave Jake a pat on the head and left him there.

Now Elkin opened the door to Studio B and stepped inside.

There was Sgt. Al, the producer, sifting through a stack of LPs. "Any ghosts?" Elkin said.

"What do you think?"

"All around, my liege," Elkin said. "It's like he's watching. Except, of course, he's not."

Elkin told Sgt. Al that they'd no longer use "Let's make it morning!" as a slogan but that they'd start fresh with "Jerry Elkin this a.m.!" Then they'd play that Sinatra song "A Day in the Life of a Fool" and after that Elkin would do the Bloomingdale's spot and have Chip Chopper come in with a traffic report.

"Mr. Nosh on Bloomingdale's?" Sgt. Al said.

"Excellent idea, my liege," Elkin said. And he arranged the two microphones so that he could use his own voice as straight man on one of them and on the other, Chip Chopper or Mr. Nosh or Coach Bruce Bruise or who knew who else would stop by.

I'm my own Ted Fox now, Elkin thought. To every man, his own Ted Fox. And his own Jerry Elkin, Elkin thought. And he signaled for the engineer to throw him the mike and put him on air.

The routine where Jerry Elkin ate his breakfast on the air and somehow managed also to talk to Mr. Nosh was the first time Max Rosenbloom had laughed since he'd put Vee away. Well, maybe that wasn't quite right, he was thinking, he had laughed at Sari's party when his son got drunk and threw up in the Carlyle Hotel planter. And would the little schmuck let him give a helping hand? No.

Max Rosenbloom sat in his favorite chair downstairs in his den, dressed in his dark brown bathrobe, noticing that the paneling was coming loose on the wall opposite, sipping Scotch now at nine a.m. His new standard had become "never before ten" but since Vee was at the clinic and Sari was in Paris and his son never spoke to him, that one took a lot of moxie. He was trying, though. Max Rosenbloom hoped that Vee would be well enough to come home soon but he wasn't sure the marriage would hold up after what happened. "Do something about it, Max!" He could hear her. Max Rosenbloom could see her, too, wandering across the lawn without any clothes. To get it like that, shit. Well, fuck it, there was never any dignity, not at the end, anyway, not from what Max Rosenbloom had seen. The marriage? He'd give it a shot, he could say that, he'd give it his best.

The little brown box where he kept World War Two when it was not a part of him lay in his lap. He was staring at the photograph of the other Max Rosenbloom, the one who'd held a submachine gun in his hand and had grenades hanging down his front and worn a helmet on his head. The patches he'd torn off his uniform, also, they were arranged on his thigh and he was touching the pages of the little diary in which he'd written things like, "Today I killed another Jap." I can live through anything, Max Rosenbloom was thinking. But then, for a moment, he got back a feel for what The War was really like and he smiled. "If you stay lucky," he said out loud.

On the radio, Elkin went into a live spot for Eastern Airlines doing the commercial in the voice of a new character: Maxie Futzer, Professional Schlub. The voice was low-down and gruff and this Futzer was sort of a nogoodnik and Max Rosenbloom thought it sounded a lot like him, Max Rosenbloom, but you're hearing things, Max, he said to himself, so don't go around with a big head, as my mother used to say.

Max Rosenbloom was thinking about the Elkin kid, Jake, and how he'd driven away while they were putting Vee in the ambulance and the rabbi was marrying Sari and Dr. Lévi. Never see that little schmuck again, Max said to himself, and it wasn't a very pretty goodbye. He wondered if 25 years from now, Jake Elkin would be sitting in his own bathrobe in his own basement den, drinking Scotch at nine in the morning and looking at pictures of Sari Rose-in-bloom, thinking that if he could live through her, he could live through anything. Or if the whole bad business would just become a funny story and he'd move on.

"God bless him," Max Rosenbloom said out loud.

Upstairs, he walked through his living room feeling the thick yellow carpet between his toes, finishing his Scotch and looking at the painting collection he'd put together over the years. All in all, in every way that people count, he'd done all right for himself, Max Rosenbloom had, not bad for a little Jewish schmuck from Bensonhurst. He looked over his canvases in blue from the years when he was sad and his canvases in red from the time when he was always angry and the canvas he'd bought that was all dark swirling browns and blacks for when Vee had been put away. Also an original Chinita Sari drawing. Sari as an artwork, Max Rosenbloom's own artwork that celebrated Sari and all the time they had spent here, under this one roof. Things were going to be different now, he could feel it in the pit of his stomach. Max Rosenbloom went into the kitchen to pour another Scotch.

That's when he heard the car pull up. Max Rosenbloom looked through the little round window of his front door to see Larry

Passoff, Boris Jampolsky and two men in dark suits coming up his front walk.

Max Rosenbloom opened the door and stood there in his bathrobe with the Scotch glass in his hand and waited for them to come closer. OK, he was thinking, OK, I see what it is. He took another sip and then they were standing in front of him below the brick stoop. They stared.

"That's him." Larry Passoff said. "That's Max Rosenbloom."

"It is Mr. Max Rosenbloom," Boris Jampolsky said.

"Max Rosenbloom?" said one of the men in the dark suits. A skinny little guy with a face that looked like he picked his zits for fun.

"Yeah, I'm Max Rosenbloom," Max Rosenbloom said.

The man with the pitted face told Max Rosenbloom that he was with the FBI and he showed Max an I.D. then told Max Rosenbloom he was under arrest. He told Max he had the right to remain silent. He had a lot of other rights, too, but Max Rosenbloom didn't hear them. He was too busy finishing his Scotch, then setting down his glass on the floor, then, when they gave him the order, turning around so they could put on the cuffs. The pitted-faced man snapped them on tight with a vengeance like he was the Angel of Justice himself come to earth and Max Rosenbloom could feel the sting as the metal pinched his flesh.

And as they walked Max Rosenbloom, in his bare feet and his brown bathrobe, to the car that was waiting at the curb, Max Rosenbloom got that certain look that he sometimes got that showed mostly at the corners of his eyes and the way he held his mouth, the look that told the men who were holding tight to his arms that Max Rosenbloom had been to where there was no yesterday or tomorrow, Max Rosenbloom had done things and seen things that would make all these little schmucks melt into the ground with their own drool and tears and if this was a time when balls were called for, if now was when you had to show 'em that you got a pair, well then, Max Rosenbloom thought, you son-of-a-bitch schmucks are holding onto the right man.

★ ★ ★

The only part of the show that he heard that morning was OK, it was pretty funny but not as funny as Jake thought it could have been. It didn't really get to the meat of things, it didn't have any teeth, it was pulling punches. The Maxie Futzer, Professional Schlub, all right, that was good, could be better but it was good as it was, and Jake knew who it was based on. He thought that maybe his father was doing it for him, Jake, to stick it to the enemy. Even so.

That's what Jake usually told Elkin anyway. That the show was just mashed-potato, middle-class comedy, it wasn't Lenny Bruce or Mort Sahl or even Jean Shepherd, a true radio genius, and Jake always got a rise out of Elkin over that, it made him stomp away mad.

"What the fuck is Shepherd doing that I'm not doing?" Elkin would shoot back.

"Sticking it to the man," Jake would fire back. "He's incredible and he's got real balls." Then he would launch into how Elkin and Fox and now Elkin alone were just ways to make the commercials longer so the sponsors got more time than they paid for and the sales department popped a cork because the sales people were the most important people in the world, anyway. Right?

"OK, wise guy," Elkin would say. "Call me when *you* have to make a living. Schmuck."

"That's not what I'm talking about," Jake would say, on the verge of tears. "I'm talking about America."

"I know exactly what you're talking about," Elkin would shoot back. "I damned my father's generation because they made the world that ended in The War. OK, so you can damn my generation for making a world that ended in commercials. And your kids will damn your generation, too, you can count on it."

"Yeah, for what?"

"Jake, it's just the way it is. The only things that get better are food and electronics."

Jake waited for the end of the show when Elkin said "Jerry

Elkin this a.m.!" and then he took the LIRR into the city and headed uptown to the Metropolitan Museum of Art. There had been a
piece about the exhibit in *The New York Times* and it was listed in
Cue Magazine. And when he got to 81st Street, Jake saw that the
museum had hung a huge purple banner across the stone façade
that read "The Chinita Saris" and it flapped a little in the breeze
over the helmeted head of Athena.

He walked up the steps. For an instant, he stopped and looked
around, taking in the sea tint of the sky and the traffic on Fifth
Avenue and the people milling all around him or sitting on the
steps, and he saw that there was a mime at the base of the steps
entertaining them. The guy was in traditional black tights with a
very white face and he was imitating people who passed him on
the sidewalk.

But Jake couldn't stall anymore. He went inside and took the
stairs to the second level slowly, concentrating on the pull in his
calve muscles, sucking in deep breaths and telling himself it was
because of the physical effort. Then he was inside the gallery.

And there she was.

Jake hadn't heard from Sari Rose-in-bloom since she'd gotten
married and moved overseas and he didn't expect to hear from her
ever again throughout his entire and now probably shortened life.
But this? What had he done to deserve this? How was he going to
live with this? How could he have been such a schmuck?

There was no air in the museum. He was going to choke. It
smelled of dried-out cloth and dust and memories and all the voices mingled into one muddy clod of distant echo. Jake wanted to get
out but he couldn't, not yet, he stood and looked up at her.

Sari was posed there in marble, maybe 15, maybe 20 feet high,
Jake wasn't sure, and he couldn't see well enough to read the little
information card. All he could see was Sari. She was even more
perfect than he'd ever seen her in the flesh, the carving, the marble
somehow bursting with the bloom that was Sari Rose-in-bloom,
budding with the rose that was Sari blooming, the curve of her

arm, how her leg bent, the slope of her hips and ass, her breasts and the hair between her legs, Oh God, Jake was thinking. Well, I've really learned something from this, Jake said to himself.

And I'll never forget it.

That's right. It's—what do they say?—a new day, a new life, it's all new. He was starting over clean. And he had all the answers, he knew just what to do. It was all right there in front of him in marble, but it was there in a way that made Jake understand that he had been in touch with some strange mystical force, don't tell him it didn't exist—this was Sari Rose-in-bloom. She had nothing to do with what his father had talked about or what Max Rosenbloom had said. This was not a person but a power beyond comprehension that was now lost forever. It was lost to Jake, at least. And as Jake stood below her and let his gaze drift over every inch of this miraculous Sari he thought that now he would always remember the horrific fact of losing her. And if he ever forgot, he could come here and make it real again.

Jake stumbled outside and sat down on the stone steps. My life is over, he thought. There was nothing left to do but push on and have the courage of his own special sadness. People who met him from now on would wonder why he was a Sad Man or a Man of Deep Sorrow and he would never tell them because there was no way to explain it. It would have to remain his secret. He would be the Secretly Saddest Man Who Ever Lived and he would visit the Sari statue every year as a kind of religious devotion.

The mime was now in the middle of Fifth Avenue, in the center of downtown traffic, and he was holding up his hand to stop a bus. When the bus halted, the mime hooked an invisible rope to the front and then he turned around like the invisible rope was over his shoulder and he began pulling, making all the grimaces and bent-back footfalls of a great effort but also turning to the crowd to smile and wave. And the bus moved slowly behind him. The mime was pulling the bus down Fifth Avenue on an invisible rope. Jake could see the driver laughing. The crowd on the steps applauded.

I hate mimes, Jake said to himself.

The mime kept pulling the bus on the invisible rope down Fifth Avenue and Jake sat there on the steps of the museum thinking about Sari Rose-in-bloom, thinking that he would never stop thinking about Sari Rose-in-bloom, that everything in his life until the day he died would dance around a Rose-in-bloom Sadness and that he would face the world as The Secretly Saddest Man Who Ever Lived, Who Always Thinks About Sari Rose-in-bloom. Then he thought about Max Rosenbloom and what Max had said to him and he thought about his father and what his father had said to him.

Jake sat there thinking. He lit up a cigarette.

He was seeing the Sari statue in his mind and he was thinking about his father and Ted Fox and Max Rosenbloom and he was thinking that every moment of his life from now on would be a Sad Moment of Rose-in-bloomism.

Jerry Elkin and Ted Fox and Max Rosenbloom.

What the hell did they know? Jake thought.

What the hell did they know, anyway?

ACKNOWLEDGMENTS

My deepest heartfelt thanks to the more than excellent friend and writer Charles Salzberg, a man of talent, generosity and insight and a fine lunch companion. He also runs Greenpoint Press, which made this book possible. Thanks, pal.

Charles had the wisdom to call upon the incredible skills of Gini Kopecky Wallace, who did the best editing job I've ever seen. Gini's understanding of human behavior and her hard work on history added to the book in so many ways. Likewise, the very talented Bob Lascaro, whose cover art was beautiful, knowing and perfect for the story.

Beyond thanking is the terrific painter Mary Jones, also my wife, who put up with me and in her work and career showed me what it means to be an artist.

A number of comrades read early drafts and offered extremely important and helpful advice, warnings and threats: writer David Feinberg; filmmaker Ian McClellan; psychoanalyst W. M. Bernstein, PhD; writer John Bowers; therapist Sharyn Wolf, CSW; actor Sidney Williams; author, playwright and brother Laurence Klavan; Navy officer Alysha Haran; and my manager, Judi Farkas, of Judi Farkas Management. Believe me, I was listening to all of you and took most of your advice.

And for that very important moral support, I want to thank owner Steve and bartenders Steve, Hazel, Norma and Jeff of the very fine Knickerbocker Bar & Grill on University and 9th.

Photo: Mary Jones

ABOUT THE AUTHOR

Ross Klavan's work spans film, television, radio, print and live performance. His original screenplay for the film "Tigerland" was nominated for an Independent Spirit Award, he recently finished an adaption of John Bowers' *The Colony*, and he has written scripts for Miramax, Paramount and TNT, among others. The "conversation about writing" he moderated with Kurt Vonnegut and Lee Stringer was televised and published as *Like Shaking Hands with God*, and his short stories have appeared in magazines and been produced by the BBC. An earlier novel, *Trax*, was published under a pseudonym. His play "How I Met My (Black) Wife (Again)," co-written with Ray Iannicelli, has been produced in New York City, and he has performed his work in numerous theaters and clubs. He has acted and done voice work in TV and radio commercials and has lent his voice to feature films including "Casino," "You Can Count On Me" and "Revolutionary Road" and the new Amazon web series "Alpha House," written by Gary Trudeau. He has worked as a newspaper and radio journalist in London and New York City. He lives in New York City with his wife, the painter, Mary Jones.